FREEDOM FOR THE WOLVES

By the same author

The Horse of Darius

FREEDOM FOR THE WOLVES

Justin Cartwright

Hamish Hamilton London

First published in Great Britain 1983
by Hamish Hamilton Limited
Garden House 57–59 Long Acre London WC2E 9JZ

Copyright © 1983 by Justin Cartwright

British Library Cataloguing in Publication Data

Cartwright, Justin
  Freedom for the Wolves.
  I. Title
  823'.914[F]   PR6053.A746

ISBN 0-241-10963-9

Phototypeset by Tradespools Limited, Frome, Somerset
Printed in Great Britain by Billings, Worcester

For Penny and the boys

The notion that history obeys laws, whether natural or supernatural, that every event of human life is an element in a necessary pattern, has deep metaphysical origins.... It occurs in many versions, but what is common to them all is the belief that men, and all living creatures and perhaps inanimate things as well, not merely are as they are, but have functions and pursue purposes.

... If the belief in freedom – which rests on the assumption that human beings do occasionally choose, and that their choices are not wholly accounted for by the kind of causal explanations which are accepted in, say, physics or biology – if this is a necessary illusion, it is so deep and so pervasive that it is not felt as such.

> Isaiah Berlin. *Four Essays on Liberty.*
> Oxford University Press, 1979.

Foreword

I would like to acknowledge an intellectual debt to Sir Isaiah Berlin. I would also like to thank the Oxford University Press for permission to quote from his work *Four Essays on Liberty*. Of all the attempts to deal with this intractable subject, his is the most profound.

The historical characters in my book have been treated in an unsystematic fashion. Some are dealt with more or less accurately, others have imagined characteristics and qualities or failings. I make no apology for this.

I would like to thank Christopher Sinclair-Stevenson for keeping faith, Bob and Coral Stephens of Swaziland for many kindnesses, and I would like to remember my father's interest in this book. Sadly he died on the very day I finished work.

Justin Cartwright
London, January 1983

PROLOGUE
1960

Dawn makes little impression here in the big, dusty, cool, creaking bedroom. The intensity of light outside is here transmuted into little seepages of brilliance between the heavy curtains (in fact old bedspreads pinned to the window surrounds) which in turn are dissipated into pools of lesser brilliance, lying irregularly and weakly upon the naked forms of the two on the bed.

One of the policemen, the one not driving the first Chev pick-up, is humming a tune. It is called 'Living Doll'. Behind the first police vehicle comes another, identical. The back of the pick-up truck is covered with canvas, stretched over a frame. Inside this frame, inadequately protected from the dust, silent, sit three more policemen, black, their khaki uniforms already tinged with the dust from the rich, ferrous red soil. This little scene is repeated in the second van, also piloted by a pair of white policemen. The effect, were anybody about to observe it, of the two vans driving at high speed down a dirt road with the sun behind them, the dust spreading outwards, billowing into the sky, the blue of the distant mountains, the village of round thatched huts, with a solitary square hut, its roof of corrugated iron weighted down with stones, the dancing river below – the effect of all this in the golden dawn is congenial.

Behind the vans, at least half a mile, the dust they have thrown up is beginning to settle, slowly. It coats the trees along the road, track really, and it coats the old man who is now, at last, remounting his bicycle after the passage of the police vans. His soft felt hat is tinged rufous, the little twists of a beard on his face grey and red by turns. His eyes are yellow. His face is curiously oriental, high cheekbones, simian; he pedals with difficulty on the rutted track, the heavy balloon tyres of the old Hercules cycle ploughing through the deep dust of the road, but barely. He is too late.

The girl on the bed is too late. She hears the police vans approaching. She jumps from the bed. Her first, culpable, reaction is to throw the wig which is lying on the floor, on top of a cupboard. It is a cheap cupboard with a mirror, oval shaped, on the outside of each of its doors, yet it has been lovingly polished with beeswax until it has an unnatural gloss, like a corpse laid out. She opens the curtains and sees the approaching dust storm following two speeding vans. It is biblical. Twin whirlwinds merging into a great exploding cloud. She pulls on her housecoat. Her hands are trembling so much that she can hardly button up the front over her purpuric nipples. She ties the cloth, the doek, around her head. It is too late for such subservient gestures. She knows. She runs.

The man on the bed does not stir, even though he regards himself as a light sleeper. He does not reach out for the empty space next to him, in the prescribed fashion. He breathes evenly and deeply. He is running slightly to fat around his naked middle. His buttocks catch a little of the available light, whitely. The sheet is twisted and crumpled, just covering his ankles. In this position he looks very boyish. He is, in fact, thirty-two years old.

In the short time that it has taken for the police vans to approach the old farmhouse, the sun has risen above the distant mountains. The water, as a consequence, no longer dances in the river in the valley far below. The whole scene becomes more prosaic. The police vans slide to a halt on the dusty earth in front of the house.

As the vans stop, the cloud of dust that has been dutifully trailing them up the narrow track now continues on over the vans and up the valley. The black policemen, with a show of eagerness, clamber out and quickly surround the house. They hold their fighting sticks ready, as their forbears have done for years. These particular policemen come from a distant country. They are not local people.

The girl breaks from the house running for the village. One of the black policemen grabs her roughly. She immediately becomes quite submissive. She does not call out for help. She does not call to the man asleep in the house. She climbs into the back of the second police van meekly. Three black policemen climb in after her. Sergeant Retief waves. The van's powerful V-8 engine surges and powers away, down the track. As it approaches, the old man on the bicycle dismounts again and stands wearily aside, his eyes downcast. He waits until the dust has yet again dispersed. He turns the Hercules round and faces in the direction from which he has come. He mounts the cycle and sets off again. He is the girl's father. His name is Tshabalala. It is eight miles to the police station in town.

No instinctive sense of disquiet possesses the man on the bed. His name is James Thompson. It is his farmhouse. He was left it by his grandfather. He intends to farm, to dabble in conservation, perhaps to breed some rare species here. By the standards of this area it is a very old house. It was built in 1890. It has a low verandah running all the way round and a tin roof which becomes fiercely hot in the middle of the day, yet manages to allow the inside of the house to remain dark and cool by shielding all the windows from direct approaches by the sun. Despite this, he sleeps with only a sheet on the bed, now, as already mentioned, crumpled over his ankles. Most nights he sleeps with Daisy Tshabalala.

Retief looks at the house with distaste. Despite the expensive car standing under the kaffirboom beside the house, despite all his money, Thompson has done nothing with the house in the four months he has lived here. The door has an old flyscreen on it; some of the windows have shutters. A few pathetic succulents in old jam tins, catering size, stand on the verandah. A meat chest – nobody has them any more – stands on a table, the focal point for the many flies which strive to get in through the fine mesh which covers it. In the distance away to the river a few cattle graze, but fences are still broken, the borehole shed near the house is overgrown, the windmill is rusting. The place smells of khaki weed, a sure sign of neglect. He hammers on the front door with the butt of his pistol.

Daisy Tshabalala exchanges no words with the three policemen in the van. One of them, in an excess of zeal, has put his huge brass handcuffs on her so that, unable to brace herself, she is bounced painfully against the side of the van as it speeds towards the town of Trichardt's Rest. The three policemen seem as listless as she. They all sit in silence; one has his head on the backs of his hands, supported in turn by his sticks which he cups in his huge white palms. The dust swirls behind the van so thickly that they cannot see out. They all stare at the floor. It is a very mournful company.

The banging on the door wakes Thompson. One of the reasons why he considers himself a light sleeper is that when he wakes he wakes instantly, from deep sleep to alertness, even anxiety. That slow fuddled, drowsy time between sleep and wakefulness is denied him, even on those mornings, like this one, when he is suffering from the effects of drink. As Retief hammers on the door again, he pulls on a pair of shorts, does them up and hurries along the corridor. The builder of the house had many shortcomings as a draughtsman. The corridor is long, it occupies far too much of the floor space. Rooms lead off it like cells in a prison. Thompson's plan is to open the house a bit, to thatch the roof with reeds from the river, to paint all the walls in ochres and browns, to rip up the linoleum which is everywhere. A probe has shown hand-sawn yellow-wood planks underneath, priceless and as yet untouched by termites. The banging on the door is not African. In this part of the world the natives are not assertive. They shuffle, they cough discreetly, they wait patiently for him to get up. They do not bang on the door as though they want to break it down.

'Stop beating the fucking door down, I'm coming,' he shouts. He stumbles against a cardboard box that contains his accumulated school photographs and albums, recently sent to him by his mother, whose past life is whirling endlessly before her these days, prompting curious, atavistic rituals (like packing up all his school trivia). He sees Retief's pistol before he sees the rest of Retief. He wonders which of the servants Retief has been pursuing for some small offence or other. Then he realises. Daisy. Retief is pursuing him now.

'Hello, Sergeant. What can I do for you?'

He speaks English. Retief is not comfortable with English, but his office demands that he speak the language of his customers.

'I would like to talk to you.'

'Come in. Let's sit in the kitchen, I'm not feeling too good this morning,' (he smiles winningly) 'my head, I need some coffee.' He would prefer the orange juice, which Daisy laboriously squeezes for him each day. They sit down at the rough table (also covered in linoleum, nailed with myriad nails) while the kettle boils on the old stove. Gas from the cylinder, which fits imperfectly, tinges the room with the unhealthy odour of decomposition. He must do something about it. Retief takes off his hat, and lays it on the table next to his massive, stagey pistol. Thompson wonders why he doesn't put it back in its ample holster. He can't believe that Retief would indulge in so theatrical a gesture consciously. It unsettles him. So perhaps Retief has done it consciously. He would like to say, 'Please don't point that thing in my direction,' but does not. Instead he says, 'So, what's all this about?'

Retief appears to be finding the words difficult to assemble. He says: 'This is one hell of a business, Mr Thompson.'

At that moment the kettle begins to whistle stridently. Thompson stands up, smiling apologetically, rather inanely.

'Black or white?'

'White, please. Three spoons.'

The little task of mixing the coffee with the boiling water is interminable. Thompson sits down, the untended pistol again pointing at a spot just below his sternum. Suddenly he has an urge to laugh. But he manages to compose his features into a serious but relaxed arrangement; at least that is the impression he hopes he is conveying. Retief wonders why he is smiling like a moron.

'Yes, Mr Thompson, this is one hell of a business.'

'What is, Sergeant?'

'Mr Thomspon, listen, you're a man of the world.'

'Well ...'

The phrase is so outlandish here in this run-down farmhouse it seems probable that Retief has been rehearsing it.

'Yes, you've travelled to other countries, been away for quite a lot of years.'

'Ja.'

'I suppose coming back here things are, sort of strange?'

'No, not really.'

Retief looks faintly hurt or puzzled.

'In that case I don't really understand why you did it.'

'What?'

Thompson knows perfectly well what Retief is talking about. All too well; he is talking about the fact that he has been shacked up with Daisy Tshabalala for some months, with less and less regard of secrecy, despite the rumours, despite the veiled warnings, despite the dangers.

'Mr Thompson, don't play silly buggers with me. You've been screwing that black girl. What's the matter with you?'

Retief regrets this outburst. But he can't bear to see the place falling apart, this rich, spoilt bastard sitting here acting dumb, his stubby little hands resting on the table insolently, the trashy African artefacts scattered about, pathetic soapstone things, a smile meandering over his soft face like water in search of a furrow, pretending he doesn't know what it's all about.

Thompson stands up. Retief picks up the pistol. Thompson sits down again.

'I want to call my lawyer.'

'Hold on, Mr Thompson. I don't think that's going to be necessary. I think we should discuss this thing first. We don't want to stir up any trouble.'

'Where's the girl?'

'We've taken her away.'

'What do you mean?'

Thompson feels a tide of anger rising dangerously. Retief has the gun in his hands.

'I mean we've taken her away. What happens to her depends on you.'

Thompson sips his coffee, which is watery and unpleasant. His head is thick. Retief appears to be about forty. Thompson has seen him before in the town, even spoken to him about some irregularity of reference books for one of his workers. His face is very solid, chiselled, yet red and sun-flushed as though he were a new arrival to these sunny climates. In fact there is a horrible solidness about all of him. He is built like a weight lifter, without muscular definition but with a layer of solid flesh wrapped closely around him.

'Oh that this too, too solid flesh would melt.'

'What?' asks Retief.

Thompson realises that he has spoken out loud.

'Sorry. How does it depend on me?'

'Mr Thompson, we want to be reasonable about this whole business. Really. It's not the sort of business you, or us, want to come out, do you follow me?'

The old man cycles steadily at slightly faster than walking speed towards the town of Trichardt's Rest and the police station where his daughter is held. The track gives way to broader road, which will eventually join up with the tarred national road. Below him is his village. He is the headman although to be headman of six men, twenty women and fifteen children is a small affair; his father commanded three hundred. The young men threaten him with contempt and leave for the mines or cities whenever the opportunity presents itself. They come back only to flaunt their new acquisitions, shoes, alarm clocks, briefcases, suits. Boredom overtakes them after the vibrant world they have seen. They leave again, although many, significantly, marry girls from these parts. His own daughter, Daisy, the youngest, is married to a man on a long contract. He cycles past his village, sweat standing on his brow and making clear paths through the dust on his face, so that his face aquires a streaky aspect, which some might find comical.

Daisy's handcuffs are taken off. She is placed in a cell. There is no one else in it. The cells are at the back, smaller in scale than the rather grand police station. Two convicts from a nearby prison farm, in long shorts of khaki, bring her some porridge and tea. She does not speak to them and they offer no comment. She sits on the floor of the cell, which is spotlessly clean, and waits. Listlessly she dips her fingers into the porridge. She drinks a little tea. Outside she hears the noise of lawn clippers; two more convicts are trimming the edge of the patch of grass near the cells while a guard, armed with two sticks and a spear, watches over them. Daisy, naturally, cannot see this, but the patch of grass has large, bare spots, where energetic harvester ants are doing their own clipping, taking the blades of grass down their burrows busily. The police station was opened by the Minister of Justice himself only four years previously. Sergeant Retief was presented with a medal at the time, a routine enough award. He wears it on the annual holiday which commemorates the Battle of Blood River: there is a parade of the local school boys in their cadet uniforms at which the police force is present. It is a moving occasion. Possibly the blacks present think they look like a bunch of cunts, and remember that their ancestors won most of the battles, prior to Blood River. But if they have these thoughts, they keep them to themselves.

Thompson finds blackmail a relief. It bridges the moral gulf between him and the police. Retief is coming to the subject by a devious route. Thompson watches him, his large, red, honest face forming the words.

'We don't want something like this to come out. I understand. Your grandfather was a very respected man in this district.'

The implication that he is not in the same elevated category as his grandfather does not surprise him. He is not.

'It would be difficult for him, difficult for us and you.'

'Yes.'

'So I think we should talk about this like men of the world.'

'Right.'

Who is going to make the offer? Retief waits, toying with his gun absent-mindedly. A bluebottle fly in its death-throes flings itself repeatedly against the glass of the window above the sink. The noise is surprisingly sharp.

'Some of the boys at the station think we should bring charges.'

'Against the girl?'

'You, man. Against you. And the girl.'

Retief would actually like to charge Thompson. But he would get some Jewish layer down from Johannesburg, some deal would be made, they would all get their knuckles rapped for going in over their heads. So the sensible thing is to get rid of the problem. Make their own deal.

'Do you have something to propose, Sergeant?'

Arrogant bastard. Retief would love to put the cuffs on him and throw him in the back of the van. A couple of days of mealie porridge would change his attitude.

'I would like to buy this farm one day,' says Retief.

'I'm going to do it all up.'

Retief breaks the pistol open and removes one of the heavy, stubby little bullets. He weighs it in the palm of his hand and puts it back in the gun.

'I wish you would stop playing with that fucking thing!'

Retief jumps up and hits Thompson with the half clenched palm of his hand. His chair is knocked over. It breaks. Thompson lies on the floor for a moment. He sits up. Warm blood trickles down his chin and on to his bare chest. For some reason he smiles. He begins to pick up the bits of chair, which have come quite apart, one from the other, as in a Western. Termites probably.

'You stupid little cunt.'

Retief speaks Afrikaans now.

'You come here, sit on your arse all day long, screw black maids, the whole fucking district knows about it, and then, you cheeky little bastard, you sit there telling me what to do. Look at this place, it's like a slum. I am going to arrest you and then we'll see what fucking happens to you. You deserve six months' hard labour alongside your kaffir friends.'

Thompson stands up. He has no chair to sit on. Retief sits again. He shouts out of the door. A young constable arrives, his pistol drawn.

'Watch him. Don't let him move.'

'Yes, Sergeant.'

Retief goes out. The young constable looks nervous. His face is fair, Germanic, with the ends of his hair, just visible under his cap, combed back behind his ears. It was he who was singing 'Living Doll'. His friends call him, 'Ducktail', in jest.

'He hit me,' says Thompson, wiping his mouth.

'Keep quiet.'

Thompson is shocked. He has not been struck since his school days. His lip is swelling; he feels it gingerly with his tongue. He moves to the sink and has some water from the tap. It is clear and cool and faintly brackish.

Retief at that moment is on the radio to his colleague. His colleague advises caution. Retief gets out of the van and walks down towards the river. He pauses on an outcrop of rock. He looks towards the village. On the roof of the headman's hut are six huge pumpkins, drying.

He should not have hit Thompson. The Thompsons are too powerful to monkey about with. Van Rensburg was right. A business deal is what they understand. He walks back to the house, little tenacious burrs of the khaki weed clinging to his serge trousers.

The old man has gained the tarred road. It stretches only a few miles on either side of Trichardt, though it is to be extended shortly – all the way to the Reef. His legs are aching. His heart is aching.

He stops to adjust his bicycle clips. He draws into his lungs some cleaner air and wipes his face around the eyes. Cycling is easier on this section, although whenever a car comes hurtling past he is forced to leave the tarred road and cycle in the red, fine dust beside it.

As he laboriously pushes the heavy pedals down, the Hercules finally mounts a small hill. Below him, surrounding a completely arbitrary little hill, which appears to be made of huge boulders piled randomly one on top of the other, now the centre-piece of the town's park, lies the town of Trichardt's Rest. He hardly has to pedal at all now. Despite the massive balloon tyres, the Hercules gathers speed. The tyres hum. A cool breeze, as a consequence, dries the sweat on his face. He heads for the police station, which is at the end of the main road, past Potgieter's butchers and the Indian store. The Indian is reputed to be the richest man in Trichardt, but he and his vast family live in a modest house behind the store. He sells meat pies in one part of the store, designated 'café', and blankets and paraffin lamps, blue soap, buckets, overalls, wheelbarrows, rice, maize – all the staples – in the other. He has recently installed a machine which toasts sandwiches. He is going to buy a cappucino machine when the new road finally comes through. The old man cycles down the hill, past the church and the school, past the post office, past Potgieter's, past the Indian, and dismounts outside the police station. A convict is watering the cannas, soft, lush, flowering vegetable-like plants. They appear to need constant watering at this time of year, for one of the fixtures of Trichardt is a convict pointing a hose at these thirsty plants.

The old man enters the non-white charge office. He sits on a wooden form, waiting for someone to appear. There is a bell on the counter, the electric cord leading over and down, out of sight, but he does not use it. He takes his hat off. On the walls of the charge office are pictures of wanted men and many government information posters. They are all incomprehensible. Eventually a black policeman comes walking through. He stares at the old man for a moment and goes out before the old man can say anything. Another policeman returns, a sergeant, very large but gentle.

'What do you want, old man?' he asks respectfully.

The old man stands up, hat in hand, and shuffles to the counter. He explains his mission. He has come to see his shameful daughter. Although the sergeant comes from a quite different tribe, he listens to the old man's story without comment, attentively. Eventually he motions the old man to sit down and goes to see Lieutenant Pretorius. Pretorious is anxious about what Retief is up to, but he allows the sergeant into his office.

Thompson and Retief are sitting, as before, at the kitchen table. The young policeman, Ducktail, has been sent outside to listen for the radio. The black policemen are sitting on a log under a blue gum tree. They would like to get back for their breakfast; Retief has been inside the house now for a long time.

'We will have to get rid of the girl.'

Thompson starts. 'Get rid of her? What?'

'We'll have to send her away to another district.'

'Oh.'

'These things aren't so easy to arrange. Passbooks, transport. You know what I mean?'

'Yes.'

'They cost money.'

'I can imagine.'

Retief finds it distasteful. But Thompson's obstinacy makes him more determined to see that he pays the full price for his folly.

The blood on Thompson's face has stopped flowing; he passes his tongue over the cut on his lip; it is beginning to swell so much that his speech is slurred, as if drunk.

'It would be better if you left too, in a while. You can understand that we can't have this sort of thing going on here.'

Thompson does not confirm this. He is experiencing a profound sadness. *Daisy, Daisy. Poor Daisy.*

'What about her husband?'

'Her husband?'

'What are you going to tell him?'

Retief finds this concern barely credible. He wonders what Thompson is getting at.

'He can't make trouble. We'll take care of that.'

'And her father?'

'Her father?'

'He's the headman.'

He gestures out of the window in the direction of the village.

'So?'

'What are you going to tell him?'

'Just leave him to me. He's not going to tell anybody. Who can he tell?'

Thompson gives up this line of enquiry. He has no doubt at all that Retief will take care of details like that. If he tells Retief that he has, in the past few months, begun to think of the old man as his relative, Retief will surely think him crazey.

Pretorius calls in the old man to his office. How does he know his daughter is locked up? Who is he? What does he want, exactly?

These questions take a while to unravel. The black sergeant helps.

'I want to beat her, sir.'

'Why?'

'She has been very bad, sir.'

'She must go away, old man.'

Tshabalala considers this carefully. He takes out a notebook, an indelible pencil, and writes something on a page of square rule, after first licking the pencil. Pretorius smiles indulgently to the sergeant. They send the old man back to the charge office.

'Take him to see the girl. He's harmless. I want to know where he lives, everything like that. I don't want any problems.'

The sergeant takes the old man round the back to the cells.

A torpor is settling upon the farmhouse. The soft light of early morning has become harsh and relentless. The black policemen are now lying on their backs on an old mattress. A small child, wearing khaki shorts and shirt, appears; he is carrying a billy can to the dairy. As soon as he sees the policemen he runs back down the path to the village, the billy swinging wildly, his skinny legs scuttling febrilely.

'I want the farm myself,' says Retief.

'All right. You can have it.'

The enormity of Retief's demands mean nothing to Thompson. A bargain price for the farm, paid out of Thompson's own money.

'Where are you sending the girl?'

'Don't worry, it's arranged.'

'I want to know.'

'Don't you think it would be better for everybody if you forget about all this business?'

'Yes. You are right.'

They discuss details of the cash payments. Retief is awed by the casualness with which Thompson regards large sums of money. He seems not to care about the difference between five and ten thousand pounds. He should have pitched his terms much higher.

'When are you sending her away?'

'Tomorrow. As soon as you fix the money.'

Retief and his colleague have worked out a meticulous plan. The deeds of the farm are to be conveyed to a cousin of Retief, using some of the money to give the transaction legitimacy. As soon as the money is received, the girl is to be taken away to an unspecified district, where a job as a maid has been arranged. Papers will be provided. Speed is essential.

The large sergeant takes the old man into the cell. Daisy sits on the floor, cowering. The old man shakes his head and clicks his tongue sadly. His pain is very evident. He bends to hit his daughter, once hard across the back of her head. Before he can repeat the blow, the sergeant leads him away. Daisy sits very still on the floor of the cell, the porridge spilled out on the red, polished cement, the enamel bowl upside down. She does not weep. The old man walks outside with the sergeant. They stop for a moment near the moribund lawn, and the old man writes something in his notebook carefully. He replaces his hat, skirts the convict with the hose, who is still watering the cannas, and mounts his bicycle.

The police vans have gone. Thompson dabs his lip with Germolene. He turns on the radio. Jim Reeves is singing 'Distant Drums'. The programme is called Hospital Request. 'And now for little Gary Malan who is in the Durban General Hospital, a special hello and hope you're right as rain soon, Gary, from your Mom and Dad in Newcastle. And they've requested for you any disc by Cliff Richard. So here's 'Living Doll', just for you, Gary. And from me, your Auntie Esmé.'

Thompson walks aimlessly about the house. No servants appear. The old man, who comes for a briefing every morning, stays away. The briefings have become increasingly desultory, yet religiously observed. Usually by this time the immediate vicinity of the house is alive with Thompson's dependants. The tame guinea-fowl cackle hysterically, wanting their dole of crushed maize. They are given to sudden panicky gallops, alternating with periods of quiet foraging, in the dust around the house. He goes to the larder and takes the can of maize outside, calling, 'chick, chick, chick, chick.' The mad creatures rush towards the food. He scatters it around in a semicircle, to give them all room in their frantic greed. Ring-necked turtle doves and sparrows appear, and a yellow weaver bird. Daisy normally does this job, although she regards it as senseless.

He goes into the house and at last picks up the telephone to call his bank. It is a party line. He waits for his neighbours to finish their conversation with the grain merchant in another town. He makes the arrangements. He feels tired, completely drained of energy, of will. He sits down at the kitchen table, and sips the remains of his coffee. The pale brown liquid becomes livid from the blood on his lip. He rests his head on the table and weeps.

Daisy, Daisy, poor Daisy. What will they do to her?

He sleeps, his head on the table.

The old man, now in the full heat of the sun, reaches the farmhouse. The demented guinea-fowl have retired. There is a stillness about the place, broken only by the shrieks of the cicadas. He goes to the kitchen door, presses open the flyscreen. Thompson is lying with his head on the table, inert. The old man waits minutes.

'Master.'

He shakes Thompson's shoulder gently. Thompson wakes, his eyes wild, disoriented.

'Yes?'

He sits up.

'What is it, Ephraim?'

'I got the name of the place, sir.'

'What place? What do you mean?'

'The place for where they send Daisy, sir.'

The old man proffers his notebook. In his careful, childish script he has written an address. The name of the place is unfamiliar to Thompson. It is called Sharpeville.

PART I

CHAPTER 1
1879

Africa. It lay there, basking malevolently in the blue-green waters of the Indian Ocean. Its coasts were rocky and lush, stark and thickly wooded by turns. In the woods, presumably, the kaffirs lurked. If so they had made no impression on the landscape: no fields tilled, no buildings squared, no roads levelled. Occasionally he could see paths meandering up hillsides or along river mouths, the paths of kaffirs pursuing game or game pursuing kaffirs, who knew?

The steamer, the *Arab*, made its way cautiously towards the hills and point of Durban. Now he could see buildings of a reassuringly English sort, solid structures of stone and thatch and galvanised iron clinging to the bluff. The *Arab* made anchor. The new port was not yet ready for large vessels. They waited for the surfboats which they could see skipping to meet them; they leaped across the breakers foaming on the sand bar at the entrance to the harbour.

He went below to his berth to collect his belongings, excited and made nervous by the proximity of Africa. He was about to embrace this Africa.

The previous day, 10 July, had been his birthday. He spent it vomiting helplessly as the steamer butted awkwardly up the coast against the Benguela Current. This current produced, probably because of its tropical provenance, an exotic rhythm in the *Arab*, which even the most experienced sailors found echoed in their gut. The Enos (highly recommended to gentlemen leaving for the colonies) had not helped much. His twentieth birthday was so miserable that he had not unpacked the cake his mother had made five weeks before. He could still feel the insidious motion of the current as he went below to fetch his few belongings up on deck. He had left his chest in Cape Town with a German merchant called Watermeyer. Watermeyer was saving to open Cape Town's first modern department store. The reason he had left it was that an old soldier, who had allowed Frank to buy him a drink, had said all he needed was a good gun, a good saddle and some good boots. This soldier had fought with General Cunningham against Sandeli at the border of the Cape Colony. So Frank Thompson carried his saddle, a light bag and his gun case only. The air was warm and rich now that the boat was at anchor. The bay was busy with naval vessels loading and unloading all around them. After his long voyage around the edges of Africa, always looking to port at the mysterious continent sliding by – the Sahara, the Gold Coast, the Congo River, the hundreds of inlets and deltas, the deserts and jungles that came right to the water's edge – he longed to get ashore finally and see the interior. The interior promised so much.

The surfboats, rowed by crews of Zulus, but skippered by a mulatto, were alongside. The crew of the ship began to unload, using small derricks. There was no apparent pattern for this; insistent passengers went ahead of bags of seed, the mails went ahead of insistent passengers and crates of Martini Henries were thrown on top of coops of chickens, frightening them. A nonconformist parson, dressed like Ruskin in a black frock coat, was knocked down by a net of flour bags swung from one of the derricks. His face was cut on a stanchion, but bravely he declined assistance as he staunched the fierce flow of blood with a surprisingly delicate handkerchief.

'The perils of Africa, my boy, we must bear them with fortitude.'

Thompson wondered if the parson always spoke as epigrammatically; he clambered down the webbing to a waiting surfboat. The Zulus suddenly put to sea, rowing mightily so that their muscular bodies, clad only in little leather aprons, which hung down between their legs, began almost instantly to sweat and glisten. The Zulu were not a seafaring race; they believed, he had read, the sea to be a potential source of medicine whose foam was particularly efficacious, but for all other purposes they regarded the sea simply as an end to the land. They could not swim and they did not fish. And yet here were Zulus rowing a boat, chanting as they pulled on the long oars. This was the beneficial effect of a few short years of contact with the white man. The last few hundred yards, approaching the sand bar, were exciting, the spray breaking over the boat and its passengers as they left the still water of the deep anchorage for the turbulence of the breakers. All up the coast, all the way from Cape Town, these breakers had lined up to fall hopelessly on the beaches. The two other passengers, a Boer and his wife, ducked to avoid the spray. It fell on the sacks of grain, but the Zulus rowed on heedless. They put on a final spurt, catching a wave at the right moment so that the boat crossed the bar with a rush. Instead of heading for the dock they beached the boat and jumped out and began to pull it up the sand. The three white passengers sat tight, unsure of their exact status now, for the last laborious yards of the journey.

Thompson clutched his gun case, worried that salt water might damage his guns.

'Ah, a sporting man,' said the Irish proprietor of the Royal Hotel. 'Do you have any more luggage, sir?'

'Not a great deal, I left my belongings in Cape Town for the most part.'

'If you don't mind my asking, sir, why would you do a thing like that?'

'I was advised that that was the best thing to do.'

'Have you a commission, sir?'

'Frontier Light Horse. Bettington's Horse really.'

'Well, you'll be needing every damned thing under the sun. Now, sir, would you like a room at the back, sharing, or one in the front to yourself?'

'I think I would like one in the front, if that's all right,' said Thompson quickly.

'It's dearer, I'm afraid, sir.'

Two kaffirs stood, silent witnesses to this conversation, waiting to carry the light bag and the saddle wherever they were directed.

'Frontier Light Horse. My, oh my.'

Thompson wondered what he meant, but did not like to ask. The black men carried his things up to his room. He gave them three pence each. From the ecstasy which scudded over their faces for a moment, he deduced that this was excessive. He must learn about these things. He did not want to appear green. The windows of the room were shuttered, presumably to keep out the glare of the afternoon sun. He opened them. The air was heavy with strange scents. Unlike the air of home which sometimes wafted a discreet smell with it – jasmine, baking bread and so on – here the air ferried a rich exotic fragrance of things unknown.

The small town itself was busy. There were stores being drawn by oxen up the road towards the interior; military supplies, farming equipment, stamp batteries for the gold mines, grain, saddlery, tents, field kitchens, corrugated iron, bathtubs, small animals. Trade following the flag. And the town was full of horses; sensible, brown and bay re-mounts all on a suicide mission because of the War Office's ignorance of the African horse sickness. Somewhere to the north lay Zululand. Its proximity threatened no more, since the power of the Zulu nation had been broken in April. It was all over. He had arrived too late, unless the Zulu were massing again secretly, for which he hoped in the privacy of his thoughts.

He watched a team of oxen, mostly lustrous brown but interspersed with speckled animals with curious, feral, upstanding horns, waiting politely by the road while crates were loaded on to the long heavy wagon they were to drag into the interior. There were thirty-six of them, in the charge of a small boy wearing a loin cloth and a cast off bumfreezer. He carried a long whip. As Thompson watched, he squatted in the dirt and peed. The oxen were unmoved.

From the window he could see the green ocean of the interior and the track away from Durban that led there. He was to journey that way himself soon, to plunge himself into that vastness.

Out to sea the over-ripe sun began to set causing the waves to become mysteriously flat. A huge flock of sea-birds, cormorants, passed across the sun's face as its edge touched the sea and began to sink. They were flying fast to some unknown destination. He passed a small market of stalls set beside the new Post Office, where Indians in dhotis were selling tamarinds, cumin and mangoes to their fellow countrymen, dark peasants from a distant continent. They were here to cut cane. Such was the commercial pressure the Empire could exert, to move whole peoples, to create new industries (running along the Bluff to the Point he saw at that moment a little steam train, as if to lend weight to his geopolitical reflections) to fight against the barbarous, and to bring, ineluctably, stability, peace and progress. Other people laid greater stress on the importance of Christianity, but he saw the process as one in which superior techniques and philosophies replaced the inferior with an irresistible logic. In the evening air (for the sun sank alarmingly fast) he felt an elation. The Empire was designed for the likes of him. He bought a mango and enquired how it should be eaten. The Indian cut into it with a small knife. The yellow integument came away in strips.

'Bite, bite,' he said sharply, baring his teeth encouragingly.

'Thank you, my man.'

He bit into the yellow, yielding flesh. The taste itself was aromatic, like the sub-continent from which its vendor had sprung.

He felt pleased with his neat analogy.

A troop of horse, commanded by a sergeant, came by. Each man led two horses; they were a colonial force by the looks of them, their feet thrust forward comfortably, soft hats on their heads, rifles slung over their shoulders alongside cartridge belt. By contrast the sergeant of horse was stiff in the saddle, his back straight, his hands still, his glossy boots geometrically arranged, his face grim and set. His men chatted amiably amongst themselves as they passed. Farmers? Zulu fighters? Thompson walked a little further, out of the town. The heavy evening air was full of the cries of insects, roosting birds and unidentifiable animals. He looked back at Durban and beyond to the deep blackness, pricked by the fires of camps and villages. The scent of woodsmoke was strong and pleasant. Beside the track ahead were some rough huts, and from them came singing; it was low and harmonic, nothing he had ever heard before. He came close enough to see a group of about twenty men crouching around a fire, on which stood a huge black cooking pot, stirred by a girl naked to the waist. The men sang the intricate and repetitive refrain, filled, he imagined romantically, with a longing for Zululand, now lost to them. The girl began to ladle out whatever it was they were to eat.

Thompson hurried back to the Royal Hotel. It was lit by candles and crude lamps, which smoked. Gas lighting had not yet arrived. As a result the hotel seemed, in this light, pleasantly old-fashioned, although the fabric of the building was new. Thompson went to dress as best he could, which was not very well because of the distance between him and Mr Watermeyer in Cape Town. But he was able to change his shirt. In another part of the hotel he heard a gong being bludgeoned to summon them to dinner. He walked down the staircase, young and self-conscious in a strange land.

The dining room, too, was lit by flickering candles. Before he could sit down he was invited to join a party of soldiers, some in uniform. They made a place for him amiably. There were only four courses, but they made up for their fewness by being extremely ample. The Indian waiters brought in a mountain of oysters, chickens and venison. But there were no savouries or cheese or proper puddings. Some of them were young men like him who had come out for adventure and experience, and others were colonists of longer standing, serving with the Buffalo River Volunteers. They had all seen action against the Zulu. The English faces and the colonial were quite different. The colonials were coarser, more solid, with narrower eyes from, he speculated, a lifetime of screwing them up against the sun. The English sported more elaborate and complicated moustaches and beards, where the colonials seemed to be either clean-shaven or to have a simple, untended growth.

Thompson wanted to know about their adventures and the circumstances of the death of the Prince Imperial, Louis Napoleon. The *Arab* had passed the ship bearing the body of the luminous young prince south towards Cape Town. The bows had been decked in black crêpe and the Prince's standard flew at half mast. It was a dreadful sight; if anybody was touched with the charm of immortality it was the Prince, you would have thought. The boat had passed them not two hundred yards away, scything through the water with its awful cargo, disappearing over the rolling sea like an illusion of death itself.

'What has happened to Carey?' Thompson asked.

'Ah, Carey. He is going to be court-martialled because Chelmsford allowed the Prince to gallop all about the place without protection.'

'Now hold hard, Consett,' said another man. 'That's not completely fair. Carey is being court-martialled because of cowardice in the face of the enemy.'

Consett was a farmer, a major in the Buffalo River Volunteers, originally from Lancashire.

'The Prince gave all the orders. The Prince ordered them to mount up. The Prince would not wait for the escort. But now poor Carey must be damned for coming back alive. You know it. The catchfarts around Chelmsford are frightened, and rightly in my view, of being blamed for allowing the Prince to stray into danger. Carey must be pilloried for it.'

'He should have made an attempt to rescue the Prince.'

'How would you rescue a corpse?'

'Did he die bravely?' asked Thompson tactfully.

'He died with seventeen stab wounds in his front. He was a brave boy but a rather foolish one, if you ask me, too filled with notions of La Gloire.'

Consett was a bluff sort of person who would never have been commissioned back at home. Things were very different in the colonies; here everybody spoke his mind. He had a kind of burning anger and resentment directed against the class which had never embraced him in England.

'What is the state of the war?' asked Thompson.

'The war is over. It was never a war. It was Lord Chelmsford's shooting party.'

'What of the Zulu? Will they rise again?'

'Finished. They're finished.'

'They will take the King soon. He's hiding up country somewhere,' said a young man with a scarred face.

'How did that happen if I may ask? Was it a spear?'

'No, it was a cow that wouldn't be milked.'

They laughed. It was good to be included in this comradeship. He drank his sweet Cape wine and thought of the King of the Zulus hiding in a forest, his glorious regiments broken, his family and councillors scattered, his vast, beautiful herds of cattle stolen, his huts burnt, his children indentured and his country squeezed like a sponge; and going now up the coast of Africa towards England, the body of the Prince of France, killed by a handful of Zulus who surprised him drinking coffee by a mealie field.

'I would like to propose a toast,' said Consett.

They raised their glasses.

'To Prince Louis Napoleon, killed by the Coon, Lord Chelmsford's final blow to the Bonapartist party.'

They drank, some happily, some drunkenly and some reluctantly. Thompson was drunk. They talked and talked until the candles died with a little plop. One man slipped on to the floor to be carried to bed.

'To you, sir,' said Consett. 'Welcome to Africa. Welcome to the continent of infinite darkness.'

Thompson thanked him uncertainly.

'Shall we meet tomorrow, sir?'

'It is already tomorrow, my boy.'

Indeed, insistent light was pushing through the shutters and under the door. Thompson went to bed and never saw Consett again.

It was winter but fiercely hot. Nobody had any idea of where he should go or to whom he should report. Pietermaritzburg. Up country. To the Tugela. To Ulundi. Thompson decided on Pietermaritzburg, because that was what his letter of introduction said. He bought a horse, a poor thing, but salted. It appeared to have suffered some deep pathological disturbance in the course of surviving the horse sickness; its ears had become unhinged so that they flopped like a mule's when it walked and its head hung rather low, as if dispirited by its unexpected triumph over disease. It was called Chaka, because it was of a darkish colour, although speckled and pockmarked from the bites of insects. 'Chaka', he was soon to discover, vied with 'Snowball' in popularity as a name for horses; dark for the former and of course light for the latter.

He changed its name to Khelim, because it reminded him of the rug in front of the fire at home: old, lifeless and worn. Khelim (né Chaka) was a salted horse, that was the important thing. It cost £200. The question now was whether Chaka/Khelim possessed the strength to carry him to Pietermarizburg so that he could find the doughty Colonel Redvers Buller and the Frontier Light Horse.

He instructed the livery stable to feed the horse as much good corn as could be found. He ordered the horse to be shod and groomed and the heavy coat to be clipped from its belly and neck, a trace clip. It was newly imported from the Orange River Free State where the weather was extremely cold and it had belonged to a Boer, now dead. The groom, an Indian syce, unaccountably separated from his regiment, got to work on the animal, clipping, pummelling and massaging its insensitive skin. Thompson imagined he saw a look of incredulity on the animal's face as he left it, its brown, whiskery muzzle deep in a feed bucket. The fortunes of war.

When he got back there the hotel was empty, its cool lounge room peopled only by waiters standing silently with their backs to the walls, small round trays at the ready. Thompson wanted to talk more to Consett, but the Buffalo River Volunteers had performed an amoebic re-shuffle and split off in various directions. If Consett were to be believed the whole war was unnecessary. Thompson wanted to tell him, now that his thoughts were clear, that there was a certain inevitability about such things. A great head of steam had been getting up in Europe and America which drove on a magnificent Leviathan, clumsy but unstoppable. At Rorke's Drift this careless beast had merely stepped on a sharp pebble. It was difficult, but essential, to see these things as the spirit of the age.

Consett, in his cups, had offered a glimpse of something else, of a great unknown. He had spoken of Chaka and Dingane and a dark but thrilling world now lost. Consett regretted the loss of the magic and ritual of the Zulu deeply.

'And why are they lost, my boy? They are lost so that the likes of you and me can be free.'

Thompson went up to his room to write home.

> *Dear Papa and Mama,*
> *I have arrived safely in Durban which is a small but busy port, showing every sign of the advent of progress. I came up from Cape Town on the* Arab *and passed the body of the Prince Imperial being borne South and eventually to England. There is much controversy here over the blame for this terrible event, as no doubt there will be in England. From men I have met who were there, it seems the Prince Imperial took orders from no one and subjected himself to risk gladly. Captain Carey is now to take the blame.*
>
> *Tomorrow I proceed up country on my splendid new horse, who would not be passed fit to pull the baker's van in Northleach. But he is a salted horse, which means that he has survived the mysterious African horse sickness and thereby achieved immunity and a vast increase in his price.*
>
> *Could you consequently forward to me some money as the war seems to have made things here very dear. The Zulu King is to be captured soon and I am proceeding to Ld. Chelmsford's headquarters in the hopes that I may go along on that expedition. I think there will be many opportunities here after the war.*
>
> *I am very well and hope that you are all the same.*
> *Your affectionate son Frank.*

He felt a small shaft of sadness as he sealed the letter. His brother and sister would be home. His mother would be spending long hours in her beloved garden. Over the whole village at this time of year hung a mid-summer torpor, broken only by the terrible noise of the new McCormick reaper. His father would be wheeled out into the sun in the hopes that the warmth would somehow thaw the paralysis that gripped him – now in its twelfth year. He had left home partly to carry on for his father who had been struck down in his prime.

Outside his window, thousands of miles away from Gloucestershire, a detachment of naval gunners passed by, grouped reverently around two seven-pounders on gun carriages. Perhaps the noise of the cannon would frighten the Zulu; there was surely no other use for them now.

He slept, with the wooden shutters closed for coolness. As the afternoon drew on he went back to the stable to see his newly refurbished horse. Khelim had a surprisingly jaunty look, his belly and neck much lighter in colour and his mane and tail properly neat and sparse. Sadly his temperament had not changed. As they plodded down the beach, the sea pounding savagely on the sand made him merely mildly suspicious. In the scrub on the dunes were monkeys with little black faces and sometimes little black faces of children, but these disappeared even faster than the monkeys at the sight of man and horse. The sands seemed to stretch forever. He managed to coax the horse into a trot. It would take nearly two days of hard riding to get to Pietermaritzburg. He returned the horse to the stable where the syce led it away and began immediately to groom it again before it had finished the first deep draught of water. Out to sea the sun was setting as full and lurid as yesterday. Nature had acted here in Africa with great profligacy.

He passed a tavern on his way back and saw two very young mulatto girls go in the door. He wanted to follow to see what went on in there. He could hear a piano seeping out into the evening air, playing a tune that had been popular in England some years before. He paused uncertainly before striding on. He was lonely but there was a certain satisfaction in it. Tomorrow the interior.

CHAPTER 2

It was surprisingly misty and cold in the hills. The horse shivered in its new tropical coiffeur.

Also it seemed to be mostly uphill to Pietermaritzburg, the staging post for the Zulu War. In the hotel at Pinetown, where Thompson stopped for tea, a few officers on their way back from Pietermaritzburg told him that Buller's Horse had long since left for the Umfolozi River. He would have to hurry to Maritzburg to get his orders to head for the Tugela River and the new pontoon bridge at Middle Drift where the massive army was crossing into Zululand. The sun was breaking determinedly through the mist, which still lay over the low ground. The horse plodded onwards, its ears flopping forwards and backwards alternately, an African Rosinante.

Ahead of them stretched rolling hills; there were hundreds of them undulating gently all the way to the interior. The whole of Africa lay beyond, vast, unknown and unknowable. Into this wilderness a stream of traffic flowed to feed the imperial engine. All wars could be measured most accurately in their tributaries and backwaters; there were no wounded being ferried back to Durban, only colonial irregulars leaving the front now that the danger was over. But in the other direction a tide was flowing, unbidden, unstoppable, to flood Zululand.

The higher into the hills they rose, the more brown and dry the country became. There were great splashes of colour from bare trees with red flowers, but the tropical lushness of the coast gave way quickly to the aridity of the interior. Distant hills were choked with the smoke of grass fires. A kraal of rounded beehive huts clustered together came into view clinging to a hillside almost directly below the road. It was quiet apart from a few dogs scuffling about and two children playing in the dust. He longed to see some real Zulu in their full regalia. The Natal kaffirs, so far as he could see, were a beaten lot. He was impatient to get to Zululand. He dug his heels into Khelim. The horse ignored the suggestion that it hurry, but nonetheless they made steady progress. By nightfall they had covered thirty miles.

Thompson was able to find some mealies for the horse at a store. These mealies loomed very large in the lives of the Natalians. Kaffirs ate them in a stiff unpleasant porridge, horses ate them cracked, chickens fed on them crushed and the Dutch farmers planted acres of them; at Rorke's Drift the South Wales Borderers had sheltered behind sacks of them. The Zulu had been foiled by their own staple. These mealies had, in short, achieved a central role in the mythology of South Africa.

They reached Pietermaritzburg the following morning, late. The town had a settled look with pleasant houses surrounded by wide verandahs. The civic buildings were strong and assertive, suggesting a commendable confidence in the future. The streets of the little town were dusty and rutted with the passage of oxen and soldiers. He was fortunate to find a hotel room and a stall for Khelim before going in search of Lord Chelmsford's staff. A Cape Boy in a cart took him at a brisk trot around to the headquarters. The place was largely deserted, the theatre of war having moved far north. The new commander-in-chief had bypassed Maritzburg altogether. It was reported that Sir Garnet Wolseley was so eager to see action that he had landed up the coast from Durban and headed straight for the Ulundi, which he had re-occupied long after Chelmsford had burnt it. A young captain said that he should head up there immediately.

'Were you at the battle?' asked Thompson.

'I was. It lasted for one hour and ten minutes and was conducted for the sole purpose of vindicating Lord Chelmsford. Gatling guns against naked men.'

Disaffection with Chelmsford seemed to be epidemic. There was a new order of course. Chelmsford belonged to the old, just as certainly as Cetewayo. Nothing could ever be the same again; witness the tumult in the streets outside the headquarters. Was it always this way, or was this, as he suspected, the start of an entirely new era?

'Do you want to draw a uniform?' asked the captain.

'Yes, sir.'

'Well, go down to the stores with this chitty.' He wrote on a piece of paper and handed it to Thompson.

'You'll be wanting a pistol and a sword too, I shouldn't wonder.'

'I think so, sir.'

The captain wrote another line with no show of interest.

Thompson went off to draw his uniform. It was a good fit, particularly as it had not been made for him. It was a sort of hussar's outfit which had undergone some colonial metamorphosis, giving it a rakish, irregular look.

'Bettington's Horse, sir,' said the Indian tailor who was pinning the jacket.

'Buller's Horse?' he asked the tailor apprehensively.

'All the same, sir, all the same.'

His sword and pistol completed the outfit. He was glad to see his name in a ledger when his pistol was signed out. He had begun to feel that no one knew about him. Certainly no one cared.

'Have you a horse?' asked the staff officer.

'Yes, sir.'

'Salted?'

'Yes, sir.'

'Capital. Take this good-for with you to Ulundi and some desk wallah like meself will pay for the waler.'

'Right you are, sir.'

He was handed another piece of paper with instructions to persons unknown to reimburse him for his expenditure on a horse.

'You'll get your insignia there, too. You know about horses, eh? The Boers say you shouldn't let them graze the veldt in the early morning. And of course it's tsetse fly country up at Ulundi. But if you've a salted animal it'll live through worse.'

What could be worse for a horse than two fatal equine diseases?

'Buller's got the VC, you know. And Wood. Wood's now Major General.'

'I had heard, sir.'

The papers at home spoke of nothing else, although the news had been a long time arriving. The man wanted to talk. He was going home soon.

Thompson left as soon as he decently could. He would set out with a Naval Brigade in the morning, standing to at four. He studied a map in the hallway; Ulundi was a long way off. It would take days to get there if he were tied to the Naval Brigade with their heavy guns. He wandered around the town in his new uniform. Men saluted him and he returned the salute with as much nonchalance as he could. Yet even as he walked, the breeches stretched tautly across his buttocks, he felt uneasy, like an actor in a play which is not fully rehearsed.

At the Post Office, a handsome new building, he sent a letter to his mother, urging her to send him the money he needed. She would do it.

'*Mother, I am in Pietermaritzburg, some fifty miles into the Interior. Today I draw my uniform and receive my orders. There are a great many opportunities opening to me I feel, but my expenses are high. Could you help me out yet again? You know I shall repay you one day. It is remarkable to see the men and material gathered in this little town. It signifies to me the irresistible march of progress. To you I dare say the tragic element, the collapse of the Zulu Kingdom, would be uppermost. But I console myself by thinking that it is inevitable, the spirit of the age manifesting itself. Nonetheless I am longing to see a true Zulu and I am hoping to get to Ulundi before next week is out. How is Father? I think of you all often. Kiss the girls for me. The farmer in Burford is NOT suitable.*'

The town smelt of horse dung and woodsmoke. It was powdered with dust; dust even rose into the air and coloured the sunset.

They stood to at four in the morning. It was bitterly cold and Thompson was obliged to wrap himself in a very unmilitary coat, so that his new uniform was lost from sight. He had to stand for an hour while every last man in the Brigade and his Martini Henry was inspected. Finally they were away with a great stamping of boots, the jingle of harness, the snorts of horses, the groaning and squeaking of the gun carriages on which the beautiful seven-pounders were mounted, and the shouts of the horse masters. Within minutes the guns, the men and the horses were finely dusted with the reddish soil of the road. In addition to its guns the Brigade had thirty teams of oxen pulling wagons fitted with field kitchens, a hospital, the equipment for the officers' mess, ammunition, buckets, tin baths and tents. The convoy stretched back at least a mile, the oxen plodding so slowly and leadenly that every stride of the horses put them further and further ahead. Even the sailors in their Gilbert and Sullivan left the oxen behind. Thompson found himself with a group of three colonial guides, one the son of a Norwegian missionary, one a local farmer and the third a half-caste son of John Dunn, the white chief of Zululand. Joseph Dunn was a man of about twenty-five. He spoke contemptuously of the kaffir, already prey to doubts and fears about his position in the burgeoning white man's world. He told Thompson that the new commander-in-chief was going to make his father the most powerful prince in Zululand after it was all over. Physically, Thompson thought, the Zulu and white blood had not mixed well in this man. There seemed to be a lack of resolution about his face, so that he had become aboriginal in appearance. He told Thompson about his hunting exploits.

'Lions. Plenty lions.'

'Do they charge?'

'Yes, sir. But my father taught me to shoot. He is the best shot in Natal.'

'Can I meet him? I should like to.'

'Maybe. He's very busy now because we had to leave our land before. I must go to help him.'

'May I come with you?'

'You can, sir. I am leaving this people at Middle Drift. My father wants to talk to me, and then I must go to Ulundi with the Scouts.'

'Which scouts are those?'

'Dunn's Scouts, sir.'

'Have you seen Cetewayo, Mr Dunn?'

'Yes, sir. Too many times.'

'What is he going to do now?'

'He can't do nothing now, sir, he's hiding. He is too fat to run. Mr Oftebro' – he pointed towards the Norwegian – 'knows him well. He must speak to him to tell him what to do when they catch him.'

'Do you know the place where the king is hiding?'

'Too far, too far. Ngami. Bad place, but plenty elephants. I have shot too many elephants.'

He used the African phrase, 'too many' to mean a great many. Dunn approved of his horse. He said that the walers were no good here. His father had tried to explain this to Chelmsford's staff, but they were not listening. Dunn senior, it seemed, had suffered many frustrations in his attempt to serve the Crown.

They rode slowly up country for two days. Thompson and Dunn made little excursions to see things of interest and to bag a few francolin or guinea-fowl. He also talked to Oftebro who knew a good deal about the history and customs of the Zulu. Dunn taught him to shoot from the saddle with the reins loosely knotted on the horse's neck. Khelim took this with equanimity, no doubt a product of his service in the Orange River Free State, mentioned by the vendor. As their caravan approached the Tugela, Thompson became fully aware that they were merely a part of a gigantic force. Behind them, over a hill and out of sight, stretched the Naval Brigade, but ahead of them, waiting their turn on the ferry, were thousands upon thousands of oxen and horses, covering the hills and valleys. Strings of wagons and huge piles of equipment and weapons waited, too. It provoked the melancholy Oftebro.

'Look at this. For one old man hiding in a forest. I must hurry. God forgive me, I must hurry.'

The magnitude of the invasion of Zululand – the engineers, the traders, the officials, the carpetbaggers, the transport riders, the journalists, the tons of tinned beef, the sheets of iron, the gleaming guns and the bustling confusion – was in sharp contrast to the impermanence of what the Zulu had created: huts woven of reeds, a little unconvincing tilling of the earth, stockades of thorn trees to corral the cattle at night and a few pits to trap wild animals or store grain. The Zulu left little behind them when they moved on. The white man felt impelled to impose some order and solidity and above all meaning on this vast continent of impermanence. It could not be allowed simply to drift on in its haphazard ignorance. Their King possessed nothing but herds of cattle and scores of wives and a few sacred pots and embrocations. And even these had gone, swept away by the war like twigs in a flood.

'What are you going to do with them now?' asked Oftebro.

'How's that?'

'What do you give them now, your Zulus?'

It was, in truth, the great imponderable. But Thompson was not perturbed. At that time it was clear to him: they must be shown the way. Oftebro had little faith, either religious or material. He seemed, tall and fair as he was, to have been unable to shake off the Nordic melancholy, the melancholy of dark forests and long nights. Or so Thompson fancied as they stood waiting for the pontoon. Thompson tried to tell Oftebro about the great Tay Bridge which carried whole trains twenty times further than this, as an antidote to his despondency, but Oftebro was unimpressed.

His father had been a friend of the King. He had eventually given up trying to evangelise the Zulu. Instead he had tried, with only some small and temporary success, to convince the Zulu that arbitrary killing was wrong. Unfortunately, the King and his councillors, so young Oftebro said, had pointed out that killing for witchcraft and evil thoughts, far from being arbitrary, was a far better way than that adapted by the great white queen, who, they had heard tell, put all the miscreants in her territory together in one prison where they could compare notes and perfect techniques. What could be more illogical than that? Oftebro Senior had been torn between the desire to explain that he was a Norwegian (and therefore no part of the great Queen of England's unenlightened penal policy) and his Christian duty to explain the beneficent effects of the exercise of love. The King could not understand how a person who aided his subjects' enemies could be said to love them. He, Cetewayo, loved his subjects; consequently he put to death their enemies. Having neatly rounded off this argument to the delight of his council and the discomfort of the missionary, Cetewayo went off to inspect a young girl brought for his approval. Oftebro decided, philosophically, that the time was not right to broach another subject on his agenda, the evil of polygamy.

Young Oftebro had evidently acquired a certain pessimism about the perfectability of human nature from his father. Thompson explained to Oftebro the logic of materialism, the irresistible logic, which was, from its birthplace in England, sweeping the whole world dressed in many fancy guises. Thompson explained candidly that the noble service of the Empire was in fact not so much the service of an ideal as of a logical imperative. Oftebro's thoughts were elsewhere. He turned away from this eager, rather angular young officer, the two of them isolated for a moment in the midst of a seething landscape. To Thompson this creaking, groaning and bellowing landscape was his argument made manifest.

Suddenly Oftebro recited:

'To watch the corn grow and the blossoms set; to draw hard breath over ploughshare or spade; to read, to think, to love, to hope, to pray ... the world's prosperity or adversity depends upon our knowing and teaching these few things; but upon iron, or glass, or electricity or steam in no wise.'

'That's your own Ruskin,' said Oftebro, evidently as a riposte to Thompson's tales of engineering marvels. He was to remember the conversation with Oftebro at Christmas when news arrived that the Tay Bridge had fallen down with the biggest splash Scotland had ever experienced, taking with it a train.

Dunn's encampment on his old hunting ground of Emogeni was acting as a vortex, drawing in his retainers, his children, his rivals and his new colleagues, the British. Zulu chiefs waited patiently for him in the shade of giant blue gums planted many years before by Dunn. Innumerable children, many of them half-caste, played in the dusty compound at the back of the ruins of Dunn's house. John Dunn himself, the centre of this attention, sat at a table in the middle of a bare, swept piece of earth. His features, familiar to Thompson from the papers, were meaner and more pinched in real life, with rather disturbing blue eyes. Eyes that had seen too much bloodshed. On either side of him, sitting in the dust, were two of his sons, dressed in city clothes, with brown bowler hats. Lines of petitioners and supplicants waited quietly to be summoned. Dunn called Thompson and his son Joseph over. His disappointment on finding that Thompson was simply a young officer was quickly hidden.

'Make Mr Thompson comfortable, Joseph. In the tents. Lovely view there. We dine at seven.'

The view from Thompson's tent was indeed superb, down to a watercourse lined with trees, some of them huge and ancient and others with sleek yellow trunks like the skin of a reptile. Thompson sat on a camp chair while a servant brought hot water. Some small deer skittered beyond the watercourse and were gone. He washed himself and shaved and then lay on his bed for a few minutes. He dozed and dreamed of Cetewayo huddling in a thicket somewhere in the North. When he woke it was cold. The valley below was shrouded in a mist which had blown up from nowhere. He felt for a moment anxious and alone.

John Dunn was full of confidence. He dressed for dinner in a mess kit of his own design which combined elements of the ambassadorial with the military. His thin face glowed with the excitement of the times and his own importance. He had become famous in England and was the friend of lords and generals. He told them what Wolseley had said and what he had replied; he told them of the vast amounts of money he had been obliged to disburse to supply his Scouts, and he told them of his importance to the war effort. There was an inky blackness beyond the charmed circle of the hurricane lamps, in which Dunn, Thompson and a few officials dined, watched in silence from below the salt by four of Dunn's sons. The Zulu – all bar the servants – seemed to have vanished into the night, afraid perhaps of the spirits. Dunn himself, so his every anecdote made plain, was afraid of nothing. Here at his table, set in the wilderness with fine wines, brandy, cigars and solid silver, he was a potentate. Somewhere in the dark lurked his twenty wives and scores of children. If he saw anything ironical in playing the part of English gentleman, two imported greyhounds twitching nervously at his feet, he showed no sign of it. He was about to claim his kingdom. He now identified Zululand's interest with his own; Wolseley was about to make him the most powerful chief in Zululand; this would be good for the Empire. Dunn spoke of the great battle he had witnessed on the Tugela twenty years before, when Cetewayo had slaughtered twenty thousand men, women and children of a rival clan, including the only son of Dingane. Dunn had developed a rhetorical style which called only for the occasional tribute from the audience; in this he had aped the Zulu princes he was usurping.

'The Zulu King is surrounded by praise singers, called isibongi. Whenever the King moves or appears in public they chant his praises. What do you think of that, sir?'

'Most interesting, Mr Dunn. Most fascinating,' said Thompson, slipping easily into his new role of praise singer.

'The Zulu people are a fascinating people, sir. I have been fortunate to achieve some degree of intimacy with their ways and customs.'

And their women, thought Thompson. In Zulu fashion, women and cattle had been Dunn's interests. Both were valued for their usefulness and, metaphysically, for their beauty and their evident connection with life itself. A man like Dunn will soon be an embarrassing anachronism. How cynical of the authorities to cultivate him now. His son Joseph had begun to sense the way things were going. A more orderly, more logical world was in tow, which made few allowances. Dunn – Thompson now included him with Cetewayo and Chelmsford – belonged to a past era. Dunn saw himself as a decisive factor in the future of Zululand and Natal. He talked of his persuasive powers; his understanding of Zulu custom and law; his influence at Whitehall and so on. But what, in truth, could his future be? And what of those children? What future for them in a new world of iron, glass, electricity and steam?

But the great man exerted a powerful charm on Thompson. Truly he had had an epic life: death, battle, hunting, conquest, acquisition and gratification of the senses. God knows how many men he had killed. Certainly his Scouts had acquired a frightening reputation. Dunn's power in Zululand rested, however, on his familiarity with the white man's world. He had acquired power by using this knowledge with the Zulu, promising to protect and supply them but in the end helping to destroy them. Every day was a feast day at Dunn's Camp. Huge portions of meat were served; it was a Zulu prince's right. But Thompson perceived the irony; in destroying the Zulu, Dunn had destroyed himself. Nothing now could resist the tramp of the iron-shod boots which Thompson could hear as a refrain in the African night above the whoops and cackles of the hyena.

Dunn suddenly stood, proposed a toast to the Queen and excused himself. With Dunn gone the party soon broke up. Thompson went to his tent and smoked a pipe. Dunn saw himself as the next Zulu King. That was why he was so keen to see Cetewayo captured. To supplant a Zulu tyrant with a white king was absurd, yet Dunn's whole life had been preposterous.

It was a cold night. He had never expected Africa to be cold. His tent was comfortable with fresh linen sheets and a writing table supplied with paper and ink. The flicker of the lamp played on the canvas. He had quickly grown to like living under canvas. It was secure and intimate, yet impermanent and nomadic. It was strange that human beings could set such store by home and hearth in one country and none at all in another. From what he had seen of Africans – admittedly not much – it seemed that they had little use for buildings and artefacts. Cattle were more important; cattle supplied the link with a time past and an anchor in the present.

He undressed and climbed into bed. When he doused the light the enclosed world of the tent suddenly vanished. It became part now of the outdoors, with glimpses of lights, stars and the moonshadow of trees. As he dozed he heard a voice.

'Sir, sir.'

'Yes, who is it?'

He lit the lamp again to find a young mulatto girl standing in the entrance.

'Can I come in, sir?'

'Yes. Yes, I suppose so. What do you want?'

It was a foolish question.

'Mr Dunn sent me.'

'Oh I see. Well, sit down.'

She sat on the bed beside him.

'Have you got any brandy, sir?'

'Yes. Wait a moment. Yes, I have.'

He fumbled nervously for his flask. Her mouth was large with bruised brown lips. She was young, much younger than he. His experience in these matters was very limited. She drank deeply and smiled at him, a half cocked sensuous smile that put him at his ease.

'You like jig-a-jig?'

'Yes.'

She took her clothes off. Her body was much thinner than he had ever seen on a woman before, but there was a lushness about her all the same. He slipped his nightshirt over his head and she was on him, her brandy lips foraging over him and drawing his tongue into her mouth. She laughed as she straddled him because his feet were still on the floor of the tent. He wanted to get on top of her, he wanted to force her down, do all manner of unspeakable things to her, yet he simply gave in to the insistent rhythm of her hips grinding down and around on him. She began to whimper and laugh. He came in minutes and lay back, drained.

'You like that? White girls not so good?'

It was a comparison he could not really make with much authority.

'No, no.'

She took another deep swig of his brandy.

'What's your name?' he asked, conscious that it was late for an introduction.

'Catherine.'

'Catherine?'

'Catherine Dunn, sir.'

Her face was rather thin, with high cheekbones and pinched-in cheeks, a legacy from her father. She seemed to be drunk now. Her hard hands were urging him on. This time she lay back and he kissed her depraved child's face. She helped him in deftly and hooked her legs behind his calves, urging him on.

'Catherine, Catherine.'

'Good?'

'Oh yes.'

'Go. Go.'

'Catherine.'

'Yes?'

'Why did you come here?'

'I want nice baby like you.'

'What?'

'Nice baby. Like you. Nice baby. Go, go.'

He could not seem to help himself. She seemed to have him in a gentle but insistent vice.

CHAPTER 3

He travelled up to Ulundi with John Dunn. Dunn rode in a Cape cart driven by a liveried Cape Boy, who might well have been one of his many sons. This cart was a curious thing with large sprung wheels which provided a reasonably smooth ride over the rutted track. The countryside, if you did not look too closely at the trees, was like an English park, open with artfully placed copses and hillocks. The trees, however, were armed with long spikes in ivory white, and the grassland, as the sun rose, proved to be dry and brown. The early light played tricks upon the eye. There were broken-down kraals and the remains of cattle byres, but the Zulu themselves were not in evidence. All this was to be Dunn's territory. He and Dunn conducted a patchy conversation. Dunn would wave imperiously and he would trot over to the Cape cart to be given a brief homily on Zulu life and custom and the part Dunn had played in the last twenty years.

They reached Ulundi just before sunset. The reason for surrounding the town and bivouacking there could only have been symbolic, because the remains of the King's kraal, hundreds of huts around the royal cattle enclosure, were now no more than ashes and charred sticks. A Zulu city could be sacked and returned to the earth in a few weeks; it was made of mud, thorn bushes, reeds and branches. Only the square walls of the King's house itself still stood, closest to and directly behind the cattle byre. Dunn said that the King had favoured squared off walls as evidence of modernism and imported builders for this purpose. As they rode in, a cold wind blew and stirred the ashes.

'When a Zulu King dies, his senior wife burns the kraal and the people move on,' said Dunn.

Perhaps Chelmsford had burned the place as an intimation of mortality.

The plain around the incinerated remains of Cetewayo's city was teeming with the Army and its lately supplemented strength. Now that the King was reduced (so the spies and scouts consistently reported) to a few close retainers and wives with no armed men at all, the War Office had finally delivered the full complement of field guns, kitchens, boots, remounts, hospitals and helioscopes; the management of all this materiel was naturally keeping a large number of men busy. At the top of this pile was Sir Garnet Wolseley, the very model of a modern Major-General. As Thompson sought his place in this anthill, Wolseley rode up to meet Dunn. He stopped and talked to some men, he cocked his spry head thoughtfully, he patted the neck of his impatient horse, a horse buffed to a high gloss by his three Indian syces (souvenirs of a previous campaign); it was not so much a horse as a beacon. Poor Khelim might have come from another sub-species of animal altogether, an aardvark or a tapir perhaps. Indeed as Wolseley greeted Dunn, and Thompson straightened in his saddle, Khelim snatched the reins from his hands and grabbed at a piece of wiry grass, his stumpy yellow teeth tearing the unpalatable stuff eagerly. The Commander-in-Chief's aides winced at this homespun sight.

Dunn and Wolseley processed towards the Commander-in-Chief's headquarters, leaving Thompson to make his own way. Eventually he found a member of Buller's staff who told him where to leave his horse. Buller himself was living in a huge tent sited on a small hill – a kopje – with a view down to the plain of Ulundi. Thompson was more or less given a choice of action; the irregulars were very free of constraints and appeared to be regarded by regulars with contempt. Many of them had set off for the Umfolozi where the King was hiding. The Dragoons were expected to find him and bring him back to signal the end of the war. From Ulundi he was to be sent to the Cape for exile. If there was any resistance it was to be dealt with severely. Bets had been struck. Young subalterns were racing about excitedly with the latest rumours. Wolseley and Dunn were busying themselves with administrative matters; the turkey was being carved. One of Buller's staff invited Thompson to dinner; the chief liked to meet new arrivals.

There were Zulu to be seen but most of them seemed to have adopted a servile mien which disappointed Thompson. These were, he said to himself, merely the camp followers and deserters. He had, alas, come too late to see the massed regiments charge, their feet and the anklets they wore said to make a noise like the crash of breakers on a beach, but he hoped that he might still see the real

Zulu in all his pride, arrogance and magnificence.

He met Oftebro, wandering around the encampment disconsolately, the long frock coat he wore over his uniform giving him the appearance of an itinerant schoolmaster. Oftebro asked him if he would accompany him towards the Black Umfolozi in the morning. They were closing in on Cetewayo and needed him to interpret. The prospect clearly depressed his spirits. Thompson walked briskly through the press of men and animals to Buller's headquarters to ask permission. He found an aristocratic young captain, who seemed to find the question rather boring.

'By all means. Find Greville when you get there. He'll probably give you something to do.'

Buller could be seen sitting at a table, just inside his tent, writing. He was a reassuringly yeoman figure. There he sat, his uniform immaculate, his staff attentive, his servants hovering, writing a letter to his beloved wife perhaps, or the orders for the following day. He was, thought Thompson, the best sort of Englishman.

Oftebro was in a state of despair. He had been asked to join a pack of young adventurers, aristocrats, who seemed to think they were fox hunting. Oftebro was dreading his encounter with the King and the reproaches he feared he would have to endure.

'It must be done,' said Thompson cheerfully.

'But must it be done by an English lord who thinks he's catching a fox?'

Oftebro was not familiar with the idiom of the chase, obviously.

'My father was Cetewayo's friend,' he said sadly.

'Come, it's not so bad. Think of it this way: you are the person most likely to help this affair along to a happy conclusion.'

Oftebro had an uncomfortable penchant for debate of a high, abstracted kind:

'The commonly held view that we are wiser, more humane, and more advanced than in the past is a falsehood. If we were, we would be happier, and yet we freely acknowledge that we are no happier. What should the product of advancement be if not happiness? Please answer me that when you talk of happy conclusions.'

For a young man about to have dinner at the table of a living hero, Colonel Redvers Buller VC, it was not the occasion for an ethical debate. Had he had the inclination he would have pointed out to his mournful Scandinavian friend that it was a romantic point of view, to assume that the past was a happier time. Instead he simply arranged to meet Oftebro at first light.

The dinner was magnificent in its setting. The table had been laid outside the mess tent with a view down to the plain, a plain pricked by a thousand camp fires. Buller sat in the middle with his more senior officers. Thompson sat right on the end, facing Buller and his cronies. It was a cool evening, but Buller preferred to eat out of doors – he believed it helped the digestion – so his boys preferred it, too. For a man who inspired so much devotion, he said little that was inspirational. He spoke only of the most mundane matters. It seemed that he was not a very imaginative man. His faculties were fully engaged by military and logistic problems, leaving him no time for frivolities. He made no mention of the King and his predicament, nor had he any views on the future of Zululand. And yet Thompson could see in him the qualities of a leader. He was, for a start, a very solid man physically, a man whose very substance suggested the foolishness of the Zulu in flinging themselves against the might of the British Empire. His flesh was ample and solid, his moustache and beard luxuriant, his face, with its long, broad nose, as benign as some prodigious farm animal. His every utterance, no matter how banal, was clothed in authority and certainty. He appeared to be a man untroubled by doubt.

Down at the end of the table where Thompson sat, there was a great deal of talk of Cetewayo. The subject of Carey and the Prince Imperial was taboo, however. Buller's view was well known: Carey was a disgrace to the British Army. He should have rescued the Prince (or even the Prince's body) regardless of the danger. Buller himself was heading back home and expecting a civic reception in Plymouth.

The menservants, crisp in white, kept up a steady flow of dishes: wild duck, guinea-fowl, boiled beef, roast lamb, savouries and cheeses. Colonel Buller refused nothing. Stolidly he ate his way through them all.

The talk turned from Cetewayo to gold. One or two of the less well set up officers were planning to look at the prospects when this little war was over. As they lingered over the port it felt to Thompson as though he was sitting on Mount Olympus. From below came the perfume of smouldering cow-dung from the innumerable camp fires; the alien sound of a bagpipe floated on the air. Further away, on the fringes of the great encampment, they could hear Zulu singing. It was low and fearful.

Buller was fond of singing. One of his staff stood up and sang old music hall airs of the sentimental sort in a thin but true tenor. For half an hour they sat and listened, barely able to hold back the tears. Thompson felt unworthily swollen with patriotism and the sadness of youth.

Buller rose, toasted the Queen and thanked his men. They stood as still as waxworks as their ample chief retired to his tent. With the living hero washing himself, or saying his prayers, the officers dispersed quickly into the vast African night, dusted with stars of impossible brightness.

Thompson walked down to the horse lines where he found Khelim happily eating from a bucket in the company of his betters. He walked on towards the ashes of the great cattle byre and the still-standing walls of the King's house. He stood in the middle; only three walls and a few charred roofpoles remained. Someone had defecated in a corner. It seemed to be a small room for a king, particularly a large man like Cetewayo.

The hunting party, sent out by the First King's Dragoons, had a decidedly sporting aspect, as the melancholy Oftebro had predicted. Lord Gifford and Major Marter spent a lot of time galloping about the countryside on the scent. The King was reported to be hiding in a kraal belonging to a chief called Mnyamana, but when Gifford and his men galloped in it was found he had left. After some quiet persuasion, Oftebro was able to discover that the King had gone to ground in a heavily wooded and remote area known as Ngone. They galloped on and reached a mountain top where their reluctant guide urged caution. Major Marter and Oftebro crawled to the edge of a precipice and lay on their stomachs. Thompson was ordered to stay well out of sight with the horses and the Native Contingent, but he crept ever closer until he could see far below them a kraal surrounded by dense bush and huge boulders. Marter and a small detachment of Dragoons led their horses carefully down a ravine, while the Native Contingent fanned out on the way down. It took three hours and two horses were killed, tumbling off ledges of rock, but the kraal was captured without a shot being fired. Finally, Oftebro and Marter were led to the hut where the King lay.

'Ask him to come out and surrender,' said Marter.

Oftebro called out to the King. There was a muffled reply.
'What does he say?'
'The King wants to know your rank, sir.'
'Tell him, man.'
There was a pause.
'What does he say now?' asked Marter impatiently.
'He says he is ready, sir. He would like you to go in and shoot him.'
'Don't be absurd. Tell him we are coming in. He is not going to be shot.

Oftebro explained and the two men stooped low to enter the cool, dark hut, which had the sour smell of beer.

There was some confusion about the arrangements. A massive horse was brought forward to carry Cetewayo into captivity. He preferred to walk. Thompson and the rest of the detachment had scrambled down the mountain now.

Cetewayo was a stout man. His thighs were chafed from rubbing together with the unaccustomed walking and running. Behind him followed his ragbag collection of retainers. He had possessed absolute power and they clung to him, reluctant to let go even in the face of the overwhelming and alien force. The King did not appear afraid; on the contrary, he appeared to be interested to find out what would happen to him next. Lord Gifford was despatched (as always at a good gallop) to Ulundi to tell Wolseley that they were bringing in Cetewayo. Cetewayo was explaining to Oftebro that he had not wished for the battle of Ulundi. He had known it was hopeless to oppose the great Queen, but many of his indunas would not listen. Thompson watched Cetewayo and Oftebro, with Marter standing awkwardly at one side, from outside the ring of Dragoons with fixed bayonets. The King wore his headring and carried a slender stick. He had watched the battle from afar; he knew what would happen when the regiments flung themselves against the wall of steel and the thunderburst of lead. He wanted the Queen in England to know that he had never wished for this war; it had been forced upon him.

Although it was nearly sunset they set off, the King and his pathetic little band surrounded by armed men. The King was a massive, dignified figure, his face broad and open, with dark, amused eyes.

Oftebro said that the King had reproached him bitterly, asking him if this was any way for the son of a friend to behave towards him. Oftebro had tried to justify himself, but without success.

It grew dark but they rode on. Oftebro could not bear to ride with the King and sought Thompson out.

'John Dunn was his friend. He took Dunn in. My father was his friend, and look at him.'

He could only be seen in silhouette now, walking slowly, painfully, at the head of his little band.

'Don't take it too hard,' said Thompson. 'It was inevitable.'

'Frank, Frank, I hope God forgives us both.'

The sky, surprisingly, took on a pale gold tint, some minutes after the sun had gone down, but it did not last. Soon it was completely dark, but still they pressed on.

'What are you going to do now?' asked Oftebro.

'I am not sure, but I think I shall stay on in South Africa.'

'And I shall leave. I have never been to Norway. I am not sure if I could tolerate the cold.'

Oftebro, who had volunteered for the Army, could not ride with or speak to his fellows. He found Thompson, perhaps because of his youth, more congenial company. He seemed to need to explain himself and justify his actions to Thompson. Finally Marter gave the order to make camp in an abandoned kraal. Cetewayo and his retinue were housed in the huts; the rest of them surrounded the kraal and posted guards. Three of Cetewayo's followers tried to escape and two were shot, although it was not clear why they should have been regarded as captives at all.

'Why did they do that?' Oftebro was in tears, but Thompson guessed they were tears of guilt rather than sadness.

'I don't know. I can't say. I don't understand the military mind. They were given orders, which you translated I presume, and they tried to run away. As far as the military are concerned that sort of thing cannot be permitted.

'They did not understand the orders.'

'Is that not your fault?'

'It may be. I tried to explain that they would be killed if they ran away, but they became frightened.'

'Did you not try to reassure them?'

'I did. But by speaking of death to them it was as if we were threatening them with it.'

'So they ran?'

'Yes, perhaps. You don't understand magic. Magic is very

powerful. The King has obviously lost his command of it. His sangomas have gone. I am obliged to talk of death in his presence, which is quite unheard of, and so his people draw but one conclusion. More powerful magic is threatening them. They run and their forebodings are proved correct.'

'Yet the King does not seem afraid.'

'He is an exceptional man. He has had a prophetic belief that the white man should not be tampered with. In a fashion he understands us well. He is eager to learn more. That is why I believe he is pleased to come with us.'

They talked of magic. Neither could sleep: the bodies were being buried by the Native Contingent and piled with rocks to prevent the hyena finding them, at least while they were camped there.

Magic seemed to offer a completely different parcel of explanations for the Zulu. Oftebro explained his father's failure to replace Zulu magic with Christian magic, in particular useless magic like loving your enemy. Thompson could see this magic now as a real phenomenon, just as real to the Zulu as notions of Empire, progress and science. And yet if Oftebro was to be believed, Cetewayo had a sense that he had not seen the full picture, only shadows. Ruskin had said that shadows are the second most striking aspect of any view. You could see the magical and physical worlds in this way if you chose, as light and shade.

He and Oftebro huddled around a fire. Oftebro was only a few years older than he was. He wanted to console him, yet there was something in Oftebro that demanded this painful self-flagellation. It made it difficult to cheer him up. He said nothing.

'You are a curious person, Frank. You understand everything and yet you are very young.'

Thompson had this impression of himself sometimes. It was a burden. Eventually Oftebro fell asleep. Thompson lay staring up at the stars, but his breathing became heavy as he slipped into semi-consciousness. When they were mustered he was not sure if he had slept at all, but he must have because there was a dew on the ground and it was appreciably colder.

Oftebro wanted to continue the discussion of the previous night as they warmed some coffee, but fortunately he was called to interpret. Marter had decided to send ahead for a cart to carry the King and he wanted to be certain that the King had no objections to this form of transport. Cetewayo wore a cloak of soft animal skin against the cold as he took his place in the circle of armed soldiers.

An orderly was sent ahead on a fast horse to make the necessary arrangements at the crossing of the Black Umfolozi.

They reached Ulundi the following day. The illustrated papers recorded the scene: the King carrying his stick flanked by two young captains with drawn swords. Ahead of them walk Marter and his trumpeter. Three bare-breasted women are seen carrying some of the King's effects on their heads. In the background on a rather shabby horse, is Thompson. Oftebro is nowhere to be seen.

CHAPTER 4

The King was despatched to Cape Town by sea. He was housed in the Castle, clad in a suit made for him by a Malay tailor and introduced to the skirl of the bagpipes, which he had first heard only at a distance. He acquired a certain celebrity, although the colonial officials were not tainted by the sentimentality of the time.

Zululand, which had in truth only been a notion, became a place. The magic was lost. This sort of magic had not proved robust enough to withstand the new order of things. Cetewayo's powers became a slightly shameful secret; how these people here would smile if he explained that he was responsible in his person for the crops, for fertility, for bravery and the national dances, without which the seasons could not perform their natural roles. He learned a little English and how to write his name and asked many questions – professional questions – about the Queen in England and how she ordered her affairs. Obviously, Cetewayo perceived, pretty well. After all she was living comfortably in her own home, while he was confined here where the wind blew ceaselessly. He wanted to learn. He had obviously missed a few tricks.

By its ending the Zulu War proved to have been a storm in a teacup. What had happened was merely a demonstration of the obvious, that a lightly armed and primitive people cannot, by bravery and atavistic appeals, overcome a heavily armed force, however incompetently managed. All the men, material and ox wagons – six hundred and sixty double-teamed, that is to say forty-four thousand oxen – were no longer needed after Cetewayo's capture and the parcelling out of the country. Zululand was left in the charge of a single resident with a few policemen to back him up.

Frank Thompson's mind had turned to gold. It was found in pockets all along the lumpy eastern ridge of the Transvaal. More gold strikes were expected. It seemed to him that the whole of Africa was opening up just as he appeared. He was eager to see this treasure house. His military career had lasted only three months, but it was clear that he would have to leave South Africa and join a regiment in India or elsewhere if he wanted to pursue it. The irregulars had disbanded immediately the Zulu were seen to be impotent and their threat to cattle, sheep and womenfolk hollow. The opportunity to venture into the Transvaal soon presented itself. To the north, beyond the misty mountains where gold had been found and where King Solomon's mines undoubtedly lay, lived a chief called Sekukuni. For Wolseley, anxious to maximise his military successes after his late entry into the campaign against the Zulu, the crafty Sekukuni represented the last legitimate native opposition. He had defied all attempts by the Boer government of the Transvaal to humble him. It was this unimpressionable person, lurking on the fringes of Boer society, who had convinced the Boers that they needed protection by the British. They were menaced by the old enemy, the Zulu, on one side and Sekukuni on another. Sekukuni now had to be dealt with. Thompson volunteered.

The purpose of this expedition was to make the Transvaal safe for the Boers to continue their raids of enslavement against his people. It was an irony pointed out to Thompson by a young farmer called Rider Haggard who had recently been a member of the British administration in the Transvaal. Haggard had a talent for exaggeration, Thompson decided as they sat one evening on the verandah of his farm near Newcastle where they billeted. Haggard had seen Sekukuni and indeed talked to him briefly. Haggard's farm was called Hilldrop. The setting was magnificent, in the lea of the huge mountains that buttressed the vast central plateau of Africa. He seemed to be in a state of confusion. He no longer wanted to farm ostriches in South Africa as he had first imagined. He wanted to pursue a career in writing or journalism. Africa, it seemed, had uncorked a bottle releasing all sorts of turbulent creative vapours. It had also aroused in him a strong sense of the Empire and the Pax Britannica.

The Boer, given half a chance, will still embark on slavery. Black gold is the term he uses. We must not allow ourselves to be used to help him. Zululand should be annexed and governed firmly. The Transvaal must be opened up to British settlers. The kaffir must be governed firmly but fairly. The benefits of the Empire must be seen by all. The Boer must be anglicized. Haggard spoke in tractarian fashion. The few Boers that Thompson had so far encountered had shown no great liking for the British. Indeed they appeared to regard the refined sort of Englishman – the officers – with amusement which ill became a nation cut off from the world for two hundred years.

'This slavery you talk of, is it condoned by their officials?'

'Condoned? Its chief instigators are the officials. Every man of substance has apprentices, as they are called, children stolen from their families on raids of conquest and plunder.'

'And now we are to rid them of Sekukuni, you say, in order that they may carry on as before?'

'Precisely. As soon as they have been helped by the British Army in their present difficulties, they will agitate for independence again. That is their way.'

Haggard's convictions were fierce and his interests far ranging. He was a tall, spare young man, almost as tall as Thompson, with dark hair and a neat dark beard. Gold, he said, was to be discovered all over the interior. King Solomon's mines lay further to the north than generally supposed. He had not himself seen the ruins of a once great kingdom, but they stood across the Limpopo as a testimony of another era, when blacks had been more industrious in the service of Hammamite masters than they were now in the service of the white man.

Next to the house, in a blue gum tree, a huge assembly of turtle doves fluttered as quietly as falling petals in pursuit of their demure courtship; beneath the house stretched endless acres of rolling grassland, touched with a delicate green brought on by the first rains. It was a vantage point from which distant principles could be seen clearly. Haggard was a restless young man. He was oppressed by the multitude of opportunities which were passing him by. Even as he talked of gold in Matabeleland, he was worrying about gold in Australia; as he talked of farming in South Africa he was longing for Norfolk; as he talked of Shepstone and President Burgers, he had Westminster in mind.

On the way up to Sekukuni's country, Thompson was to meet the Swazi agent, Captain McCleod of McCleod. McCleod was gathering a force of Swazi to help in the destruction of Sekukuni. Haggard asked Thompson to take a message from his principal servant, a Swazi prince, to be passed on to the King of the Swazi, Mbandzeni.

Haggard envied him his adventure.

'I have long wished to see the King of Swaziland myself. My servant Umzilkase has told me of Swaziland. You have a wonderful opportunity to see it.'

Many years later Thompson was to realise that this strong, fine looking Swazi prince, who acted as butler and factotum, had become Umslopogaas in Haggard's writing.

They set off in the morning for the pass, Laing's Nek, not far from the farm. Haggard paced about anxiously as he waited for the little contingent to leave.

'You have a wonderful opportunity. I wish I were coming with you, but my ostriches come first.'

The mountains in the early morning wore a ruffle of moist cloud half way up their steep slopes. An eagle with sharply upturned wingtips patrolled the pass, looking down coldly on the little column. The place was made to a heroic model; it was little wonder that Haggard was becoming erratically artistic. Haggard had said that he wanted to go home to marry. 'A man cannot live in a place like this on his own.' Africa aroused, Thompson thought as they plodded upwards, a strong sense of place. The splendour of the scenery, the elemental nature of life and the primitive conflicts, all tended to produce in the outsider outbursts of philosophy tied closely to geography. The European was constantly aware of the vast skies, the empty plains, the towering mountains and the untouched landscapes. It was easy to understand Haggard's desire to marry and produce children. It was a primitive urge to huddle together in the face of so much untrammelled nature.

Two years later the Boers were to inflict a dreadful defeat on the British on this spot. Haggard was on hand to hear the gunfire and see the peace treaty being drawn up. For an advocate of Empire, he had chosen the right location to observe its workings. Later, when Haggard was famous as a writer, Thompson occasionally thought about the ironies of their meeting.

It took three days of hard riding to reach the Swazi King's territory. The main force was heading by degrees for Sekukuni's country. He was to rendezvous with Norman McCleod at the King's kraal. He found McCleod's camp at the top of a steep pass looking down to the valley where the King lived. He was expected. McCleod appeared from a tent. He was wearing a kilt and above it a tightly fitting jacket and Glengarry. His legs were pale and celtic, lightly freckled, with reddish down, the pristine version of his hair, now grown darker, almost russet.

'Delighted to have you with us. Absolutely charmed. Alister Campbell – do you know him? – Alister Campbell will be riding with us.'

Thompson guessed that McCleod was about thirty-five, but he had about him a bustle of enthusiasm and cheerfulness that was boyish.

'Wolseley is only expecting two thousand Swazi,' he said with a smile.

'How many have you got, sir?'

'Five thousand so far. Another two or three thousand tomorrow coming from the outlying districts. Wonderful fellows. Wonderful. They'll make old Sekukuni dance.'

From what Haggard had told him of Sekukuni it was a poor choice of metaphor.

Campbell walked into the camp, carrying a canvas bag and a little box of instruments. He was a much younger man, probably the same age as Thompson. He wore a shirt and breeches with brown, comfortable boots. He removed his hat to greet Thompson.

'How do you do?'

'Well, thank you. May I ask what instruments those are?'

'You may. I am studying the insect life of these parts. Would you like to see?'

They immediately got on their knees to look at the little bottles of ether, the tweezers and pins and the press. The watching Africans probably thought it was some sort of ritual greeting.

'Shall we swim? You must be tired and hot after such a long ride.'

'Oh yes, please.'

'Are you coming, sir?'

'I must work. Go ahead. Wonderful waterfall,' said McCleod.

Thompson followed Campbell along a path which led towards some thick bush, hung with creepers and vines.

'Look there.'

Below them lay a metropolis of round beehive huts set about a huge central cattle byre made of massed ranks of tall dry branches. Thousands of warriors were milling about on the dusty assembly ground in front of the kraal. Their shouts and chants could be heard here, hundreds of feet above.

'Do you want to look through the glasses?'

'What is happening there to the left?'

'I think they are killing cattle. The King gives animals from his herd for the royal regiments. In fact the main part of Captain McCleod's negotiation has been about cattle. They may keep all the cattle captured from Sekukuni. Old Wolseley had to agree. I doubt whether he realises how many Swazi are coming.'

In a small kraal six or seven warriors helped an old man marshall some animals. Slowly he walked around them and then lunged forward with a spear and buried it beneath the shoulder of an animal, which at this distance seemed barely to react. It walked on and then stumbled once before sinking mutely to the ground. Immediately two of the assistants began to skin it while the old man walked calmly after the surviving cattle until he had one cornered; he lunged again, deftly. The cattle seemed to accept the inevitable with resignation, even as two, then three of their number were skinned in their midst and the small, frail old man stalked them quietly. Perhaps it was the false perspective of distance but there was a ritual and balletic appearance to the killing far below in a light haze of dust.

'Shall we swim?'

'I'm sorry. I was caught up.'

'Come on, old fellow.'

Campbell trotted off down the path to a stream. They made their way down the side of a stream to a small waterfall which fell in cascades down the rocks into a deep pool, churned by the plummeting waters. Campbell undressed and jumped from a ledge into the pool below. Thompson was more cautious, but he also jumped. The water was so cold that it convulsed him for a moment. He struck out for the other side of the pool where Campbell was already climbing out on to a rock face, his buttocks very white and his long brown hair plastered back. He clambered up the rocks and then sat down on the slippery rocks and slid wildly down into the water, his feet in the air.

'Try it. Try it.'

They spent a happy hour swimming, sliding and basking in the sun. At the edge of the pool some small Swazi boys appeared to stare and laugh at them, their little faces serious for a moment and then split by mirth.

'How strange we seem to them,' said Campbell, 'with our pale and furry bodies and our hair like horses' tails.'

'I hope you speak only for yourself,' said Thompson pushing him off the rock so that he slid into the water. The little line of naked aldermen was beside itself at this.

Thompson felt himself seized by euphoria. It was so intense that he leapt into the air yelling, lost his footing and bounced painfully into the water below. They were children in the garden of Eden. They were young and untouched by grief.

They dressed and walked back to McCleod's camp, their recent nakedness a bond. McCleod was wonderfully well organised. A table was laid for luncheon; Khelim, brushed and curried, was tied to a tree, feeding.

'Good, good, good,' said McCleod, 'I am starving. After luncheon I must go to Nkanini to greet the regiments from Tinjojela. I am the guest of honour.'

'As always,' said Campbell.

'I saw the forces gathering below. How have you done it, sir?'

'Honestly speaking, I do not know how the message gets out, yet they have assembled in three days.'

'Why is the King helping us?'

'Why? Because Sekukuni's people are traditional enemies. And because we asked in the name of the great Queen. That's why I am wearing the highland regalia, actually. As the Queen's representative.'

'You're becoming very burnt by the sun, sir,' said Campbell sympathetically.

'Yes I am. My knees are giving me hell, old fellow, but I am doing it for the Empire.' McCleod laughed. 'Would you like to come down to Nkanini?'

'Oh yes. Yes, if I may.'

'Of course. Eat up and we'll be off.'

They mounted up and rode down towards Nkanini. From their position in the hills above it had been clear that the layout of the royal village was very orderly, geometric in its precision. But down here on the plain confusion seemed to reign, with regiments forming up and trotting forwards for a few yards and then falling back again as though they were limbering up for an attack on the great cattle byre itself. Streams of warriors were arriving down myriad paths. A detachment forded a river at a run.

Their arrival on horseback caused great excitement.

'We must wait here until the King's counsellors send a messenger to escort us to the great Sibaya.'

They stood with their horses beside a clump of thorn trees at a respectful distance. Hundreds of men, clad in loincloths of leather or leopard skin, all carrying sticks, shields and spears, surrounded them cautiously but amiably. Many knew McCleod and he greeted them in the Swazi language. An old man came forward. He spoke to McCleod and then waved his slender stick to clear a path through the seething mass of warriors. The old man walked ahead; he carried a long black feather in his hair and wore an apron of the skin of some deer; his ankles were circled by porcupine quills and teeth, perhaps of a lion.

'He is Sandlane Zwane, the King's senior Induna,' said McCleod.

Everybody stood aside for Zwane, though he carried himself humbly and even bowed his head and muttered deferentially to men of royal blood, distinguished by the brilliant red feather in their hair.

They approached the huge stockade of the cattle byre. It was, Thompson reckoned, all of twenty feet high. The horses were left outside with McCleod's servants. They followed Zwane through a narrow gap into the enclosure. Inside, the royal regiments in all their glory were drawn up facing the north side of the cattle byre. Zwane led them there and asked them to sit down. A huge, murky bowl of beer was produced. McCleod drank deeply. Thompson and Campbell, not wanting to appear green, followed. The beer was grainy and muddy in texture, with a sour taste.

McCleod winked at them.

'Nectar of the gods,' he said cheerfully.

The regiments waved their shields and began a backwards and forwards motion, the shields and sticks rising alternately. They chanted in unison, stamping their feet and hissing to produce the notorious sound that their cousins the Zulu had used to loosen the bowels of Boer and Briton alike, the sound of surf on a distant beach. Then they advanced in a line, apparently on the instructions of an old man who stood with a stick raised aloft like a drum-major's. The ebbing and flowing movements went on for an hour, the singing at times painfully sad. Was it for the death and bereavement that was sure to follow, or was it for the spirits of warriors past? Thompson looked at Campbell who sat beside him, his eyes half closed as though perhaps he were thinking the same thing.

There was a stir at the top end of the byre to their left and a surging mass of elders and counsellors appeared surrounding the King, Mbandzeni. Thompson wanted to stand but McCleod held his arm. Mbandzeni sat on the ground some yards from them. He was a huge man, stouter even than Cetewayo; on his head was a ring similar to Cetewayo's and he wore a leopard-skin loin cloth.

Some of his many wives filed in and sat on his left in a billowing mass of concupiscense, the younger ones clad only in short aprons with beads on their bosoms and feathers in their hair.

The regiment from Tinjojela arrived. It was greeted derisively by the royal regiments, but took its place beside them, forming one of the horns of the force. The dance began again. The King stood and walked forward to his regiment to stand next to his commander-in-chief, Mbovane Fakudze, a tall, dark almost Hamitic man with fine features. The King, despite his immense size and weight, danced for two hours, filling his men with the spirit and courage for the task ahead: the slaughter of the wretched Bapedi and the plunder of their innumerable cattle. Songs were sung about these cattle, their long horns and glossy coats, their beautiful spotted skins like leopards'.

Only when the sun began to sink did the King leave his regiment to watch the warriors lope past and out of the huge byre. A full moon was rising on one side even as the sun still hung bruised above the mountains on the other.

'It's splendid.'

Campbell nodded his head and smiled.

'We're very fortunate.'

'Now for the feasting. Courage, mes enfants,' said McCleod.

They were ushered out of the cattle byre by an induna to meet the King. The King was friendly and forthcoming; McCleod gave him a present, a new Lee-Metford rifle, and passed on Thompson's message from the future Umslopogaas. McCleod told him that Thompson had seen the capture of Cetewayo, but he did not want to hear details; he simply shook his head expressively. They were seated in front of the great hut, adorned with the skulls of fine cattle in token of ancestors. The King, in a mood of joviality, summoned Thompson and said that the Swazi name for him would be Ukhwalimanzi, the heron, because he had seen how still he had sat, missing nothing. The counsellors sitting nearby laughed and applauded their King's wit.

'You're fortunate, lad. He has some very cruel names for us folk,' said McCleod.

'To tell the truth, I was terrified he might see me looking at some of his young wives.'

McCleod laughed, tipsy from the beer. The head of an ox, a man at each great spreading horn, was carried into the enclosure around the hut. These men, the butchers, wore nothing but a short, leather apron; their colleagues appeared carrying slabs of meat on poles and huge cooking pots (made in Birmingham, said McCleod). The wives now began to sing, just at sufficient distance to provide a pleasant background. They shuffled and swayed to the intricate and beautiful harmonies. The meat was roasted and handed out, the choicest parts first to the King and his visitors. Thompson watched McCleod in his trews and Glengarry, the great Queen's representative, receive his meat with cupped hands, and he did the same. Mbandzeni had a ferocious appetite; he ate and drank continuously until he lapsed into a glazed, and mildly comatose state. The night above them now had a false, luminous quality like a painting by Alma-Tadema.

'When do we leave for Sekukuniland?' asked Thompson.

'Tomorrow or the day after. Another regiment is expected in the morning. I estimate we will have eight thousand men.'

'How are you going to supply them?'

'God knows. I've nothing for them. I've no transport of any sort.'

It was a long march up to Sekukuni's country, at least two hundred miles. It did not matter. They would somehow manage to get to Lydenburg where Wolseley, presumably, would provision them. Anything seemed possible.

Finally they took their leave of Mbandzeni. A young boy was delegated to lead them to their horses. Nkanini was wrapped in a blanket of smoke pungent with the brewery smell of fermenting beer and the scents of roasting meat, urine, animal skins and porridge. It was a warm blanket of intimacy, yet they were glad to be out in the open air again, stumbling in the semi-darkness to their camp. Mbandzeni was wrapped in this intimacy; even close to, he appeared to be a man in a mist, dimly perceived. His motives were a mystery. He was summoning thousands of warriors, cattle were being butchered ceaselessly, the national medicines deployed, the ancient dances performed and the terrible sharpener of death was in the air, all at McCleod's request. And yet McCleod could not explain his reasons.

'The truth is, Frank, I've lived here a year and I do not begin to understand.'

'Are they capable of civilisation?'

'There's a question. Civilisation as we know it is a very partisan notion.'

'Can they be taught, sir? There are wonderful opportunities here if they learn.'

'For them or for us?'

'For both, surely.'

'I am not sure. I cannot help thinking that their system, however imperfect, however barbaric, suits them. It has evolved that way, as has ours, our way.'

'But it will evolve further, surely?'

'I don't know. It has its own logic. If we destroy one part of it, the whole edifice may crash down.'

'It would surely profit them to learn some of the rudiments of science and education.

'I am sure you are right.'

McCleod would have been brought up on romance and Walter Scott. The irresistible nature of progress was lost on him. It was not a question of will or malevolence or altruism; a process was in motion which was inevitable; it was in an absolute sense neither good nor bad. But he did not pursue the argument.

'Do you want to turn in, you must be tired?' asked McCleod.

'No thank you, sir, I shall smoke a pipe and have a walk.'

'I'll come with you,' said Campbell.

He and Campbell walked to the top of the precipice. The royal village far below was almost quiescent, a few fires still burning but the noises of revelry faint. In the middle of the cattle byre they could see a dark blotch, the diminished royal cattle huddled together nervously, perhaps aware of the arrival of hordes of warriors eager to exploit the King's hospitality.

'Do you wonder what your family are doing now?'

Campbell, his pipe glowing, turned to him.

'My family. I love them and yet I hardly think about them. Do you find this? Days go past without a thought?'

'Yes,' said Thompson, 'this world is so overwhelming, it seems almost to blot out the other.'

'Are you staying?'

'I'm not sure yet. I have the feeling that I am fortunate to be here. History is in the making. Everything is happening. What about you?'

'I have already identified what I think are five new specimens. In a way that is epoch-making for a natural historian.'

They talked for an hour or so. At home the first snows would be falling perhaps, little flurries soon over. The harvest would be in; the Gloucestershire countryside settling down for its period of inertia, comfortably. Campbell lived in a grand house in Scotland.

They talked of their parents; Thompson told him of his father's affliction and his mother's calm strength.

'Do you know what the Swazi call their King? The Lion. And the Queen is the She-Elephant. The King is expected to be brave and perhaps something of a show-off, while the Queen is the more solid, the Mother of the nation. It goes without saying, of course, that an elephant is stronger than a lion.'

They were sharing a tent. A hyena whooped deliriously and insects, many of them large and clumsy, buzzed and shrieked and scraped around the canvas. But they were both soon asleep in the deep untroubled sleep of the young.

McCleod was wearing the full uniform of a highland chief for the send off from Nkanini: kilt, tartan jacket, scarlet vest, bonnet with cockade, dirk and claymore and the clan badge of juniper. Thompson and Campbell were dowdy by comparison, both with McCleod and with the Swazi forces, all eight thousand of them.

They were decked in feathers, necklaces and ox tail anklets. The princes and chiefs wore huge head-dresses. Thompson's rather fustian uniform was not at its best and Campbell could only muster a sort of modified hunting outfit, tail coat and brown hat, so that they felt like the poor relations. They waited while McCleod entered the great sibaya to take part in secret ceremonies which involved, inevitably, the slaughter of an ox as medicine for the King and his commanders. Eventually McCleod appeared from that direction, his face slightly rouged with blood as though he had been kissed by a whore, his jauntiness intact after whatever it was he had been doing.

'How long now, sir?' asked Campbell.

In little knots, rivers and clusters the warriors were beginning to form into their regiments.

'Hours yet, laddie,' said McCleod cheerfully.

'Hold fast, eh?'

'That's the spirit.'

Eventually the King, surrounded by an excited entourage of counsellors and sangomas, burst from the gap in the byre and joined his regiment. He was clad in full battle regalia, his head in a crown of black feathers, his waist bound in monkey and leopard skin and his arms and legs encircled by the tails of oxen. His huge frame was charged with excitement. The King had been doctored in anticipation of death; it was not so much to ward off death, as to make light of it. The regiments felt it coming. His great quivering body was bursting with the anticipation.

They raised their shield and roared 'Bayethe', the royal salute.

McCleod saluted and Thompson and Campbell stood stiffly. The King trotted now with his indunas and medicine men along the face of the regiments. Each section raised its shields and assegais and whistled and chanted. He skipped and danced along. Where he had passed the regiments seethed as the magic touched them.

'I pity the poor damned Bapedi,' said McCleod proudly.

The King was possessed. He danced with his own regiment, his body convulsed with life and energy. The regiments began to rush forwards and fall back again. They sang songs of battle.

Thompson and Campbell were unsure what to do while this was going on, but McCleod joined the King and Fakudze. He danced with them, his legs doing a modified version of a fling or a reel by McCrimmon; the Highland music skirling through his head was obviously in the right tempo.

From the side of the cattle byre the young princesses appeared wearing only beaded aprons. Their hair was spiked with red feathers in a vivid coronet; above their bare breasts were little amulets of beadwork. Each girl carried a thin white stick which she waved gently as she danced in front of the warriors, a subtle and sinuous motion which brought them ever closer to the centre of the regiments. Young men leapt out of the ranks, bounded up to them and crashed their ox-hide shields into the dust at the feet of one or other of the girls. It was a token of love, or perhaps a simple surge of emotion at the sight of such beauty. The demureness of the girls was suffused with sensuality. Thompson felt himself uncomfortably aroused. The girls danced until the sun was low above the great cattle byre. Then the regiments suddenly began to move out, so suddenly that McCleod's party was caught by surprise with their oxen grazing and horses unsaddled. McCleod had prepared a speech which he was proposing to read, promising them cattle and the Great Queen's protection if they were successful, but he was too late. The Swazi left the village at a fast trot, past their King and McCleod, their commander, who had to hurry to find his horse and get himself to the head of the column by means of a quick but dignified canter.

'Come, come, Frank,' shouted Campbell, much amused. They galloped off to join McCleod.

'Fine fellows, eh?' asked McCleod. The splendid column stretched back half a mile. McCleod's voice was choked. As they began to climb out of the valley up a steep track, Thompson and Campbell looked back: eight thousand Swazi warriors, singing, laughing, and chanting in primitive splendour. Behind them now lay the broad and fertile valley, rising sharply to the mountains of wild ravines and huge mounds of boulders. The sky was as red and dramatic as a painting by Church or Lewis, as if nature were imitating art.

Thompson turned to Campbell, his eyes pricked with tears.

'Magnificent.'

'The Bapedi have guns,' said Campbell quietly, 'and they hide in caves.'

Thompson told him what Haggard had said, that in defeating Sekukuni they would only be releasing the Boer from his fear of the kaffir.

'Yes, we have beaten the Zulu and now we must set one lot against the other for their own eventual destruction. Poor devils.'

Looking back over Khelim's wiry, pock-marked rump, Thompson felt some sympathy for the romantic view of god in nature. If it had any truth it must find supporting evidence here as the sun set and the clouds hanging over the mountains bled bright portentous blood on the heads of the eager Swazi. The Swazi were animists, it seemed, curiously similar in their view to the romantics.

To keep up with the Swazi, Khelim had to jog from time to time; they half trotted and half walked up, ever upwards, until they reached the top of the escarpment where they rested awhile, drinking from a stream that tumbled down to the valley below. The Swazi had no provisions at all apart from some dried meal in little pouches, so McCleod decided that their white leaders would not eat until they made camp later that night. He quickly changed from his kilt into breeches and boots; the three of them – McCleod, Thompson and Campbell – sat against a huge boulder still pulsing with the heat of the sun and sucked their pipes while the horses were fed surreptitiously with the ubiquitous mealie.

'I can hardly believe it at all,' said Thompson.

'Nobody could believe this. It is too fantastic,' said Campbell, moved.

McCleod smiled smugly.

'I hope Sir Garnett appreciates your work, sir,' said Thompson.

'Ah, Sir Garnett. I am afraid he has not our innate interest in all this.'

The implication was clear: they were closer to the real Africa. But which Africa, Thompson wondered? For Alister Campbell it was a vast new field of natural history, of finding God in the particular; for McCleod it was Walter Scott and the Faery Flag writ large. And for him?

'Have you been in a battle?' asked McCleod.

'No, sir.'

'It will be hot. It will be hot. Last time they repulsed the Boers.'

'Were there many casualties?'

'Not many. They have a hill beside the town, full of caves and huge boulders. No one dared approach too close. The Boers packed up and went home when they saw that.'

One of McCleod's Swazi servants, dressed in a discarded Norfolk jacket and wearing a soft brown hat approached.

'Tshabalala was there,' said McCleod.

He spoke to the man in Swazi. Tshabalala sat down in front of them, hunkering respectfully.

'He says that they are cowards but cunning. They have knowledge. By that he means of medicines and secrets.'

'Does he think our medicines are strong enough?' asked Campbell.

'He says our sangomas have different medicines. Medicines for bravery and battle. But he is doubtful. They have secrets. Sekukuni can transform himself into various animal forms.'

Secrets like little Chinese boxes. Under the everyday appearance of things are spirits and secrets.

'What about Sir Garnet and his field guns?' asked Thompson.

'Guns have introduced a new element into the equation,' said McCleod. 'Guns are knowledge.'

Wolseley's field guns would blow to pieces this fragile construction of superstition and medicine, of that Thompson was sure.

There was a slight chill now. The horses had to be led down the rock-strewn track between great fortresses of boulders until finally they came out on a plateau of grassland. Far off they saw the ghostly shapes of elephant lumbering quickly away. The Swazi regiments fanned out and advanced in lines, practising their jabbing and battering as they went, their assegais attracting the moonlight.

At dawn they came to the wild Komati River, where the Swazi rested and bathed.

CHAPTER 5

Alister Campbell was one of the first to be killed.

The battle – the terrifying, hectic, throat-rasping and hysterical few hours – was ferocious.

It started in acrimony with Wolseley accusing the Swazi of cowardice when they refused to attack before dawn. McCleod stood before him, defiant in his Highland fancy dress.

'I've given the order, sir, go to it.'

'Excellency, with respect, the Swazi do not care to advance in the dark. It is their custom.'

'It is a matter of cover. Cover, sir.'

'They don't mind, Excellency. They prefer to be seen.'

'They prefer to be killed?'

'I believe they prefer to fight as they always have, sir.'

The shells from Wolseley's nine-pounders made the conversation doubly difficult. They crashed into the huge kraal and on to the hill to the side of it, where many of the Bapedi had retreated for their last stand. It was at this self-same hill that the Boer commandoes had failed previously, refusing to support the Swazi and leaving them exposed and forced to withdraw. The Swazi had now decided that it would not be sensible to attack until their allies were properly committed. As Fakudze explained it to McCleod, a man who has crossed a river and seen a crocodile lurking there, goes by another route next time. McCleod did not think Wolseley was in a mood for this sort of allegory at this moment, so he simply stuck to the argument about daylight, larded with mystique.

Wolseley found the whole thing unsatisfactory and irregular, but he saw that McCleod could not be expected to have complete command over eight thousand befeathered strangers; he acquiesced and sent in Ferreira's Horse first from the plain, followed by the Border Horse and the Foot. From the South, where the Lulu Mountains gave them a chance to get close, the Swazi rushed the hill in waves, led by McCleod, sword in hand and pistol blazing. It was on the lower slopes that Campbell was killed scrambling after the Swazi who were soon ripping and tearing the Bapedi to pieces, as they tried to retreat up to their caves and redoubts. The Swazi were irresistible, despite terrible casualties. They vaulted over the bodies of the dead, they ran into the gunfire, they laughed at the dangers.

As the Horse galloped across the open veldt to get to the hill, Thompson lay low on Khelim's scrawny neck. Khelim galloped the same way as he walked; unconcerned, fatalistic, even now as the bullets whined past like lethal bees in the early light. It was a short frightening gallop. The hill was soon reached, a tangle of boulders thrown up by some volcanic exertions of previous aeons in the middle of the plain. Where was Sekukuni? Where was the simian little schemer? Was he up there in the heights planning – as Tshabalala feared – their destruction by the exercise of his arcane knowledge?

They reached the cover of the lower slopes. He left Khelim behind a boulder, tethered lightly to a spiky tree with leaves like cow's ears, and he began to mount the hill. They fanned out. There was no plan now. 'Take the hill' was all Wolseley had said. He had not given any indication of how to avoid being killed. Rocks began to roll down from above, shattering into shrapnel as they hit the huge boulders below. Already – it was only five o'clock – the sun was above the hills surrounding the village. He scrambled upwards, his pistol in his hand but unable to fire because he was behind many of his own men. He came upon a body; for a moment he thought of stopping to try to drag it behind some rocks. He carried on because he could see that the man was dead. In peaceful repose with only a blood stain under his head on the grass, he looked out of place, a man having a nap at Armageddon. It was hot and he found sweat pouring into his eyes. His heart was bouncing alarmingly in his chest. He caught up with some of the Foot, firing from behind a natural fortification of boulders up towards a thickly covered ravine. They were firing at the smoke and flashes of flintlocks. Thompson used his pistol wildly, aware even as he did it that it was useless at this range.

'How do we know who we're firing at?' Thompson asked.

A sergeant laughed: 'Anybody firing down is against us, sir.'

It seemed logical. They moved forward again. The 80th fixed bayonets. He wondered if he should draw his sword in his other hand. If he did that he would not be able to climb. He took a swig of water and followed the regulars up. From ahead there came some screams. Suddenly, over on his right and way above them he could see a swarm of Swazi appear from the ravine and scramble upwards. He began to run and scramble after them, desperate to be there, uncertain of why he was running and slipping and gasping, sweat pouring from his face, his boots giving him no grip at all on the loose rocks and dry grass – upwards, upwards, his breath scouring his lungs painfully. A rock struck him a glancing blow on the head and blood streamed down his face. There was little gunfire now. Up there the natives – the Coon, the Kaffir – were fighting each other in the old way; the short, satisfying plunge of a stabbing spear; the wrist-jarring thud of sticks on bone and cartilage; the blood thick and dark on glistening brown skins; the sheer animal joy of killing. He passed bodies now and men dying quietly from hideous wounds. He gave this man some water, that man a piece of bread and hurried on. A wounded Pedi crawled out of a crack in some rocks and tried to roll a large boulder down on him. He shot at the man; the bullet succeeded only in tearing open his cheek; still, cataleptic, the naked man tried to reach him. He ran and crawled away from this implacable lunatic; soon he reached a small cliff face where hundreds of Swazi surrounded the entrance to a cave. They were tearing branches and grass to start a fire. God knows who was in the cave on the point of being roasted. There were bodies everywhere – at least a hundred – and above them on a plateau, perhaps the summit of the hill, thousands of Swazi were gathering.

'It's ours, it's ours,' yelled McCleod as he appeared from the midst of the Swazi. His face was scratched, his legs torn and his kilt soaked in blood.

'What, what do you mean?'

Thompson choked. He did not know what McCleod was talking about.

'The hill, Frank. We've taken it. Come on, boy, come on.'

Thompson followed blindly, tears, blood and sweat meeting above his mouth in a saline confluence. McCleod's face, with the effects of the dust, blood and sweat, was almost unrecognisable. He looked like a creature straight from hell. The Swazi cheered them – they loved them in the consanguinity of death.

'Why are they doing this? Why?' Thompson asked as the Swazi rushed forward at the last Pedi redoubt.

'Where's Sekukuni? I want to see him,' he shouted. 'Where is he? I must see him.'

Nobody was listening.

He sat down shaking and trembling. His calves were twitching involuntarily, and tears were flowing uncontrolled from his eyes. He stood up again. The Swazi were clambering over the last barrier of rocks and mud walls. He must be with McCleod when they captured Sekukuni. But he could not find McCleod now in this dreadful charnel house. Instead he attached himself to some of Ferreira's Horse who had arrived here somehow on horseback. They were trying to bring some order to this primitive drama now. The white men always did this. In their heads they carried a master plan which could be imposed on all the random, confused activities of the natives. They were shouting and galloping amongst the battle-crazed Swazi. Thompson could see no sign of Alister Campbell either. The air was thick with smoke; from the caves below came a terrible appetizing smell, the smell of roasting flesh. The Swazi were jubilant as coughing, suffocating, seared Pedi began to emerge from caves and crevices. They cuffed them and prodded them and killed those who resisted; they challenged them to produce their vaunted magic.

Suddenly McCleod appeared from above with Fakudze. The Swazi drew back and formed up loosely as Fakudze raised his stick.

'We've got him surrounded. He's in there.'

McCleod put an arm around Thompson's shoulders.

'Are you all right, laddie?'

'Yes, sir. Thank you.'

McCleod conferred with the Horse who sent word back to Wolseley that Sekukuni was surrounded and that the Royal Engineers with their dynamite were required, as the Swazi method of slow asphyxiation was perhaps insufficiently scientific for a modern military engagement.

Somewhere in this last redoubt of granite boulders, twisted roots of trees and deep caves, Sekukuni and his counsellors were hiding. He would have to have quite a trick up his sleeve if he was to prove Tshabalala right now, surrounded by thousands of Swazi, Ferreira's Horse, the 80th arriving stolidly and the Engineers with their strange little packages and wooden boxes expected.

'We've lost Campbell,' said McCleod.

McCleod led him to a rock where they both sat down. It was only mid morning. The whole thing was over. Campbell was dead. Hundreds, perhaps thousands of Pedi and Swazi were dead. Below them Sekukuni's well-ordered town was no longer burning fiercely.

It was smouldering.

'Shall we look for him?'

'Yes, we must,' said McCleod. 'As soon as we've taken Sekukuni.'

The Engineers arrived and began to unpack their boxes according to the prescribed routine. Some of the Swazi lost interest in this painstaking end to a glorious fight until the first explosion split a vast granite ball in two and sent dust, trees, fragments of birds and burning grass high into the air. When the smoke and dust had cleared, only two Pedi emerged from the depths of the cave. They were questioned roughly about Sekukuni's whereabouts. It seemed he was hiding somewhere deep inside the hill. Deafening explosions and a rain of organic matter, diced fine by the force, produced more trickles of the Pedi during the morning, but Sekukuni was not to be found. Thompson feared he might have been buried alive by now, executed and interred in one move, a scientific advance.

McCleod summoned some Swazi and asked them about Campbell's death. The reports were conflicting but all agreed that it had happened early. The Swazi, regardless of their own losses, helped McCleod and Thompson search for Campbell. They spent the whole day looking, but his body could not be found. It had vanished. Campbell may have crashed into a ravine or a hole. Or perhaps the Pedi had stolen his body for medicine. He could not be found.

Death, it seemed, walked hand in hand with life, smirking. Alister Campbell with his new German microscope and his love of plants and insects. Alister Campbell showing him the scarab beetle which rolled up balls of dung with its hind legs. Alister Campbell showing him the ant-lion cunningly catching ants in its trap. He was interested in the springs of life. Cruelly, pointlessly, he had lost his own. His death made Thompson feel immeasurably old, as if he had seen that youth was merely a mask in a grotesque pantomime. So much for Campbell and his natural history; he was the victim of no natural law but of absurdity advertising itself as history. He gave up looking for Campbell. He had known him only a few days and yet he had loved him.

'We must need die and are as water spilt on the ground, which cannot be gathered up again.'

There was an impromptu service for the dead, accompanied by a homily from Wolseley. Here in the middle of godless Africa they stood in the fast-thickening twilight, the bodies neatly lined up, covered with blankets. There was a glorious sense of sacrifice in the air. Sacrifice was in itself good, Wolseley seemed to suggest in his short speech; it did not matter, presumably, in what cause. 'Sacrifice,' he said, 'makes men of us.' This was at odds with the chaplain's contention that the death of one man diminishes us all, an adaptation of Donne. No matter. Nobody required that they should make sense.

Thompson felt bitter, as though his brief friendship with Campbell had been perverted deliberately. He was disturbed too, that these few men should be remembered particularly, when the hills and ravines were still strewn with Swazi bodies. Somewhere, too, lay Campbell's body, his life literally spilt on the ground, neither to be gathered up nor even to be seen again. Hyenas whooped in the distance, the bacchanalia of the undergrowth about to start in earnest. Campbell would probably be torn apart in a tug of war between two hyenas.

'How do you feel, laddie?' asked McCleod.

'I'm all right, sir.'

'Oh, away with you.'

McCleod affected this rough, Highland camaraderie habitually, it seemed.

'Away with you. Death is always so, first time. The fighting was terrifying. You wanted to be brave but you could not think clearly. Am I right? And then we lost Alister Campbell. A terrible loss. It is always so.'

Even his reaction to these awful events was ordained; his lack of courage, the weakness in his legs, the sense of loss of innocence, which hurt more that the loss of a limb. He felt as if he had been defiled.

'Now the Swazi. They're not sad. No, no. They know you cannot have life without death. Fakudze's people boast they would go willingly, singing, into the grave of their king. They will not have to be pushed.'

'May I ask you something, sir?'

'Certainly.'

'Do you really become used to this?'

'I'm afraid so, laddie.'

The Swazi were singing now, a quiet song. McCleod took his arm and led him towards the Swazi regiments, to where Fakudze and his lieutenants were sitting beneath a bulbous tree which appeared in the firelight to be suffering from a deformity, a sort of elephantiasis of the plant kingdom. The Swazi had had nothing to eat at all for four days. Now they were preparing to feast on captured cattle. Their encampment was a galaxy of pungent camp fires. Some of the Swazi were already stupefied with beer. But McCleod was right; they were not downcast. For them death in battle was not to be feared or mourned; it was simply a fact. McCleod with his medieval passions had wanted to impress this upon him. The Swazi danced and sang and laughed as individual warriors re-enacted their triumphs.

He drank deeply from a gourd full of the grainy beer. Perhaps it would help him shake off the heavy hand that rested on his shoulder. The Swazi were celebrating death. They were glorying in the details. Livingstone had found this kind of thing hard to stomach; the absence of compassion had appalled him at first. And yet were they wrong? When you set out to kill and maim a whole tribe, should you be surprised that your comrades are killed? McCleod put these questions rhetorically.

But Campbell's death was quite another matter. He was not mourning Campbell. He was mourning himself. He felt insubstantial, an empty space through which the wind blew. It was the feeling of the god-forsaken.

Thompson knew then that he could never be a soldier. War was not necessary to produce a change of heart. The evidence of industrial superiority was sufficient. Wars were a relic of another age. Sekukuni, like all things African, had been blown away on a breeze. The officers were celebrating their victory over Sekukuni. Who was Sekukuni? He was merely an aboriginal hovering uncomfortably on the fringes of a new order. The band of the 80th played light and cheerful airs as Thompson lay on the ground with a blanket, too tired to remove his boots from his swollen feet. They did not understand. This country would be conquered by the manifest advantage of civilisation, not by the awful symbolism of death. Death, seen like this close to, death in pursuit of military honour, was evil because it was the product of ignorance. He fell asleep, soon to wake, sobbing in catches of breath, like a child in a tantrum.

Three days later Sekukuni was finally captured, a wizened,

cunning man, disappointingly small and frail looking, with yellowed eyes. Despatches were sent back to London to make the whole exercise appear more creditable; nobody had the least idea what to do with Sekukuni. The Castle in Cape Town could soon be full of confused, harmless African chiefs. Perhaps the great Queen in England would begin to wonder why all these petitions flooded in from her captured territories, imploring justice for this coon and that, apparently quite innocent of the crimes in whose name wars were started. But the wars were never started in response to crimes. Thompson saw that they were in response to a law, the law of natural selection. These curious anomalies dressed in their smelly animal skins were clearly unfit.

First, Sekukuni had to be transported to Pretoria to provide the citizenry and the Press with tangible results of the campaign. The fighting itself had lasted from half past four until half past ten in the morning. However you looked at it, it was not much of an achievement.

Thompson decided to travel with the Swazi and McCleod. He would pass through the goldfields on his way from Swaziland. McCleod was able to make the necessary arrangements without difficulty. They were given a rousing send off by the 80th and Ferreira's Horse. The Swazi left at a trot, making the earth throb. McCleod saluted. Wolseley saluted, his keen little face stiff and composed. Thompson saluted. The cattle had already been sent ahead so there was nothing to delay them. The Swazi took with them a few captives, *souvenirs de la guerre*, whom they treated kindly, like backward children. These captives trotted too, self-consciously, away from their country.

Up the hills they ran, Khelim jogging reluctantly to keep abreast. Thompson looked back at the scene of triumph. The village – the knowledgeable called it Sekukuni's 'Stadt' – lay devastated, the ground pockmarked with craters. Children and dogs wandered about the wreckage trying to find the familiar. Sekukuni was reported to chew leaves continually. Perhaps they were hallucinogenic, for certainly his power seemed to have been an hallucination from this vantage point, dreamed by the Boers and Sekukuni himself.

They reached Swaziland in three days. The cattle were following behind at their own pace; they were fine animals, with exceptionally long horns. The Swazi were highly delighted with their demeanour and appearance. It was believed that the finest would find a place in the royal herd; there they would stand proxy for the souls of departed warriors.

They rode down the steep track back towards the valley where the King waited for his victorious regiments. The rains had come in earnest and the little waterfalls were savage torrents now. The huge, bulbous rocks glistened, seeping water from their inner recesses into the bright morning sunshine. On their way down they passed through a patch of mist which hung about the mountains uncertainly; then below them was the glorious valley, the Swazi paradise, a river meandering along its floor, bare broken mountains on either side and little kraals dotted about. The Swazi began to sing again as they saw it, the halt and the lame hopping and jogging as best they could, the captured Pedi dared to scorn this Shangri-la, their cowed faces trying to register the desired emotions. Brilliant loeries, widow birds with improbably long tails and gemmological sunbirds floated and fluttered in the air. Little boys appeared from the kraals on the hills and ran feverishly alongside the great heaving mass of the regiments. Their wiry, powdered legs were inexhaustible. Pure joy filled the air; McCleod waved happily and exchanged greetings; yet Thompson could not share it, his loss was too great.

The next day the newly returned regiments had the place of honour in the cattle byre. It was the season of Ncwala, the first fruits ceremony. Once more the regiments danced, but this time there was a deep melancholy in their singing.

'Perhaps they are sad after all?' asked Thompson.

'No, laddie, This is a sacred ceremony. They are not mourning their losses, but cleansing and renewing their King. The King is the life force of the Swazi. Every year, like the seasons, like the crops, he must be renewed.'

McCleod loved the ritual. He was unhealthily taken up in it. There was of course a strain of medievalism in it all. Walter Scott had single-handed cooked up the myth of The Faery Flag and Dunvegan, the McCleods' dearest possessions, so it was understandable. But Thompson was growing impatient with him.

The King himself was not visible. He was housed in a shelter of waxen green leaves at one end of the cattle byre. McCleod and Thompson sat with other notables on the ground on the King's right. Between this shelter and the subdued warriors, the royal cattle stood uneasily. If they had forebodings they were well-founded because, at a signal from one of the elders, a hundred or more boys, all stark naked, rushed in from one of the side entrances of the byre and waited near the cattle, which began to mill about. One of their number, a black bull, was separated from its fellows. The boys moved towards the animal. It tried to join the rest of the herd, but this had been driven over to the byre. The animal was now alone, surrounded by ten thousand warriors; it quickly realised that it had been elevated from the role of placid ancestor-substitute to something more numinous. It stood at bay for a moment as the boys closed in and then it charged headlong towards the royal regiments. They raised their shields, but the animal drove right through them knocking a few men to the ground. The naked boys were now divided into two groups, those who were pursuing the bull from behind and those who were trying to cut it off in its panic-stricken gallop around the kraal.

It took a few minutes before one of the pursuers grabbed the animal by the tail; he was pulled along until another boy grabbed his feet. They slowed the bull down sufficiently for the group which had been trying to head it off to close. The bull tossed its head and gashed one of the boys in the stomach. Three other boys seized a massive horn and were tossed about and banged on the ground. It was an error of judgement by the animal, for now its head and neck were seized from all sides; its hind legs were splayed out and its movements became more and more laboured until it fell, toppled over by the swarming Lilliputian mass of boys, who began to hammer and tear at the animal with their bare hands. It bellowed as it was hammered into unconsciousness. Before it was dead the medicine men came, in their finery, to cut open its stomach and remove certain parts, highly efficacious (said McCleod) for the sustaining of Kings. It seemed that there was no escaping the relationship between death and life in these parts.

'Do you think it is mumbo jumbo, to use a modern expression?'

'I would like to presume ...' began Thompson.

'Do you see them now? They're taking the organs in to the King to doctor him. The regiments are fearful. This is a worrying time for them. It is ritual. Do you know the meaning of ritual?'

'Not exactly.'

'Ritual is what makes life real and therefore understandable. Do you follow me?'

'I don't believe I do, sir.'

'Let me ask you a question. Suppose life were no more than a ritual played out for a purpose we do not know?'

'Yes?'

'Just as this Ncwala, we perceive clearly, is a ritual played out for a purpose the Swazi do not fully understand. They gain reassurance from it even though we recognise it to be mere superstition. Do you follow me? Good. Does it matter that the Swazi fail to recognise this ritual as mere mumbo jumbo, to use your expression?'

'I don't believe I said ...'

'No, it does not. To them it is life writ large. Do you see my meaning now?'

'Are you saying that all life is ritual?'

'In a manner of speaking. Yes. We are all engaged, consciously and unconsciously in ritual from cradle to grave.'

'Would you suggest, sir, that science and the demonstrable cause and effect of empirical studies, like Campbell's scarab beetles, is mumbo jumbo? Can you compare that with the killing of a bull and the eating of its vital parts for strength?'

'I can. For all we know the whole body of science may be an elaborate deception or mumbo jumbo. Certainly its effect on the world is more evil than those of Ncwala.'

Poor McCleod was deceived. Material progress rested on demonstrable facts; it was not merely desirable, it was inevitable. They stood at a watershed of understanding. But McCleod preferred the comfort of the Paradise lost, the axe in the primordial wilderness; god-in-nature.

The King appeared from his shelter. He threw something to the regiments. There was a seething eruption in their midst. It was dark. Behind the lumpy mountains the sky had a brick glow still but here on the valley floor an inky night was developing. The warriors dispersed. Nobody came to bid farewell to McCleod and Thompson. But McCleod knew the form; it was time to leave the royal village.

One ruler renewed, another destroyed. Alister Campbell gone.

And I am only twenty years old.

CHAPTER 6

Everything in Africa happened at daybreak or sunset. No tampering with natural time was possible. The nights were dangerous and restricting. So it was dawn when their parting took place.

'Goodbye, laddie,' said McCleod.

'Goodbye, sir.'

'Here is the letter I promised. The world must know that the Swazi were the first up. Will you take every care with the parcel?'

'Of course, sir. Gladly.'

Frank turned towards his horse.

'Frank, you think I am a romantic fool, I suppose, living in the past?'

'Not at all,' said Thompson, guilty.

'You do, laddie. And maybe you are right with your Darwin and your natural selection and your progress. But, Frank, just remember, nobility and bravery are enduring qualities. They will survive our changes, the ones you so eagerly desire.'

'Perhaps you are misrepresenting me, sir. I do not despise these qualities at all. Nor do I think they will become superfluous.'

'Before you go, will you permit me to say that I know how keenly you felt Campbell's death.'

'Yes, sir,' said Frank reluctantly.

They were standing awkwardly outside McCleod's camp, with a few blacks gathered solemnly to watch their parting.

McCleod held his arm firmly.

'His death was noble. In battle.'

'Yes, sir.'

'It was noble. Nothing in his life became him like the leaving of it.' He said this without apparent irony.

'I was very fond of him, sir. But I am afraid that I cannot agree that his death was in any way his most noble act. On the contrary, I believe it was an awful and cruel waste.'

'Of course. You are upset. Poor Alister.'

He wanted to get away from McCleod now. McCleod was

perhaps trying to tell him that everything, even in the modern world, was subject to death and decay. If that was the case, he knew it already.

'I must go, sir,' said Frank firmly, mounting up. 'It is a long ride to the goldfields.'

'Go, laddie, and God go with you. Go with care, as our Swazi brothers say.'

'Goodbye, sir.'

He left McCleod standing there, smiling and waving in a distracted manner. He had been cruel to him. He could just as easily have left him with the comfort of agreeing that Alister Campbell's death was in some way a necessary sacrifice. Freedom in the truest sense could only come from understanding. He left McCleod as much in the mist as his Swazi allies.

It was impossible to travel in South Africa without acquiring retainers. He had acquired two. One was a half-caste called Kriel who was travelling only as far as the goldfields, and the other was a man of his own age, the son of Tshabalala. Kriel rode an old horse but Tshabalala walked, at first shyly behind the horses, but soon alongside.

'I have my servants now, Mama. We are travelling grandly to the goldfields where I shall make my fortune. We got back to the Swazi country thoroughly tired with travelling. The Swazis are splendid fellows, each one of them. In my little band I have the son of one of their important men. He is to travel with me to learn something of our ways. I was in the party of Captain McCleod and became friends with Alister Campbell; he was killed along with five other white men in the attack upon Sekukuni's Stadt, as they call it. We estimate that five hundred of the brave Swazi were killed, yet they walked cheerfully back to their own country. I was very fond of Alister Campbell.

I am seeing life and death out here. From discussions I have had I believe that great opportunities lie in the goldfields. It seems certain that we are now only at the beginning of an age of discovery. I am indeed fortunate to be here. Please pass my fondest wishes to Papa when he is able to receive them. Sometimes I long to be with you, seeing as if in a photograph the church, the old farm, our beloved house, all no doubt framed in frost now as I labour here under the sun. You would not recognise me. I have grown taller and thinner and nearly as brown as the unfortunate Coon.'

He composed the letter as they plodded along. The vastness of the landscape, the unpeopled valleys, the rolling purple mountains, (now becoming hard and bright as the sun rose) could not be captured in a letter. Nor could he say what he felt as a result of Campbell's death: a certain inner coldness, which had expressed itself in his farewell to McCleod. The coldness was accompanied by a sense of loss, the loss of his own substance.

Tshabalala walked next to him, holding on to Khelim's mane now. He pointed things out to Frank and gave them their Swazi names. Thompson tried to learn them. They appeared to have different names in different contexts. Kriel interpreted impatiently. The context which interested Tshabalala was the magical. Trees had magic properties. The roots of this tree were used to doctor the King. The trunk of this tree contained the spirits of people who had died by violence. This river was full of evil because of the way the rocks were strewn. The world for Tshabalala was not a fixed place with clearly defined properties. Not at all. The natural world, it seemed, was a slippery and evanescent article, hard to grasp or pin down. Tshabalala was learning the magic of the Swazi. He was to be one of the King's special counsellors, following a family bent. Along with this interest he had a great fascination with guns. Thompson showed him the workings of his guns. Together they stalked some francolin. They camped that first night beside the Lomati, and Kriel caught some fish.

Kriel built a small stockade of thorn bushes on a piece of flat ground above the ford. He said there were lions everywhere. They ate well on francolin and fish, grilled in the glowing embers of a fire. The wood burned almost without smoke, so hot that it was sufficient to allow the fire to smoulder. Frank took the first watch. He was alone at last. The Army created its own metropolis wherever it went; it was wearying.

Down below at the river he could see the shapes of hippos emerging for their anxious nocturnal ramble: they grunted and snorted one to the other before ploughing through the reeds and sedge on the banks. Kriel had told him that lions did not roar when they were hunting. They called softly to one another. Kriel had made the noise for him. Frank thought he heard it, in some bushes near the horses. He loaded his shotgun. The horses were knee-haltered within the circle of thornbushes. He stood up and walked a few yards from the fire. Suddenly he heard a low, bronchitic cough, nearer now. He fired at the bushes. Something rushed away but he caught only a glimpse of it. He fired again. The night sounds had died; Kriel and Tshabalala were building up the fire.

'I chased off a lion,' he said, 'your turn now.'
Kriel laughed.
'It was baboons in those bushes, Master.'

Frank lay on the ground with his head on his saddle. He had no tent, but he covered himself with a blanket and a sail, a piece of canvas which had a variety of uses as makeshift shelter, groundsheet or wrapping. He soon slept.

It took two days to reach the goldfields. On a hillside a small town had, as they say, sprung up. It consisted of a row of makeshift houses, clad in tin and timber, and a hotel. The miners themselves had spread out into the endless ravines and canyons on the surrounding mountains. It was a hand-to-mouth operation. He booked himself into the hotel and had the horses turned out in a pleasant field by a stream to recover from the journey.

At first sight the prospects for a young man seeking his fortune were not good. The dusty little street of Pilgrim's Rest was busy enough with crates of machinery as shiny as spittoons, ox carts, transport riders, farmers with produce and blacks sitting watching the spectacle from the side of the road. The problem, really was to find out how to start. He walked up the street and back again.

The exact circumstances of his meeting with Winkelmann were, like many momentous events, remarkable only with hindsight. Frank was sitting in the Royal Hotel reading an old copy of *The Times*, so old that it was still dealing with the fall of Ulundi seven months earlier, trying to catch up with the cricket scores (it was a good season for Gloucestershire and W. G. Grace) when he heard someone shouting in the hall. It was Winkelmann. His transport for Delagoa Bay had not arrived from Lydenburg. Winkelmann spoke English in a fashion that Frank had only heard parodied in music halls, with a strong cockney accent underlaid with German.

'Excuse me, sir,' said Frank, 'but I will do the job for you.'
'What do you know about transport riding?'
'Not much, sir, but I am willing to learn.'
'Do you know who I am?'
'No, sir. I am afraid I have only just arrived.'
'I am Ernest Winkelmann.'
'How do you do, sir. I am Frank Thompson.'
'You're from the old country?'
'Yes, sir. If by that you mean England, I am.'

'Of course I mean England. What are you doing here?'
'I am just out of the Army, sir.'
'Army. Army. *Sheiss.*'

Winkelmann was a good-looking man of about forty. His dark features were strong, so that there was no part of him that was not pronounced. His nose was large, his eye sockets protectively pouched, his chin sharp, his cheeks high and his eyes, very prominent, perhaps exaggerated by the thickness of his glasses. He wore a neat, closely cut beard. Here, in little Pilgrim's Rest, he wore a modish dark suit with a huge diamond tie stick. He might just have been off to the City.

'All right,' he said, 'I'll take a chance. Have you a wagon?'
'Yes, sir.'
'Meet me here with a wagon at five and I'll give you your instructions and load for Lourenço Marques.'
'What about pay, sir?'
'The usual rates.'
'Thank you, sir.'

He spent the rest of the day finding a wagon to buy. Wagons were expensive. The frantic activity of the interior, the search for gold, ivory, diamonds and minor chiefs to conquer had created a seller's market. He was finally able to buy a small outfit which came with two appropriately sized black youths, one to lead the oxen and one to goad them from behind on the carrot and stick principle. He had to part with all his cash and one of his guns, redeemable, to make up the deposit. He retained Kriel to manage the horses, because now that he had arrived at the goldfields, his purported destination, Kriel had no further plans. Tshabalala asked no questions with a certain African stoicism, although he was concerned that Frank had had to pawn the gun. It would be needed in the wilderness.

The road to Delagoa Bay was not unknown. It had simply not been mapped because it suffered severely from the weather and from the fever, so that huge detours were made to avoid sickly areas and flooded crossings and malarial swamps. Lions preyed upon straggling horses and oxen, always eager for an easy kill; dying animals were simply cut loose. Hasty enquiries revealed that a few wagons were leaving the following day, but he could not equip his wagon. He would have to obtain an advance from Winkelmann. He discovered what the rate for the job was and then sought Winkelmann out. Many years later, Winkelmann would recount the conversation with the eager young man.

'Sir, I am prepared to offer a discount on my rates, in return for an advance.'

'That's decent of you. Why would you want an advance?'

'I want to equip my wagons more fully.'

'How many wagons do you have?'

'One at present, sir.'

'And you have only had that for an hour or so from Mr Vermaak, from what I hear.'

'That is true, sir, but capital is what is required here, sir.'

'Now I take notice of what you are saying. I like it. You are a clever boy.'

'Yes, sir. I have been meaning to set up on my own, but I appreciate the necessity of capital.'

'Finance. Money. Capital. Yes, yes. These people' – he gestured expansively out of the window of the hotel – 'think you can make money by panning gold. Sure you can make a small fortune quickly if you are lucky – maybe – but what is needed in this country is machinery, capital, resources, do you understand me? To buy leases. To finance mining. That's it.'

'That's it, sir. That's my feeling exactly.'

Winkelmann gave him half the money and a great deal of advice.

The road to Lourenço Marques started with a dreadful downhill lurch towards the fever country below. The oxen slipped, the wagon slithered and turned over taking the best part of a morning to right. By the time they reached the bottom of the escarpment they were in disarray. Down here it was hot and steamy. The air carried disease; it carried the tsetse fly which simply enervated oxen, killing them in days. There were theories about beating this lethal insect: travel only at night, stick to high ground, avoid belts of trees, travel in cool weather only, and so on. Sometimes transport riders got through without a death; on the same route in the same month, whole teams could be destroyed. The tsetse, Glassima Palpalis, caused sleeping sickness in humans, a Rip Van Winkle affliction without the charming sequel. One of the early Boer pioneers had disappeared with all his family and followers on this route. Only recently the Swazi had returned two white people to the authorities in Lydenburg. These middle-aged Boers, captured as children, had suffered a fate at the hands of the Shangaan worse than death: naturalisation. They had become true Africans, all trace of their Calvinist election lost in their long steep in Africa.

Tshabalala, too, regarded this country as malevolent. The few trees with their yellow and poisonous-looking bark, like a reptile sloughing off its old skin, contained powerful medicine used by the Shangaan. The clouds of mosquitoes, never dispersed by cooling breezes, the endless wheeling in the skies of vultures, the startled, anxious animals in the bush, gave to the area the quality of uneasy dreams. The rivers redeemed the landscape. Around them were pleasant parklike growths of huge trees. On this road to the Malala Poort there were many beautiful camping places where wagons outspanned and oxen refreshed themselves. Outspan, after the first grinding day which had seen all the brake shoes smoking and useless, was a blessed relief. The oxen – his heavily mortgaged oxen – were led down to the river by one of the boys who banged the water with a stick to frighten off crocodiles. Frank could not help thinking that it might be akin to banging the dinner gong in the crocodilian world, but he kept his counsel, eager only to get to Delagoa Bay and learn the ropes. He sat down beside his wagon with some coffee, exhausted. Other members of the convoy were going through the same rituals; fixing the sail to make a tent; hacking wood; corraling the oxen; cooking coffee in old battered coffee cans; roasting meat on the fires and repairing wagons. Frank went to check on Khelim. He was, as ever, content, eagerly eating the dry hay that was considered an antidote to the horse sickness, a disease which flourished in the damp grass at night. He tugged the horse's coarse, powdery mane affectionately, but Khelim merely shuffled away from him, impatient with this sort of endearment. He walked around the other wagons. The drivers were a motley lot: some Portugese who were chopping onions and spoke no English; a young Australian who gave him some coffee and a Boer who had lost his farm. He talked to the Australian about the road ahead. It seemed he was optimistic.

Loneliness is mercifully transient. Since Campbell's death he had often felt lonely, even in the midst of many people. Down here in this flat, unhealthy country the very landscape was indifferent; Tshabalala seemed to be as distanced from the natural world as he was. This country was new. The kaffirs here were milling about to escape death and enslavement. The animals had a haunted, doomed look. Roads vanished overnight. Wagons were plundered. Settlements were ravished. Streams of disinherited white men were trickling out into the unknown, only to get themselves killed under the unseeing gaze of blind, cruel Africa. Loneliness crept up on him each day as the sun set and work was done. Loneliness is the realisation that life is finite. You are alone and moving on well-greased wheels down a straight path. *Ne pourrons-nous jamais sur l'océan des âges Jeter l'ancre un seul jour?* Lamartine, schoolboy French. It made keen sense here under the dreadfully impartial gaze of myriads of unnaturally bright stars. What little was left of Campbell lay out there. He thought fancifully of a few bones arranged with careless symmetry.

And yet loneliness sharpens the mind and the perceptions. He was perversely proud to be alone and lonely, moving through this restless wilderness, thousands of miles from home. It made the well-ordered certainties of life in England appear to be artifice.

He longed for a woman, for children, for possessions, to fill the void.

Lourenço Marques had a ramshackle, unorganised, shabby vitality. The houses were roofed with terracotta tiles. The harbour was full of craft. Two steamers were tied primly to a dock, away from the medieval shuttling and bustling of the dhows, dinghies and fishing boats. Here he could see it: creaking timber and sail beside iron and demonic steam. To accommodate this steam a huge mountain of coal was piling up on the spit of land next to the harbour itself. Beyond the harbour was an island, Inhaca, a refuge from the heat and squalor; a place it was said, where you could swim in clear waters, drink cold Portuguese wine and make love to beautiful girls of all colours. On the journey down the Australian had spoken of little else. Even here in town, as they outspanned near the market square, whores solicited him. Before he had had time to take Winkelmann's packages to the assay office, he had heard women say 'Fuck' many times; in his whole life he had never heard the word uttered by a woman. They said it like an incantation. He walked through this vicious undertow, until he found the agents. A black guard in an opera bouffe uniform struck the last woman, who was still following him, as he entered the courtyard of Williamson and McBride, Agents, Ships Chandlers and Importers. These desperate black and mulatto women could sense his loneliness and youth. It was an animal instinct. As he entered the offices of Mr McBride he hoped the guilty stirring in his groin would settle.

McBride was a tall and impossibly thin Ulsterman. It took him many seconds to stand up and stretch out his hand and offer Frank a seat. His face was grey from living in this unhealthy place, his skin stretched on his cheeks, pulling at his eyes and the corners of his mouth to give the illusion that he was smirking. McBride was one of those unlikely men who are invariably found in places like Lourenço Marques. Frank wanted to know why he did it, but did not ask whether he had a black mistress, how many times he had had dysentery and fever, whether he was making vast sums of money, or whether he was ever going home. Nor did McBride seem very curious about him or his dealings with Winkelmann.

'On Wednesday we shall have the merchandise ready for you, Mr Thompson. And you may collect the money at any time.'

'Thank you, sir.'

'I hope you have healthy oxen.'

'Happily they have all survived the journey.'

'It is uphill going back.'

Was it a joke?

'I suppose it is.'

McBride stood up again.

Suddenly he said, 'Would you like some tea?'

They sat down again awkwardly and waited while the tea was brought. A fan above their heads moved lazily, creating no perceptible draught. Its source of energy was hidden from view but it was probably adapted from the Indian method.

'What are the Portuguese like, to do business with, I mean?' ventured Frank. All the time he was thinking of that teeming horde of whores and hoping at Inhaca to find himself a girl with whom he could exorcise his loneliness.

'The Portuguese are a very indifferent people, but suited to this kind of place. They have been in Africa for three hundred years, you know.'

What did he mean by this? That they had barely scratched the interior; that they had made little impression upon the landscape away from the Bay; or that they had gained wisdom through long experience?

'Is Mr Winkelmann a big customer of yours?'

McBride was puzzled by the phrase. Then after a few moments' deliberation, while his eyes seemed to lose their focus and become oily, he said, 'Yes, he is. I would say he is our most important customer in South Africa.'

There was a world of commerce here. Williamson and McBride were people to get to know, but for now he must go to Inhaca and slake himself. It was becoming obsessional.

'I must go now, Mr McBride. Perhaps on Wednesday we could meet. I have many questions to ask you and things to learn if you would be good enough to bear with me?'

'Certainly, young man. And I shall have your money. Three pounds and ten shillings the ounce.'

The slow process of unravelling himself began again for McBride. He accompanied Thompson through the cool inner courtyard, where a black man was watering exotic plants in terracotta pots and out into the cruel heat of the road. They shook hands gravely. Business complete. He had already made fifty pounds towards paying off his wagons. It was the first money he had ever earned on his own account.

Inhaca, like the sexual act itself, proved to be ephemeral. The greatest pleasure, more substantial than the others, was to swim in the clear, tepid sea and to lie on the sands; every minute he spent splashing in the water steeped away the experiences of the last few months. Death was easily forgotten in the rasping sun, the cool vinous shade and the promiscuous lap of the water. He met a girl called Consuela as he was buying some bread and she followed him back to his lodging. She lay on the bed without bothering to get fully undressed. He grasped her lean, wiry thighs and thrust himself into her. She smiled and kissed him. She was a mulatto, with a dark, smooth skin and lips which were faintly purple close to. She said her father was Chinese, but there was no sign of it. Her unthinking sensuality calmed him. She would play casually with his penis at all hours of the day and suck it distractedly when they were lying in the cool of the palm thatched hut that opened to the sea. She tried to interest him in mounting her from behind; she sat astride him and milked him with her muscular hips so effectively that he thought he would faint. The second night she brought another girl, who she said was her sister, but she too did not look Chinese. She was so young she seemed barely pubescent, with tiny breasts and a sly smile. Where Consuela had wiry African hair, this girl had long dark hair: he lay on her and fucked her, her little girl's face, her neat mouth, smiling benignly, bored, while Consuela's tongue found its way into his ears and then down his thighs and back. Consuela and her sister did all this with an absent-minded air that shocked him at first, but then reassured him. The little sister, Maria, who lay under him like a cherub, had a mullet pink mouth tasting of woodsmoke and corn beer. Her neck had a patch of white, where her pigmentation was imperfect, the size of a half crown. Her knees were speckled as though cinders had embedded themselves there just below the skin. They spoke very little English, but three days passed pleasantly, almost domestically; they became a small depraved family, lost children.

Taking leave of Inhaca was easy. He was excited by the prospects of South Africa. It was not a lust for wealth, but a conviction that he could use his talents there to good advantage. He shared a bottle of wine with the girls as they waited for the ferry. What would they be doing as he went off to acquire a knowledge of gold and the capital requirements of this raw country? They would move on blithely to other men and other secrets. He was in a fortunate position; it seemed to him sitting in this remote place with two whores. (one smiling vacantly and beatifically at the sea and the other sniffing tearfully) that he had been given the key to a new age. The wine, though light, made him heady. He stood up, for a moment trapping Consuela's discouraged hand in his trousers. He laughed. He gave them money.

'You come back. You marry me and my sister.'

He laughed again, but not unsympathetically. The boat, a cutter, which had been modified to take a paddle at the back, tied up. He took his few things aboard and sat back on the transome. The girls stood on the little jetty, Consuela weeping, her sister waving happily; with every pull and tug of the oar on the resisting sea, he saw their innocent figures receding into the past.

Before they tied up again at the bottom of the steps in the harbour, Inhaca and the two girls had joined another world as surely as Alister Campbell.

McBride moved far too slowly for him. Yet he had spent the morning politely showing Frank the workings of the shipping business and the assay office. The Portuguese, McBride explained, had seen gold simply as another product of the unknowable interior; ivory, skins, slaves and now gold. But they were worried about the newly vigorous and largely North European activity of the uplands. It was a threat to their existence here, clinging to the coast as they had done for hundreds of years, waiting for the desperate, the lunatic and the murderers – in short the only people who had a reason to venture inland – to bring them the fruits of their adventures. Gold was a profitable business, but they preferred the more haphazard trade of earlier times which had made little impression on the immemorial ways of the hinterland. Now – so McBride said – they saw the straws in the wind.

McBride knew the gold trade well, but he saw only the parochial implications. Gold, quite simply, was not an ordinary product like ivory or skins. It captured with its dull yellow light two of man's divergent instincts, the desire for beauty, the most transient of properties, and the desire for permanence, the least obtainable. Gold was now trickling to the outside world. When the trickle became a flood, then the power of those who controlled that flood would have no limits. They would have political power and the power of command.

He and McBride lunched at a Portuguese hotel where an attempt had been made to recreate aristocratic Portugal in the high, timbered ceilings and elaborate, poorly painted furniture with tassels. They ate a local fish, familiary called bacalao and some mutton stew, which Frank found oily. Kriel and Tshabalala had the wagon loaded and the horses and oxen ready. He signed for his money, shook McBride's hand and they began to trek out of town. The machinery for Winkelmann was nailed into a sturdy crate. This object, looking like a huge hat box, sat incongruously in the middle of the wagon. The oxen strained, the whip cracked and Tshabalala and the two boys shouted in high, harsh voices. The ship of Africa was under way.

Winkelmann was pleased. Frank did not tell him what it had cost in sleepless nights, sweat and the exercise of will to get back to Pilgrim's Rest two days early. He accepted the congratulations modestly. Four oxen had died of the sickness. The last three days had been a torture with Khelim and the other horse unwillingly joining the surviving oxen for the long haul up the mountains. The resourceful Kriel had bitten and burnt the tails of the oxen, while the boys goaded and lashed them repeatedly. The ox, it seemed, had hidden strengths which it was reluctant to produce except under duress. He had had no time to shoot for the pot and they had eaten nothing but mealie meal. It was a cruel, primitive struggle.

Winkelmann sent him to Pretoria to have some documents stamped by the government of Sir Theophilus Shepstone. It was pleasant to ride up there on so undemanding a task. The Union flag, presumably the very one that Haggard had raised, hung limply over Market Square, a rebuke to the Boers for their short-sightedness in allowing the British to take over. The British were busily replacing the Dutch language, smartening up the official buildings, finishing a race course and polo field, planting trees and changing the names of places. The Boers, led by Paul Kruger, were beginning to cook up all those resentments and myths which are essential to nationalism. It troubled Frank to see the blindness of the officer class in Pretoria as it blithely ignored the feelings of the Boers and welcomed the inevitable conflict. As usual it failed to see a connection between prosperity and peace. As for the blacks, in Pretoria they were an ignored people.

Nonetheless he was invited to a ball by a young officer whom he had met in Zululand. This young man's name was Richard Tuffnell. He had been a classmate of the Prince Imperial at Woolwich. The ball was for his sister, Lucy, who was returning to England in a few days.

By the time Frank had plodded back to Pilgrim's Rest a week later he was determined to go to England to marry Lucy and pursue his education in the world of finance. But it was three months before Winkelmann permitted him to leave, with letters of introduction to Dinkelsbühler and Bruns in the City and a promise of a junior partnership in the firm of Winkelmann and Brothers on his return. There were no brothers, but, Winkelmann contended, it made the firm look more solid.

He took ship from Durban on the *Arab*, by a coincidence the same boat on which he had arrived nearly a year before. It was rusting now.

CHAPTER 7

Neither family's circumstances were what they appeared. The Tuffnells lived in a huge house built for an earlier and more prosperous generation on the banks of the Avon. It was suffering from the effects of ill-advised attempts to keep up with the times. Disastrous financial speculations by Lucy's father had almost ruined the family. The Chinese garden was sadly overgrown. The stables, built for fifty horses, housed six, and the staff was reduced to the bare minimum necessary to keep chaos at bay. Most of the thousand acres were let or mortgaged. Fortunately this May fires were not needed in the main rooms because of an early and warm spring.

Sixty miles away, in Gloucestershire, the Thompsons lived in a small village in a pleasant manor house next to the church. From the steeple of this church the hills and secret hollows of the surrounding countryside could be seen, sheltering remote cottages and farms where strange practices involving barely nubile girls and their relatives were believed to go on. Or so it was said, hopefully, in the Market Tavern in Northleach. Frank's father had suffered an apoplectic seizure very early in his career in India; he had been an administrator and a scholar. Now he sat impotently in the study, the pregnant shafts of light filtered through the trees of the churchyard falling heavily on books he could no longer read. Nonetheless he kept up the appearance, being wheeled each day to the same spot, where he sat staring at pages he could not turn.

Frank's mother was a careful, well-organised woman. She knew to the penny how much money they could afford to spend. The household and the farm ran smoothly and without apparent effort. There were two other children both still at school, a boy and a girl. Frank was the oldest, the only one who could remember the happiest period of their lives, when his father had been active, energetic and cheerful. It was a memory they conspired to keep bright, like an icon in a dark room. Father playing polo; Father meeting the unimpressionable Maharajah of Jaipur; Father working on his treatise on Indian imports; Father in consultation with the Viceroy. India, with all its oriental fakery, was for Frank simply a lantern show. Even now the British were attempting to subdue the tribes in the icy hills around Kabul. It was a game of bloody chess.

Despite the air of frugality that clung to the household and the little farm, the place had prospered under his mother's guidance.

Frank looked at his familiar surroundings with a sense of surprise. Nothing had changed. He had expected after a tumultuous year to find things changed. But no whirlwinds had swept through here. The farm was orderly, the same ten cows were milked every day, and the house hung quiet in the spring air, expecting something that never happened. In his study Father sat in the thrall of his silent inquisition. He went in and shook his father's hand and spoke quietly to him.

'I'm back, Father. Back from Africa. Have you been well?'

His father appeared to struggle to speak, but he had been unable to utter a word for fourteen years. A cloud perhaps scudded over his troubled face.

'I'm back, Father. Africa is a strange and wonderful place. I wish you could have seen it. I'll tell you all about it.'

He felt a welling affection for this man, not yet old, trapped here, the weak light of May falling on his desk, the white wistaria already hanging down in rich exotic profusion outside his window.

'I'm going to be married, Father. The girl has not yet had her father's consent, but I am sure I can convince him of my worth. After all I have only to tell him who my father was.'

It was an unfortunate choice of words. He put his arm around his father's shoulders and hugged him briefly. He had never done anything like that before. Did his father notice how brown and tall he was? Did he sense that he had grown up? He turned to go; at the door he looked back; his father was nodding slightly now, his greying, thin hair neatly brushed, his hands resting stiffly on his thighs, his useless books symmetrically arranged.

'I shall read to you tonight, Father,' he said.

His mother was waiting in the drawing room, a simple room with a high open fireplace where a fire of elm logs burned and the dogs lay.

'How is he?' Frank asked.

'It's impossible to say. The years go by and there is no improvement. Come, let us have tea.'

She led the way serenely out into the garden. Tea was laid on the terrace under the Tibetan magnolia, now a substantial tree, the result of one of his mother's trips to the great botanic gardens in Calcutta many years before. It had survived the cold winters of the Cotswolds only by careful nurturing, but now in its adolescence it seemed to have acclimatised well. Against the bare stone wall of the house its white and pink flowers were as delicate and imperious as the head of a swan.

Her curiosity about Africa was peculiarly motherly. She wanted to know about the weather and the food and the means of transport from place to place. She was interested in the politics only to know by how far the beastly Boer and the savage Zulu were overstepping the mark. Frank tried to explain to her his fascination with the country and its riches, but she was more concerned that there were few hospitals, many wild animals and no reliable tradespeople.

She was a shrewd woman. Her handling of the family fortunes proved it. But when circumstance had forced her to abandon the world of ideas fourteen years ago she could no longer allow herself the pleasure of idle speculation or unreciprocated sympathies for places and notions with which she had no dealings. She had retired into the world of the material and the practical. Her retreat was the mirror image of her husband's who had sunk into a dark world where there was no reality.

He watched her as she told him of the year's happenings. She was cheerful, but her eyes were rather too bright, like a bird's, as though under the apparent serenity she was always watchful. Her hair was perhaps a little more grey, her waist a little stiffer, but he thought he could see the girl who had married his father twenty-three years earlier. She had been a beautiful girl by all accounts, blithe and generous. The surprise was that she had responded so well to his father's illness, firmly guiding them back to the draughty Cotswolds and to the small family property, and equally firmly making it prosper. In India, in the scented, dappled world of his infancy, they had had body servants, bearers, syces, and secretaries; here she baked bread herself, made butter and cooked. In the beginning old Doctor Jeakins had come to see Father, but his remedies and suggestions were ineffectual and probably painful. Now he came infrequently for purely totemistic reasons; he was the local doctor after all.

'I am dying to meet your Lucy. What is she like?'

He had her picture and a snippet of her hair in a locket. He could not tell her that he had only danced with her five times and spent half a day riding with her on the bare veldt. It was too thin an acquaintance to justify his proposal of marriage. By now Lucy might be back in the safety of her home and forgetting the foolishness of the gypsy encampment of Pretoria. They had written. Her letters were full of rather literary endearments. He showed his mother the picture.

'Lovely girl. Frank, she is so beautiful.'

He had not thought of Lucy as beautiful.

'I propose to go back to South Africa when I have finished with Dinkelsbühler.'

'How long will that be?'

'Perhaps a year. I must first meet her father and obtain his consent.'

The jam on the scones was plump with last season's strawberries. This was England; the cuckoo calling in the copse; the church clock at a quarter past three. And yet it was tied to the cries of the savage and the crack of the Martini Henry which he could still hear over the water.

Lucy was hoping that he had not regretted asking her to marry him. They both felt a great relief in finding out how anxious the other had been.

Lucy was wearing a tightly-waisted silk dress, with lace trimming over the bodice. How young she was. He felt more than his three years older than her. She was nervous about his introduction to her father; she knew that her father's confidence had been destroyed by his ridiculous speculations and she was worried that Frank, so obviously a sensible and intelligent young man, would despise his weakness, pretension and glaring guilt. He had destroyed in a few misguided years what had been built up over two centuries. It was a heavy burden. Old families were growing rich by the strange mechanics of the stock market; everone was investing money in mines in Australia, tea plantations in India, shoe factories in Nottingham, railroads in Ohio, steamships in Liverpool, diamonds in Kimberley, repeating rifles in New Jersey and factories in Birmingham. Poor Tuffnell had invested in a gold mine in Mexico, blighted by an Indian revolt before it had started its operations. The Indians had murdered the Yankee overseers and stolen their mules and guns. In Pretoria Lucy had been happy and carefree, away from the oppressive atmosphere of the family home.

She explained this quickly as they walked along the stream, diverted from the Avon, to form the Chinese garden; a small pagoda of lacquered red stood over a tributary. It was a copy of one in the gardens of the Imperial Palace near Peking, destroyed in 1860. They clasped hands. In the dusty pagoda, with the water rushing over a small weir beneath the floor, they kissed.

'Will you come with me to Africa?'

'Yes, my darling. Anywhere.'

She pressed herself against him so that he could feel her breasts and legs. He could not help comparing her embrace with Consuela's.

'Anywhere you say.'

'Shall we go and see your father now?'

'In a moment.'

She kissed him this time. He could feel the cleft in her back as he put his arms around her. It was touchingly childish. He longed for the time when he would be able to make love to her, as he had done to the depraved sisters. At least they had taught him that women can enjoy the act. At school it had been said in whispers that true ladies did not move during the act of love. Lucy pressed herself against him oblivious. He pulled away from her fearful that she would feel something untoward. They sat down, both a little ashamed of the nakedness of their feelings and watched two swans paddling, bad tempered, upstream through the overgrown plantings which no longer resembled a delicate Chinese pattern so much as the inevitable onset of oriental decay.

'It's awful, isn't it?' she said.

'What are you thinking?'

'I'm thinking that you should not see how low this place has come in the past few years.'

'What about your brother?'

'There's nothing much Richard can do. He has no fortune. It will all be sold or mortgaged soon.'

'We'll do something about it.'

As yet he had not even joined Dinkelbühler on a salary of £90 a year, but she believed him. Cheered, she led him in to see her father who was waiting apprehensively in the library, pretending to attend to his business affairs; the truth was that he had long given up looking at his papers. Whenever he had tried he had felt an irreversible despair creeping over him. He hoped that his prospective son-in-law, a young man with connections in the goldfields, could help him to sort out his affairs. He looked up at the knock on the door, one hand holding a blotter, as if caught in the middle of important work.

Frank Thompson was a tall, thin young man, with a deep suntan and intense eyes. He was dressed rather plainly, but his voice was precise and firm, hardly the voice of a young man at all.

'So you would like to marry my daughter?' he asked as soon as the introductions were over, trying to imitate his earlier manner, which had been full of bluff good will and directness.

'Yes, sir. I would. And as soon as possible.'

Lucy's father was about sixty years old, he guessed, dressed in the old fashion with boots and a stock, as if he were proposing to go out hunting at any moment. He had been the master of foxhounds in these parts; now he dressed as though he were expecting the happy clamour of the hounds and the clatter of horses' hooves in the stableyard to resume at any minute. Between his large, bucolic whiskers, his nose was laced with tiny broken blood-vessels, the product of sleepless nights and intense worry. His eyes, like his daughter's, were blue, but with a film over them as if he were in imminent danger of going blind. Perhaps if he blinked the film would become opaque.

'I must think it over, Mr Thompson. Alas, Lucy's mother is no longer here to advise me, so I must take especial care. But it seems from all I have heard of you, from Lucy and Richard, that you would make her a good husband.'

'Thank you, father.'

'Thank you, sir. I hope your estimation of me proves correct.'

'Are you proposing to go back to South Africa?'

'We are, sir. As soon as I have finished my training in finance.'

The whole conversation had an unreal character. He felt sorry for this broken-down country squire in his rambling house, the Jack Russells asleep by the fire, farting minutely and twitching, the paintings of over-bred horses and dogs and memorable days in the field. Over it all hung the tyranny of poverty.

Frank saw Tuffnell's weakness with such clarity that he wondered as he lay tucked up that night in a huge feather bed only two doors away from Lucy, why his stay in Africa had given him so cruel an insight into the foibles of his countrymen.

Lucy was not asleep. She lay awake happily. She felt slightly feverish. It had been such a wonderful day. Frank was so strong in these troubled times, so sure of his future. They had talked about Africa and Frank had explained what was taking place there in very straighforward terms. Where Henry Morton Stanley had seen the opening up of Africa in terms of human enlightenment, Frank saw it simply as the irresistible march of man's mastery of the material world. This world was producing change according to a foreseeable pattern. Lucy now regarded Frank, happily, as a product of this new age. It was different from her brother's world, which embraced ideals that bore little relation to the actual world; her father's world had passed altogether, lost in the growing welter. It was ironic that Frank should discover this in the old, dark continent.

Dinkelsbühler himself was German, a cousin of Winkelmann. He had moved easily from the world of conventional finance into the new business of mining finance, despite the handicaps of language and social pretension that faced him. His offices, near London Wall, were cramped and cluttered, but there was a sense of purpose and earnestness which appealed to Frank. From those four small rooms telegrams, bills, promissory notes, letters of credit, share issues and assay reports flowed. Winkelmann was the man in the field. He and his older cousin were attempting to gain control of these new riches; they had missed Kimberley by five or six years, but they saw that new opportunities, perhaps even greater, were open to those with a sense of occasion. Up the river, in Whitehall, they might be thinking of grand imperial designs involving the despatch of regiments, missionaries and administrators; here they thought only of the application of capital.

Winkelmann was the entrepreneur. Dinkelsbühler was the provider. He sat all day long at an uncomfortable, high, roll top desk, smoking turkish cheroots which cloaked his little office with a Byzantine fragrance, a fragrance which clung to the place even when he was not there.

'The reason we have employ you, Mr Thompson, is simple. Mr Winkelmann and myself need someone who can talk with the English.'

They wanted him to be a front man. Trade and the flag were, for better or worse, inseparable. Frank was slighted, but he said nothing, sure that Dinkelsbühler would see his worth soon enough.

Winkelmann must surely have told him that he had some good qualities.

That first day he worked, with Dinkelsbühler's guidance, through five huge ledgers which detailed all the transactions, all the borrowings and lendings, for the past four years. So far Winkelmann had spent nearly three quarters of a million pounds and there had been few returns. But they owned jointly and through public companies, twenty-four leases, eighteen farms and vast amounts of plant.

'We must buy. We must control. We must not sell.'

In another huge ledger all the assay reports, with Dinkelsbühler's comments in German, were neatly written. Dinkelsbühler showed him this briefly and then locked it away in the safe which stood huge and immovable beside his desk.

The next day he was sent to the assay office with some samples that Winkelmann had forwarded to London. He was shown the laboratory at work. It was a simple enough process; already Winkelmann had portable kits in the field, but with so much salting of claims going on, the prospective subscribers wanted the government certificate. Dinkelsbühler knew just how to use assay reports in his prospectuses. He enlisted Frank's help in writing the prospectus for the 'New Goldfields Chartered Company of South Africa.' It was rushed to the printer. They would have virtual control of a new rash of finds south of Pilgrim's Rest by the end of the year. Each day was filled from eight in the morning until nine at night with these dealings. He crept home to an Islington rooming house, exhausted but exhilarated.

He and Dinkelsbühler soon became firm friends. The older man became quite indiscreet in telling him of their dealings. They had raised the first hundred thousand pounds on the strength of two leases bought from a bankrupt prospector before the gold was even discovered on his properties. Winkelmann simply felt that the small canyon where the farm *Allesverloren* stood, must harbour gold. Fortunately he had been right. They had moved very fast to secure more leases in the area cheaply before news of the find became common knowledge. Dinkelsbühler was not interested in the politics of Pretoria, but Frank told him of Haggard's fears and the need to be ready.

'You should be right. The Transvaal must remain in the hands of the British. And if not, we will become German again,' he said with a smile.

Dinkelsbühler had developed a great love for England; Frank found it incongruous because he spoke English poorly and was completely German in his personal taste and habits. But, as he pointed out, Prince Albert was little better.

Lucy found it hard to understand Frank's preoccupations. Other young men went to Henley or to balls or to Ascot, but Frank preferred to work. As often as he could he would take the train down to Salisbury to see her, but it was not often and Lucy suffered, imprisoned at home in a state of suspense. Frank was able to persuade Dinkelsbühler to buy some of her father's more pressing debts, which eased the atmosphere at River House considerably. Lucy and Frank's mother made plans for the wedding, while Frank and Dinkelsbühler worked on the enthusiastic subscriptions for the Goldfields Chartered Company day and night. By carefully including various holdings and excluding others, Dinkelsbühler and Winkelmann would retain overall control, although they had invested virtually no money of their own. The Goldfields Chartered Company had no charter, but Dinkelsbühler believed, like his cousin, in appearance. It was important that it should appear solid, Frank realised, because in his rather quiet, unimpressive way, Dinkelsbühler was taking stupendous risks with huge sums of other people's money.

The wedding took place in November. Dinkelsbühler did not come; Frank had made sure he was invited over his mother's misgivings. She feared that a hairy Israelite, complete with Merchant of Venice wardrobe, would appear from the City and begin to eye the family silver. But Dinkelsbühler was a sensitive man. As well as his glaring foreignness, which he knew would make the guests uneasy, he explained to Frank that he would not want to spoil the day for the bride and her father; his presence would be a reminder of their indebtedness. Let them have their day.

'It's our burden, you understand. We are supporting half the nobility of Europe, so they don't want to see us. *Natürlich.*'

It was the only time Dinkelsbühler ever talked to Frank about the burdens of being a Jew.

His gifts to the young couple, a set of silver candlesticks and a letter formally inviting Frank to become a junior partner on his return to South Africa, were generosity itself.

Frank stood at the foot of the three low steps leading up to the altar. The harvest festival had given way to the elaborate flower arrangements of the wedding. As he stood, waiting for Lucy to appear on her father's arm, he saw a large rat, sleek with its gleanings from the harvest festival, appear for a moment beside the altar, look coldly out at the congregation and vanish under the altar cloth.

He thought suddenly of Tshabalala and his magic. What would he make of a rat at a wedding?

The organist began to play frenetically. Frank turned. Lucy and her father stood for a moment at the entrance to the little church. He had pretended not to listen to the details of her dress. It was very simple; in her hair were tied some short satin ribbons, which gave her a carefree pagan look; she held a small bouquet of lilies of the valley; her veil was studded with seed pearls. She was intensely happy. So small was the church, with its rough flagstones and poor stained glass window, that she was soon beside him. At that moment he loved her with unbearable intensity; all this dressing up, coming together of families and singing of psalms was a ritual, in McCleod's words, that made it real.

'With my body I thee honour.'
'With my body I thee honour.'
'I Lucy Mary Christina.'
'I Lucy Mary Christina.'
'With my body I thee honour.'
'With my body I thee honour.'
'I Frank Edward.'
'I Frank Edward.'

He would never be lonely again. The corn-fed rat appeared. He hoped Lucy's father did not see it; he was a disciple of Frederic Myers and might imbue it with undue significance. It was chewing something, its cheeks puffed with contentment.

Lucy tugged his hand gently. They were man and wife. He walked with her to the vestry to sign the register. He looked at her blue eyes, so young, so happy, so innocent and kissed her formally. He noticed, for the first time it seemed, her small mouth, pink and well fleshed; it reminded him irresistibly of Consuela's little sister, Maria.

CHAPTER 8

Sir George Colley was killed courting death or glory at Majuba. Glory evaded him. Poor Colley had proudly attacked the Boers without regard for local conditions and without listening to informed advice. Perhaps he was trying to make amends for his previous blunder. Death or glory boys. He was shot sitting on his horse in the open. The Transvaal was lost to the British. Frank and Lucy Thompson landed in Durban a few weeks later. In Durban the defeat and the incursion of the Boers into Natal were regarded as a catastrophe. In London Gladstone was delighted. He was able to get rid of another expensive and irksome problem. A few thousand backward and troublesome Boer farmers could now be left to the freedom of their rural ignorance without expense to the Treasury. The argument that the Boers' freedom would prove inimical to the freedom of others, notably the blacks, cut no ice with him. On this principle Her Majesty's government would have to intervene in almost every country on earth.

When Frank Thompson finally arrived in Pilgrim's Rest, he discovered for himself that things had changed. The town had lost its attractive bustle; there had been few new finds and the existing holdings were almost worked out.

Lucy was shocked by the primitiveness of the place. She had been expecting something like Pretoria, not big but somehow substantial, in keeping with its status as the richest gold mining town in the world. It seemed absurd that this little village, with one street of flimsy houses could be the eldorado that Frank had spoken of. To add to her sense of dislocation, they were greeted at their new house by Tshabalala, who wore only a leather apron under his Norfolk jacket, and had his hair in greasy plaits. Round his neck were amulets of beads and porcupine quills. His role in the household was not clear, but Frank said he was a good man. Winkelmann had found a gardener and a cook for them, and Kriel soon returned from his aimless wanderings to complete the household.

She liked the house. Winkelmann had discovered it and made all the arrangements. It was a low building of stone, with an iron fretwork balcony and galvanised iron roof. In the garden was a small clump of indigenous trees with strange thorns and nobbles. Winklemann appeared to her an outlandish character at first, certainly a charlatan, with his curious accent and sharp's clothes, but he quickly won her over. He had put interesting books by her bed and bought her a horse as a wedding present. He took her into his confidence and explained that things had taken a dangerous turn in the last few months, but said that this presented even greater opportunities for them. Frank was a young man with a lot of promise. They would have to work hard, but it would be all right in the end. Despite his look of a confidence trickster, she found she believed him.

At first Lucy cried at night, from homesickness. Frank made love to her desperately to comfort her and keep at bay the anxiety which she had brought with her. They would fall asleep exhausted and sweating, her tears of loneliness joined by the tears of ecstasy. Frank sometimes missed the carefreeness of his previous stay in Africa, but as Lucy began to flourish in her new home, he became almost unbearably content. The knowledge that she was at home, waiting for him so that they could go out riding, or supervising the garden, or playing the piano happily, was so precious to him that he felt as if he were the possessor of two lives rather than one, the second granted to him quite arbitrarily and undeservedly.

He and Winkelmann spent long hours together planning; they were precariously balanced.

'We have leases, properties and resources, but we do not have income.'

'Do you really believe more gold will be found?'

'Who can say? There must be more. It is very unlikely that this is the only place in the whole continent where gold is found. But then I may be meshuga myself, after too many years here. If we want to go on we must give our shareholders and subscribers something. If we can't get gold we must get leases. I would like you to go to Pretoria and promise the Boers some concessions in Swaziland in return for more leases here. They only want land. They want winter grazing in Swaziland. Mbandzeni will sign anything.'

Winkelmann himself was negotiating with the diamond magnates in Kimberley, offering them participation in the new company in return for some cash producing assets in Kimberley to satisfy the subscribers in England. Their terms were harsh, for they were already millionaires with mansions in Cape Town and Mayfair, racehorses at Newmarket and the certain prospect of titles. But Winkelmann had played on their fears of missing out on any new gold strikes. Rhodes despatched his brother to strike some sort of bargain and soon Winkelmann was able to send back to London the reassuring news that Mr Cecil Rhodes would be taking a substantial interest in the new company. The ship was leaking, but Winkelmann was adept at plugging the holes.

Lucy had brought some seed from England. It took only a few weeks for this seed to produce lettuces and cauliflowers that were the envy of Pilgrim's Rest. She began to make a collection of the trees and flowers of the area; she and Frank would ride out into the surrounding hills and collect cycads, orchids and the seeds of trees which came in pods and oyster-shaped cases and winged boxes; Tshabalala knew many of these plants, although he had never tried to grow them himself. She went with Frank on a trip to Pretoria, to establish contact with the new mining commissioner. Paul Kruger, the Boer leader, had left for Europe, and Pretoria was in a confused and inert state, with the British residents resentful of the new government and angry with Gladstone. Lucy and Frank bought a few articles for the house and had their picture taken by Mr Gros, the photographer in Church Street. The photograph shows Frank and Lucy standing frozen with – respectively – a masterful, confident stare and a sweet but resourceful smile. Frank Thompson has already begun to Africanise his dress and holds a soft felt hat of the sort worn by the irregulars. His waistcoat and jacket are trimmed with thin satin braid and he wears riding breeches. Lucy Thompson carries a parasol and wears a small flowery hat from which three small ribbons hang. It is very dashing.

When they were last here, Pretoria had been the scene of balls and rudimentary polo matches and all the gaiety of a military encampment. Now the town was quiet and morose. Grass and weeds had grown in the streets during the siege. The road from Pretoria to Lydenburg was still littered with the bones of the horses and cattle belonging to the 94th Regiment. The number of British dead was a cause for alarm not only to the British, but to the Boers themselves. It might well bring massive retribution one day. The first, shocking, puddles of blood on that dusty road had ensured that there was no going back to a state of innocence.

Frank and Lucy met the new mining commissioner. He was

flattered and charmed by this young couple so fresh from Europe, so keen to succeed in this far-off country. He signed some papers carelessly and promised to look favourably at the grant of new leases in return for grazing concessions in Swaziland. The truth was, the Boers thought that gold was played out and were glad of it.

'What are these leases worth?' Lucy wanted to know.

'Nothing much at the moment, but Winkelmann believes there is gold in the south.'

'Does the commissioner know?'

'He does not. Nor does he care. They are interested in land. They would like to take the Swazi country now.'

'Why do you want yet more useless concessions?'

'When the next finds are made, we will have control. Do you see? Mr Winkelmann and Mr Dinkelsbühler believe that they can become as powerful as Mr Rhodes.'

'And you?'

'Ah well. I believe we should wait and see.'

Winkelmann was well pleased with the concessions.

'Now, my boy, all we have to do is find some more gold. And you must court the new commissioner. Give them something in Swaziland. Go and see the King.'

The remaining prospectors in Pilgrim's Rest were sent out on salary to look for gold in the hills in the south. The two workable mines, the property of the Chartered Company, were placed on a more systematic basis with new stamp batteries. The town had lost half its population; the remaining half worked for Winkelmann and his junior partner, Frank Thompson, who, in keeping with his extreme youth, behaved quietly and respectfully but began to display an iron determination which appealed to Winkelmann. It was essential to the whole operation to keep the exploration and assay reports flowing in. They both believed that there must be more gold; small finds confirmed this; Winkelmann wrote home to Dinkelsbühler; Frank composed letters to newspapers and financial journals, well salted with technical detail; the subscribers continued to subscribe.

'I must go to Swaziland next week, dearest,' he said.

'I wish I could come with you.'

'I will only be gone a fortnight. Do you know what the Swazi King named me? The Heron.'

'Why?'

'Because he said I was watchful.'

'You are watchful, Frank. I sometimes think you are too watchful. Too much the observer.'

Frank deflected her from this line of conversation. Since Alister Campbell's death he had felt a detachment which only now was beginning to fade.

'Are you happy?'

'Frank, I am so happy. I thank you for it. Frank, it is much too early to be sure, but I think I may be going to have a baby.'

'Oh, my God, I hope so. I long for it.'

They embraced. Frank was amazed, and stunned, that new life could be created with so little experience or premeditation.

The signing of the papers was the least important part of the whole process of negotiation. It appeared to have become meaningless routine to Mbandzeni. Frank had to guide his thumb from the ink to the bottom of the lease, where it produced a smudge. The sovereigns Frank had paid for a huge tract of grazing and some leases near Phophonyane Falls in the northern part of the country were left lying on the ground in their little bag, in danger of being forgotten while the cattle Frank had presented were slaughtered.

Mbandzeni had grown fatter and less alert since their last meeting. McCleod had long since gone and the Swazi King's affairs had sunk into confusion. Parts of his country had been granted two and three times over to different speculators. The path to his royal village was well trodden by white men. He had forgotten Frank, it seemed, until he was reminded by Tshabalala of the name he had given him. Mbandzeni wore a bulky necklace of wooden blocks, which looked very uncomfortable. He sat on the ground and stared vacantly at the mountains, rousing himself only as the meat was brought for their approval. The royal women danced and sang in the background, which appeared to comfort the King.

Tshabalala explained that the King was bewitched. He was no longer himself. The confusion the clamouring white man had brought to his life was merely a symptom. The disease itself was far more serious. The King ate greedily. Tshabalala explained which parts of the ox he might eat to fortify himself. All the organs had properties. Everything had properties. Tshabalala wished to acquire a knowledge of these properties. The King needed medicines that were very powerful. They talked long into the night after the King had retired stupefied and fearful.

There was a disturbing fecundity about the place. Her mare was in foal. The plants she stuck hopefully in the ground sprouted instantly. Black girls wearing only tiny leather aprons walked insouciantly about the town, breasts bobbing jauntily. And she was now sure she was pregnant, although it was too early to call in Doctor McAllister.

She longed for Frank. It was almost an obsession. She longed for his body and the feel of him. This desire could afflict her for days on end from waking to fitful sleep. Their bed was draped with a mosquito net to form a private tent. There the unthinkable, unspeakable madness took place. Her breasts prickled as she thought of it. She loved Frank and now she understood what it meant to honour someone with your body.

Frank and Tshabalala rode up towards Phonphonyane to look over the claims there. Gold had been found higher up the river, but their claim looked promising, huge pools gouged out of the rock by the falling water. The problem with this alluvial gold, however, was that it had always proved to be limited in quantity. The action of water washing particles minutely down to low ground over millenia was strictly finite. The question was whether or not there were great storehouses of gold, locked in caves or in quartz or in veins of rock. This was a geological problem which no amount of haphazard fossicking would solve. They must invest in trained men; they must be scientific.

They camped beside the stream, not far from a Swazi village, and Frank bathed in a turbulent pool and thought of Campbell. If it were true that Lucy was pregnant his wholeness would be restored.

They rose early, setting off before sunrise, Frank with his pieces of paper, regarded so lightly by the King, and Tshabalala with a little bag of bark begged from one of the King's own sangomas. Two pieces of magic.

When Frank arrived home two days later, they embraced and went straight to the bedroom, although tea was laid and Frank was expected at the office. She did not have time to undress completely before they were locked together. She groaned and called out as he quickly spent himself. The shutters allowed fierce bars of light to fall on them, young and inexpressably happy. On Frank's brow tiny beads of sweat stood. He smelled of horse and leather, and she smelt of lavender and the semen which smeared her belly and thighs in libation.

'I love you, Frank.'

'I love you.'

'I think it is true, I am going to have a baby.'

'Lucy, Lucy. How do I deserve such perfect happiness?'

Now they were completely naked. They made love again, Frank with exaggerated tenderness. Lucy began to weep and he kissed the tears from her eyes. The sunlight fell more weakly through the shutters. The sun set in these parts with alarming speed. Outside they could hear the clatter of a milk pail on the verandah and the guinea-fowl calling excitedly.

Frank stood up and washed himself in the flowered bowl that stood on a chest of drawers. She watched him. He was lean and thin, perhaps too thin. He turned, ever sensitive, and smiled; she thought her heart might burst with the love she felt for him. As he pulled on his moleskins and a clean pair of boots, she jumped off the bed and embraced him from behind, squashing her breasts against his bare back.

'I love you, Frank. I had to tell you again.'

'You wanton woman. Mr Winkelmann is waiting.'

'Tea is waiting. Do you like cold tea?'

'I am afraid you have made me too late for that.'

He pinched her sharply.

'But you have ridden miles.'

'I shan't be long.'

He pulled on a tweed jacket and his favourite hat.

Winkelmann was pleased to see him. Frank told him how it had worked out. He did not attempt to describe to Winkelmann, however, his rambling discussions with Tshabalala. Nor did it seem appropriate to ask Winkelmann about the propriety of their dealings with the King. There was no connection between Tshabalala's world and Winkelmann's. It was a dark chasm that could never be crossed.

He and Winkelmann strolled in the evening air, scented with the blossoms of flowering trees. This rich scent, the warm air and the distant lights of a prospector's camp, the cries of the tumultuous insect world and Winkelmann's approval, on top of the almost unbearably sweet love of his wife, produced in Frank a delirious sense of well being. England with its formal notions of Liberty and Restraint, Propriety and Conviction and its rigid, self-imposed castes, seemed as far away as the lip of the moon which was now rapidly changing from the colour of Cheshire cheese to a glacial blue-white as the night got properly under way around them.

'Wonderful girl, your Lucy.'

'Thank you. You have been more than kind to her.'

'Wonderful girl. She is an expert on the trees already. She is writing a monograph.'

'She even surprises me.'

'Before you go home to her, walk with me to the end of the road.'

'Certainly.'

The little town dwindled into darkness very quickly just past the bank. Was he lonely? Winkelmann gave off a sense of self-satisfaction and a completeness at all times. Yet for four or five years he had been living alone here away from his family – if he had any – and away from his race. But he had great strength of mind and purpose. He would not, perhaps he could not, go back to England less than a gentleman and he could only be that by the acquisition of wealth.

'Do you ever intend to go back to England?' Frank asked.

'I have been asking myself that. It is different for you, but I feel free here. Do you know what I mean?'

'I believe so. It is a tabula rasa.'

'Yes it is. Except for the poor schwartzes.'

The benighted coon, out there in the primeval blackness.

Lucy waited for him in the glow of the new oil lamps from Cape Town. Her face was composed now, without a hint of the frenzy which had possessed her a few hours before. She was wearing a simple dress, almost touching the floor, her shoulders covered in a shawl, her arms bare and her hair tied back. They sat down to dinner.

'Two days ago I was eating for my dinner the liver of an ox, freshly slaughtered and served on a stick.'

'Frank, really.'

The lamp light kissed her face.

'Are you as happy as I am?' he asked inanely.

'Anywhere you are, I shall be happy.'

The lamb curry was served with bananas and dried coconut and dishes of chutneys from the Cape. It was his favourite meal.

When Lucy woke in the night, complaining of a pain in her stomach, she blamed the curry. But she was sweating and her face had become very pale, not at all like her habitual fairness, but grey and lifeless. It looked to Frank like the colour of tripe. He rushed to call the servants and sent Kriel for the doctor while he bathed her face. Her body was swelling, blowing up from within. Her eyes were nearly closed.

'I'm dying, Frank.'

The doctor came, his breath smelling of whisky. He played billiards every night at the Royal Hotel. He fumbled in his bag. He withdrew a long silver instrument, something like a stiletto, quickly swabbed her distended stomach which he had roughly bared, exposing her legs and belly and her small, glossy pubis, and plunged this instrument into her stomach without saying a word to Frank. There was a release of gas so pungent and sudden that Frank choked. It seemed quite impossible that such a noxious substance could have formed in the body of someone so young and lovely.

'I'm afraid she will die,' said Doctor McAllister.

'What? What are you saying?'

'It is gas gangrene.'

'My God, my God.'

Lucy seemed easier when they went back into the bedroom. The doctor gave her a draught which he mixed with shaking hands. Frank opened the windows. Outside, on the verandah, stood Tshabalala. His face was painted and he wore his porcupine amulets. Frank wanted to drag him inside and ask him to employ his little bag of precious bark, to do something, anything. Tshabalala simply dropped his head so that he was looking at his feet. Frank turned back to the doctor.

'Can you do nothing?'

'Nothing except make her easy. I'm most dreadfully sorry.'

Winkelmann arrived, wearing a striped dressing gown. He spoke sharply to Doctor McAllister, but the doctor showed surprising firmness and asked Winkelmann to sit down. Frank stood, uncertain, at the entrance to the bedroom while McAllister mixed another draught with a little glass rod that tinkled as he stirred. He held it to Lucy's lips. Frank came and knelt, holding her hand as she sipped.

'You are going to be all right,' he said without conviction.

He wished he had said nothing.

Lucy smiled gently, understanding his dilemma.

'I've lost you, Frank, everything that was precious to me.'

Her eyes closed and she seemed to sleep peacefully in that hideously stinking room. From outside the window came a great pained cry and the sound of bare running feet, slapping on the slate of the verandah.

CHAPTER 9

The discovery of massive amounts of gold near some barren ridges in the veldt, ridges that resembled the spine of a bony dog, finally made Thompson, Winkelmann and Dinkelsbühler wealthy. The actual discoverer of this gold-bearing reef was believed to have been eaten by a lion while carrying the news back to Barberton.

Barberton had become the new centre of the South African goldfields. Thompson and Winkelmann lived there in a rambling house on the outskirts of town. The myths that grew up around them in those years were largely the product of a misapprehension. For some years they had been perhaps the most powerful figures in the goldfields, yet they were teetering on the edge of collapse; as a result they had become secretive and autocratic. Nobody must question them. Nobody must know that Frank's letters and articles, describing new explorations and new prospects, were being returned unread and unpublished. Nobody must know that Dinkelsbühler had had to go to New York and beg the Seligman brothers to take an interest in the company on the sole grounds that their mothers had come from the same village in Germany. Nobody must know that the money invested in Chartered had so far failed to yield a return. Barberton, too, had a limited life: already stamp batteries were idle. Gold, it was now said, would never be found in appreciable quantities. The few freak nuggets and pockets, washed down by the immemorial streams, were a thing of the past.

Frank had become a rather silent man. He went for weeks with Tshabalala at his side, prospecting, inspecting, writing reports and occasionally shooting. He thought of Lucy often. At night in his tent he was tormented by grief, although daybreak brought some relief. But on his visits to Pretoria and in all his dealings in the field he displayed skill and determination. He spoke the Boer language fluently; he steered clear of the contentious issues that vexed the Boers and he travelled and worked ceaselessly. With Tshabalala he spoke only Swazi now. He was party to many mysteries, but he never spoke of them. Tshabalala was frequently called to his King's side. His influence was growing, his knowledge of the outside world seen as an asset in the straitening circumstances the Swazi found themselves in. Frank bought a large tract of land ten miles from Barberton, near a settlement called Trichardt's Rest. He built a small house of reeds and thatch by the side of a waterfall, and planted trees there in memory of Lucy. Monkeys and baboons played and squabbled on the rocks and in the undergrowth. Whenever he could, Frank would go to this little retreat and work with Tshabalala on the creation of a simple garden with a view of the waterfall. In Barberton it was said that the death of his wife had broken his heart. It was not true. He had drawn within himself, the better to carry on. He and Winkelmann hardly spoke. It was not necessary; they knew what had to be done. Lucy's death had given Frank an even keener vision, because he had so little to distract his mind and his emotions.

Frank had made two trips to England in the intervening years. The first, shortly after her death, was the more painful. He could not avoid the opprobrium which attached itself to him. He had taken her away and forced her to live in a disease-ridden township ... he had allowed his vaunting ambition ... and so on. Lucy's father had been so stricken that he no longer made any pretence of keeping up appearances. The joint effort of Dinkelsbühler and his former son-in-law had restored the family fortunes to some extent; the gardeners were back at work and the threat of sale had been lifted, but he could not enjoy it. His son Richard had been wounded in Afghanistan and Lucy's death had been the final straw. He walked around his estate sometimes, but failed to see it; it might as well have been sold.

The second trip had been in connection with an extension of the Seligman loan. The Seligmans were deeply interested in railroads, so Frank had taken Isaac Seligman, the London representative of the bank, a detailed plan of a railway to Delagoa Bay. With this he had baited the hook. Seligman took to Frank. He had started life in America as a peddler and Frank was just the sort of Englishman he wanted to cultivate. Dinkelsbühler's family connection had been good for the first hundred thousand pounds; Frank's sophisticated plan for exporting the raw materials of the African treasure house, supplied the second. The Seligmans underwrote the issue on America and Europe, and saved the Chartered Company. His dealings with Seligman – the argument, the manipulation, the risk, the tactical deployment of imperial and idealistic motives – excited

Frank. He was made a full partner.

So it was that when the Australian, Harrison, discovered the greatest store of gold the world was ever likely to see, only to become a lion's breakfast shortly afterwards, Frank and his partners were suddenly rich beyond the dreams of avarice. Everybody wanted to buy shares in their company. When thousands of fortune hunters flocked to the Transvaal, digging, scouting and staking in a feverish state of excitement, the Chartered Company was able to buy up many of the best leases, move in stamp batteries, organise mining finance and grab for itself a large share of what was now called Johannesburg. Frank and Winkelmann, based in a tent on a dusty track near their biggest claim, one day reckoned their personal holdings to be worth three hundred thousand and eight hundred thousand pounds respectively. They decided to build themselves offices and majestic houses on a hill beyond the diggings, looking north towards Pretoria and a distant range of purple and brown mountains. Winkelmann took upon himself the pleasant tasks of going to England to seek an architect and to help Dinkelsbühler cope with the huge inflow of money. Dinkelsbühler had his eye on substantial offices in Moorgate.

Winkelmann was to sail from Durban in the grandest stateroom on the *Exeter*, by way of the new Suez Canal. Frank went to see him off. How happy he looked, immaculately dressed by an Indian tailor, his tie-pin glinting in the sun, his shoes shining, his handsome face plumped with grace. The ship's siren sounded the warning. They embraced. Frank hurried down the gangplank, childishly anxious that they might haul it up with him still on board. There were harsh rushes of steam, the strident scrapings of cable, and then the water below began to boil and throb. Away she went, slowly, slowly, eased by the new steam tug, carrying back to England one of her more substantial private citizens, soon to be the biggest racehorse owner in the land (after the Earl of Rosebery) and the patron of innumerable charities.

Winkelmann never returned from that trip. Everything he had ever sought had been granted him. There was no longer any need to pay his dues; he was in the club, a life member.

Frank returned immediately to Johannesburg. Johannesburg was springing up all around him, like the staging of a theatrical production with too short a rehearsal period. The silent observers of this avaricious, frantic activity were the blacks, who came to watch the show and were pressed into small parts which they accepted with bemused tolerance. Nobody asked them what they thought of all this: white men desperate to dig great trenches in the bare unproductive veldt, where only a few Boer farmers had previously scratched a living. Grand people from Europe and America arrived to see for themselves this miracle: money could be dug up by anyone with a pick and a shovel. To the immigrant whites it appeared to be proof of life's infinite possibilities. To the blacks it appeared to be a new, rather active form of religion. To the Boers it was the supreme irony. They had left the more populous and materialistic parts of Southern Africa to seek the freedom of the wide open spaces, only to site Pretoria, their new Jerusalem, not thirty miles from the greatest dung-heap of gold in the history of the world.

Winkelmann's return was at first postponed: the pressure of business, the lure of new ventures, the establishment of new contacts, the demands of new wealth. Frank found himself in charge of the operation. He employed a young man of almost his own age, an illustrator and painter, to design his house on the hill. They sent for yellow wood from the Cape, teak from Burma, Douglas fir from Oregon, marble from Carrara and granite blocks from a quarry near Pretoria. Frank and the illustrator, John Pennycuick, designed a platform with an ornate wooden balustrade, reached through a trapdoor. Frank did nothing to discourage the element of whimsy. Neither of them had much experience of running a household, so the kitchen was sited in the wrong place, a long march from the dining room (to be panelled in old oak shipped from England), and the house was so high on the hill that a huge water tower had to be built to achive sufficient pressure for the advanced system of plumbing. For all its oddities and impracticalities, the house began to take on a pleasing and attractive character.

'It is rather big,' said Pennycuick. 'What are you going to do with it?'

They sat on a rock looking at the house, now standing high with half a roof.

'I'm going to be married again, I suppose.'

They had become friends. Pennycuick knew nothing of finance or gold shares. He was preparing a book on his travels through Africa. It seemed to Frank an idyllic and carefree life.

'You built it with her in mind.'

The distant hills had become hazy in the heat of the afternoon. Who did he mean? Lucy or his next wife?

'Yes. I should like to have a large family.'

'Are you proposing to live here?'

'The gold reef may not be as extensive as we had first hoped. It appears to be just beneath the surface in a very limited area. We shall see. But certainly, I believe there is gold here for ten years. That's a long-winded way of saying, yes, I expect to live here for the foreseeable future.'

Frank was aware that, because of his wealth and his previously solitary life, he had become rather grave and measured for a man of his age. Pennycuick offered the antidote. He was interested, in a Kelmscott sort of fashion, in the aesthetic to the exclusion of all else; he dressed with a casual elegance, wearing beautiful calf-skin boots, soft white breeches and a silk shirt, crowned by a wide-brimmed hat so that in his discussions with Rowbotham and his endless scramblings over the site, he looked like an aristocratic plantation owner from the West Indies. He was a lover of fine food and insisted that Frank employ a proper cook. The guinea-fowl and the local partridge, despite their athletic life, were delicious and became fixtures on the menu. Pennycuick enjoyed sketching flowers and plants and took Frank with him collecting specimens to draw, little spiky aloes, gentians with star-shaped flowers, proteas and vivid orchid-like plants which grew near the streams which sprang in the hills beneath the house. Frank would take his gun and usually manage to bag a few birds. Pennycuick was an innocent; Frank envied him his botany and his drawing and his romanticism. They were only a few years apart in age, yet Frank felt that he must have lived his life on another planet from Pennycuick. Walking in the hot sun made Pennycuick pink in the face and his fair hair cling to his forehead. He glowed. Frank's body had long since grown used to the heat; it had become dessicated, its wells dried up. As they walked and scrambled along the course of a stream, it occurred to Frank that in their physical guises their inner natures were well depicted.

Pennycuick stopped to sketch the nest of a weaver bird, which hung over a pool in the stream; Frank walked on downstream after a francolin. He lost it in the shimmering heat. He looked back up at the hill where his house rose, the roof timbers nearly complete, the sandy coloured rock used in the building catching the sun to create a mottled pattern. He walked on towards an abandoned kraal where some old mealie fields were sure to hide a few guinea-fowl. Strangely, there were none. A feral dog, slinking nervously about, just out of range of a stone or stick, was the only sign of life. The dog had probably been left when the inhabitants had been moved on. Frank lifted his gun, fired, and killed it. It lay twitching for a moment as the last life in its wretched, starved body ebbed away.

'Did you get anything? I heard a shot.'

Pennycuick sat on one rock, his feet on a second, so that his knees formed a platform for his sketch pad. The light on the pool reflected sharply on to his face, lighting it from below like theatrical footlights.

'No, I missed.'

'Not like you.'

'Thank you, if that was a compliment.'

'It was.'

Why did he not tell him about the dog? Pennycuick lived in a charmed world; he would not disturb it.

They walked on, Frank carefully sending him on a detour to avoid the body of the dog, which was now covered in ants and flies, its blood fast congealing on the bare path where it lay. Frank had lost heart; he wished he had not shot the dog. Africa could never be tidied away. It was hopeless. Where had these people gone, whose sticks and dried mealies and broken-down huts stood here still?

'Frank, I hear some down there, by those bushes.'

'Right, go round and chase them towards me.'

'All right.'

The guinea-fowl came running in there scuttling, over-excited way. Over-excitement turned to hysteria as he stepped out from behind a rock. They began to fly, but he bagged two.

'Good work, old fellow.'

As they picked the birds up, Frank suddenly said, 'Let's go home now.'

'Oh. As you wish. I was hoping to do a bit more sketching.'

'No, let's go. Or I'll go on my own.'

'No, no. I'm coming. Are you all right?'

'Yes thank you.'

How quickly Pennycuick sensed the change Frank felt.

'It's nothing. I've just remembered that I must speak to someone about a matter of urgency.'

'No need to explain.'

They walked quickly and silently back towards the hill. Up on the hill Frank's house was touched with gold, while down here they were in deep shadow.

'It looks like the Parthenon,' said Pennycuick, smiling.

'Will you do me a painting of it, like this, with the sun going down?'

'What do you want to call it?'

'The house or the painting?'

'The house, of course.'

'Let's call it Hilldrop.'

'Not very original.'

'True, but I had a friend who had a farm called Hilldrop. And how appropriate it is.'

'Actually I like it. It is unpretentious.'

'Unlike the house.'

They laughed.

'Friendship is such a precious thing,' said Frank suddenly.

Pennycuick put his hand briefly on his shoulder in mute acknowledgement. Frank was thinking of Campbell and lost innocence, really, but he did not spoil the moment.

When they reached the top of the hill, Pennycuick started immediately to sketch the house.

'You're starting my painting?'

'Yes. I want to catch this feeling.'

Frank watched him for a moment. Pennycuick's face was flushed from the scramble up the hill and his hair was moist so that it curled; round his neck he had tied a kerchief; his shirt was unbuttoned almost to the belt. His body, exposed in this way, was babyish and pale. A servant approached and said something to Frank in a language Pennycuick did not understand.

'Do you want tea?'

'Yes, please.'

'Right. Johannes will bring you some. I must go for awhile.'

Pennycuick watched him walk away; all of a sudden he noticed a black man squatting near some boulders at the side of the house. Frank and he talked for a moment. The black man stood and they walked together round the house and out of sight. This man had a single black feather in his hair, and underneath his ragged jacket he wore a leather apron with a sort of kilt of animal skins hanging down around the back of his knees.

Pennycuick returned to his sketching, but it was too late. He had lost the light. He walked around to the front of the house, hoping to catch a glimpse of Thompson. There was no sign of him now, nor of the black man. Why, he wondered as he sat down to tea on the unfinished verandah, would Thompson be talking to this man?

Later they dined together, but Frank did not mention his visitor.

'By the way, old fellow, who was that black you were talking to?'

'Who? Oh yes. That is one of my most faithful servants. He has been with me since I arrived. He lives on the farm near Barberton.'

'What was he doing here, if I may ask?'

'He was bringing me some news.'

'Curious way to obtain information.'

'Well, you know what they are. They like to tell you in person. They don't understand the telegraph. Not many people in Barberton do, for that matter.'

Frank was nervous and ate fast. He was living in the Heights Hotel now, while Pennycuick made himself comfortable in the stable block.

'My Cape Cart is waiting, John. Will you excuse me?'

'Of course.'

He left Pennycuick on the verandah at a table, with the cheese, the trifle and the savouries still to come. At the best of times Frank was a careless eater.

Pennycuick felt slighted and abandoned here on this wild hill. Frank had about him an aura of strength and purpose. Without him the night was empty and primitive, where it had been full of promise.

Frank hurried down the rough road towards the town. This road wound between some hills, hills which were now alive with the fires of squatters come to the goldfields for a myriad of purposes. Frank had bought a good deal of this land and one day soon he would have to start moving these desperate people on.

He stopped near a farmhouse tucked under the slope of a hill, where the old Rustenburg road passed. Tshabalala was waiting. He climbed quickly into the Cape Cart beside Frank. Kriel, the driver, cracked his whip and muttered angrily as they jogged off into the night.

Tshabalala was deeply puzzled and his sense of fitness was disturbed. They had tried to arrest him. The diggers committee and the Boer police had sent for him, but fortunately he had been warned in time. It would not have happened if Frank had been in Barberton.

'Why did you do it?'

It was a difficult kind of question in Swazi. It was far too direct.

'The King is being bewitched. He has been ill with swollen feet and arms. He does not know who his enemy is.'

The nature of the illness was not so important to Tshabalala as the cause. There was no point in treating the symptoms.

'He is sick like Miss Lucy.'

The malevolent force must be identified and placated or vanquished. Frank told Kriel where to take Tshabalala. It was easy to hide him here in the confusion of Johannesburg. Before they parted, Tshabalala asked a favour of Frank. He was now in deep disgrace. The organs of the child he had killed – necessary to smoke out the King's enchanter – had, in those last panic-stricken moments as the white man's horses thundered on to the farm, to be abandoned. Frank must please send some white man's medicine to the King, more powerful if possible than those Tshabalala had left behind, with an explanation of what had gone wrong.

Frank climbed out of the Cape Cart and watched it go. He walked the last mile into town. The streets were still busy, with music and drunkenness floating out on to the night air from the many bars and hotels. A theatre was being built. There were now at least twenty hotels.

Two Boer policemen walked tentatively up and down, uninvited guests at this wedding between the dispossessed of Europe and the wealth of Africa. Their uniforms were part comic opera and part farmer. They recognised Frank. He stopped to talk to them outside his hotel, whose luminance was steeped in the smell of beer. He gave them some money to buy a drink. They were farm boys from Soutpansberg, homesick and unsure, with broad Lowlands faces from a painting by Mierevelt. And yet, like all things in this continent, they had become peculiarly naturalised, their weak European eyes permanently screwed up against the sun, their bodies swaddled in heavy muscle, their beards bleached and unkempt. They walked off down the road, cheered by their chance encounter with one of Johannesburg's leading citizens.

Frank felt alone again, as he had not done in the recent past. Tshabalala's terrible crime, the killing of a child with a knife, the slitting open of its small belly, as round and soft as a ripe fruit, was unthinkable; and yet it was no crime for Tshabalala. In truth it was his duty to his King to procure the right child and kill it. By protecting Tshabalala, Frank was certainly committing a crime.

He had a sense, anyway exaggerated by his success, that he was different from other men, quite different from the unseeing, unheeding crowd of opportunists drinking and fighting and gambling in the bars. None of them would have protected Tshabalala for such a grotesque crime. Frank did not want to go to bed, to think of a child disembowelled and emasculated, nor could he go back to Hilldrop to see Pennycuick, so he went to the office and tried to work. He could not. His office – its ledgers neatly lined up in rows, the massive rolltop desk, the yellow-wood floors, the portrait of Dinkelsbühler, the clock on the mantel, the new Bokhara on the floor, the painting of a horse and hounds, the cluster of steel pens and swart ink, the crude pressed ceiling – seemed to belong to someone else. Was he the only man in Johannesburg to see that there is not one world, one life, one morality, but many, parallel and conflicting?

Outside in the street there was a noise of drunken fighting. By protecting Tshabalala he had taken a step along a path that led away from home.

CHAPTER 10

Pennycuick too had a sister. She had had an unhappy love affair with a painter, a friend of her brother's, who believed that an artist must pursue his vocation at whatever cost to his friends, family and loved ones. She was no longer able to tolerate this presumption, the more so as she thought him a poor painter. So she was ready to accept her brother's invitation to see the house he was building for a mysterious magnate in Africa.

> 'My dearest sister Emily,
> You shall meet my friend and patron Mr Frank Thompson when you come to the Transvaal. We live in some splendour. Mr Thompson is tall and very attractive, I have been told, to women, and it is this, of course, rather than the fact that he is the fifth richest man in South Africa which will commend him to you.
> He is, I sometimes think, a lonely man without a good idea of how to proceed with his romantic life since the premature death of his wife. I have no doubt that you will be able to give him some instruction.
> My book, with which I am nearly done, has a marvellous title suggested by Mr Thompson. It is 'Travels with No Destination'. I have dedicated it to him. I talk of him as a much older man, but he is only twenty-eight years old. He has a great knowledge of the local vernaculars, one of the few people in his position, indeed in any position, to take such an interest.
> My dear sister, I am as fond of him as if he were an older brother, and I hope you may become equally fond of him.'

It did not puzzle her that her brother should have a compulsion to introduce her to Frank Thompson; he was usually impulsive and enthusiastic, and always eager to share his enthusiasms. She had read a little about Thompson in the newspapers. He was reckoned by *The Times* to be one of the coming men of the new generation that followed Rhodes, Robinson and Barnato in South Africa. She beautiful with its mountains rising improbably out of the sea, the huge breakers crashing on wild beaches, old Dutch wine farms tucked into the lea of the mountain and the happy miscegenation of Dutch and English architecture.

Emily was twenty-four now. Her eyes showed that she had been hurt. The gazelle-like innocence had gone. He knew that the painter had made love to her. Frank must never know. He would not be in sympathy with the Brotherhood's tastes and morals. As soon as they were unpacked at the Mount Nelson, Emily insisted on going swimming. She was unpredictable; at times she could be quiet and reserved and at others madly, extravagantly exuberant. She took off all her clothes and plunged into the sea. He was forced to follow, ruining a good pair of moleskins. She stepped out of the water, the boiling surf around her thighs, proudly exposed.

'You're thinking I'm a fallen woman?'

'No, I'm thinking how beautiful you are and how foolish my erstwhile friend Edward has been.'

'What a sweet prince you are, John.'

She kissed him with salty lips as the waves tugged at their legs. Her lips were plump, strangely so, because the rest of her was still childishly thin. She hugged him. The sea was icy cold; it had streamed up here from the antarctic without changing character until it collided with the tip of Africa. They climbed way up so that he could sketch the bay and mountains from a rocky promontory. Down there on a beach lay seals basking just out of reach of the urgent waves.

' "He clasps the crag with crooked hands …" ' she said.

' "Ringed by the sea in azure lands." The ghost of Nanny Donnelly haunts us.'

'Is this our azure land?'

'I think it may be yours.'

She picked flowers as he sketched and pressed them in her little wooden flower press, the latest thing for travellers. She watched tiny sunbirds, their beaks delicately curved, hover beside the huge fleshy flowers of strange spiky plants. These plants were unknown to her. This whole continent was unknown to her.

'What sort of house does Mr Thompson want?'

'He wants a large house, with a view.'

'Something grand? Something gay? Something old? Something new?'

Out to the east of Cape Town lay a shimmering range of

mountains, powdered with a haze. Beyond it lay the hinterland. She was eager to be off. But Christmas was upon them and they had been invited to the residence of the Governor, Sir Bartle Frere, for a few days.

Frank could not afford to acknowledge Christmas. He worked late into the night, writing letters, looking at assay reports, sending telegrammes to Dinkelsbühler and Winkelmann, and marshalling the resources of The Chartered Company to withstand the coming slump. The deposit, he was sure, was far more extensive than Rhodes, Rudd and Joel believed. He was consolidating his properties along the line of the Main Reef. He was also looking for a more efficient chemical process than the old mercury plates for the recovery of gold from the stamp. He wrote to universities and scientific establishments all over the world. Rhodes had started to sell, convinced that gold was unrecoverable below a certain level and that they would hit a belt of pyritic rock soon, which would indicate the bottom of the Reef. This had indeed happened on one of Frank's properties; he managed to sell off this and one or two other unproductive properties so that he could buy more of Rhodes's holdings.

Dinkelbühler cabled that he should sell as much as possible. Frank without thinking, replied:

'I am buying. We hold fast.'

That cable was neither literally true nor even honest, yet it would come to symbolise him in the eyes of his biographers: determined, brave and visionary. At the time he sent the cable he was tired and lonely. He fell asleep on Christmas Day at his desk. He woke in the early evening, sweating and uncomfortable. The telegraph office was closed, not even his retainer to the operator sufficient inducement to keep it open. He returned to the hotel, bathed, and had dinner sent up. There was a great deal of drunkenness in Johannesburg. It floated through his window in snatches of song and screams and cries of lust, like a tune played in a locked room, by an unknown musician.

He thought of John Pennycuick and his sister. They would be amusing themselves in Cape Town, perhaps stopping to sketch and paint, while he was in danger of bankruptcy and disgrace. Nor would Tshabalala be hoeing the King's gardens dutifully this year. He was an outcast, blamed for much of the misfortune that had befallen his King.

Frank went to bed, perversely happy in his self-immolation. He thought of home, his father not so much clinging to life as tied to it, his mother bustling in the kitchen supervising the Christmas dinner; his brother, now twenty-two years old, and his sister, married to a farmer – all of them drawn back to the family home, while he glided off on his own. Emily Pennycuick would anchor him in this world in the house her brother had built.

He woke feeling fresh and happy. What is the power of our dreams? As he was breakfasting the waiter placed a cable on the table. In Dutch it asked him to see the Attorney General of the Republic in Pretoria immediately. He set off by the Mail coach. It was early afternoon when he reached Pretoria.

'Good afternoon, Mr Thompson,' said the Attorney General.

'Good afternoon, sir. To what may I attribute this honour?'

'It is the holidays. Nobody is working, there is nobody about.'

'Except your good self, sir.'

'That is right.'

'Am I to take it that I am here on some sort of official business?'

'No, sir. You are here to talk to me as a friend who has your welfare at heart.'

'I am honoured.'

The Attorney General was a likeable man, self taught, but extremely diligent in the pursuit of his office.

'Sir,' he said formally, 'I have a complaint that you have harboured a criminal. This man is said to have killed a child on or in the vicinity of your farm at Barberton.'

Frank said nothing.

'Is this true?'

'It is true.'

'You must give this man up, sir.'

'I cannot. He had gone to Swaziland.'

'You can get him from there.'

'I don't think that it would be wise.'

'It is not a question of whether it's wise or not. It's a matter of the law.'

The Attorney General had worked long nights to master the law. His origins were very humble, a dirt farm in the wilderness.

'Ah, the law. I am a great admirer of yours, sir, and a great admirer of your people.'

'Thank you.'

'But I have observed a tendency on your people's part to play ducks and drakes with the law. You regard the law as a tool. Native law, if it suits your purposes is sufficient; if it does not you very quickly talk of "the law."'

'This man must be returned. People are angry. Frankly, I am doing this for you. People are saying that you have protected this man. For God's sake, Mr Thompson, a child was murdered.'

'A ritual murder was conducted as they have been for years, and despite the law, no doubt they will be for years. Make an exception as you invariably do for your own people when it is expedient.'

'Did you say you were an admirer of my people? You have always been regarded highly here in Pretoria. That is why I am trying to advise you.'

'I am an admirer of your people. I believe that I understand their feelings. But I do not ask you to place me in a position above the law, because you regard me highly.'

'This kaffir has murdered a child with his own hands on your farm. That is the problem, sir.'

'Do I understand you to mean that it would be all right if it had not occurred, as you say, on my property?'

The Attorney General was silent for a moment. His office was small, his clothes sombre, his face earnest.

'Unfortunately that has not been the case. You, it is alleged, not only failed to turn over the kaffir, but you also helped him to escape.'

'Perhaps you should charge me with being an accessory, or some such.'

'Mr Thompson. Nobody wishes for that. We simply want you to hand the man over.'

'Have I or have I not broken the law?'

'You have, but it is not for me...'

'If I have broken the law you are presumably going to charge me.'

'Mr Thompson, you are being very stubborn.'

'And if you charge me, I shall hire the finest advocates in the world, who will demonstrate that there is no clear precedent on native and tribal law to follow, you having long ago put the blacks outside the protection and constraints of your Roman Dutch law; I shall also demonstrate clearly that the laws of the Republic are habitually applied unequally; I shall make it plain that murderers of natives are infrequently charged and never convicted and that certain members of your own government have been guilty of murders in the war for which they were charged but never convicted. And furthermore I shall tell the world of my dealings with, amongst others, the dynamite monopoly. I, sir, pay an extortionate price for dynamite because certain officials of your government are growing rich at my expense. Why do you not prosecute them? Is it not against the law?'

'Are you above the law?'

'You have invited me to be so. But I do not regard myself as above the law. The law must be applied evenly or there is no law.'

'Can you not hand the kaffir over?'

'I will not hand him over so that you can hang him, not for his crime for which you do not give a damn, but to satisfy the ignorant who do not wish to see a foreigner harbour a native.'

'I thought you said you were a friend of my people?' the Attorney General asked sadly.

'I am a friend of your people. I am making them rich. May I be excused?'

Thompson went straight to the cable office in Market Square, to cable Pennycuick.

'Arrive Cape Town soonest possible. Wait for me please.'

Sir Bartle Frere and his lady presided over the many Christmas functions with amiability. Lady Frere dressed in a style favoured in large country houses during the Crimea, but she was a sensible, intelligent woman, the survivor of many gubernatorial hazards, a seasoned animal in the service of the Empire. She thought Emily's clothes were very modern, and professed to find them charming. Sir Bartle was a shrewd man, but gave the impression that he had coped with most of the problems his eminence was ever likely to attract, and so looked upon the world with amused tolerance. They were delightful hosts.

Mr Cecil Rhodes called on Christmas Day, to pay his compliments and leave lavish presents. He was the uncrowned king of South Africa, gracious and attractive in his success, but rather too opinionated. His thoughts were running wildly to a grandiose confederation of Africa, so Sir Bartle divulged when the great man had gone, and it was Sir Bartle's job to restrain him. Rhodes did not, apparently, think much of the new goldfields.

'Mr Rhodes believes that the real finds will be to the North.'

'King Solomon's mines,' said Lady Frere with a sly smile.

'Exactly, my dear. Curious how hard-headed magnates like Mr Rhodes believe in myths, don't you think?'

'Good thing, too,' said Pennycuick.

'Ah, a romantic,' said Lady Frere. 'I would love to see your painting. Is it romantic, Mr Pennycuick?'

Emily looked across the table at her brother. He was bright eyed and happy. His face was slightly heated and eager, like a schoolboy's; his habitual paleness was touched with gold, his fair hair wheaten, his moustache slightly darker. Sir Bartle wore rather baroque whiskers, very old-fashioned but comfortable.

William had once argued when they were very young that there was no truth but artistic truth. Did he believe that now? She did not. She had discovered that there are many truths and each one is the basis of a contingent falsehood.

They were talking about Frank Thompson. It surprised her that the Governor should know of him. He would love the house they had found for him, of that she was sure. It was one of the old homesteads, surrounded by vines and sited at the bottom of a steep ravine which climbed up the lower slopes of the mountain. It was in a state of decay, but it presented wonderful opportunities. Perhaps John would become an architect or designer rather than a painter.

'When are you going to Johannesburg?' asked Lady Frere.

'As soon as Mr Thompson has finished his holiday. I have been away too long already. Goodness knows what will have happened in my absence to his house.'

'Is he delayed?'

'He is always delayed, I am afraid,' said Pennycuick.

'A fine young man,' said Sir Bartle conspiratorially. 'You are going to like him, Emily.'

Frank passed two days at Kimberley waiting for the train. The Club, Rhodes's creation, was a comfortable, rather raffish building, sumptuously finished in mahogany. The mining business in Kimberley was a simpler operation. It was twenty years since the empty lands inhabited only by roving bands of half-caste Hottentots – a region in practice autonomous because nobody had wanted it – had become famous. Kimberley was still a collection of low, rather modest buildings in the middle of a vast plain; its wealth, increasingly concentrated in a few hands, came quite simply from a vast hole on the edge of town. Looking down into its depths, Frank could well understand Rhodes's reluctance to become too involved in the uncertainties of Johannesburg. Here all was simplicity; you dug and you recovered gems. It was a cottage industry gone mad, where Johannesburg (he saw it so clearly) demanded all the skill of engineering and chemistry and all the inventiveness and capital that Europe and America could produce. Not even Winkelmann was aware of the true scale of things. Ludo Stephens had mined copper and gold. Some of these mines had been driven deep into the ground. Perhaps he would have the necessary imagination.

The train journey was a tedious one, stiflingly hot as they passed through the endless scrub of the Karoo, a region which looked as if it had never fully recovered from the volcanic upheavals of earlier aeons. Little hills poked up from the flat plains, piles of disturbed boulders; what trees there were were squat and fearful. The scrubby plant life, all too visible from the slow moving train, was either fleshy with stored water or dessicated, patiently waiting for the next rain to plump out and spring to life. Darwin would have understood clearly its fitness for life in this place.

What blessed relief it was to descend, finally, the mountain passes away from the Karoo into fertile valleys planted with vines and dotted with white, Dutch farmhouses. The change was so sudden that it seemed magical, a sleight of hand. He wondered if Pennycuick had found him a house. In his imagination he had tried to picture Emily Pennycuick on the long, shuffling journey. Coming down here to the Cape was a fine idea. Kriel had taken word to Tshabalala to hide in the depths of Swaziland. He was glad to have left Johannesburg behind. As the train steamed with new vigour along a sunlit valley beside a river that was brown yet clear, like light ale, with fields of grapevines and orchards vivid in the morning sun, he felt himself solitary. It was time to slough it off.

Emily looked remarkably like her brother. She was lightly freckled from the sun now, and her hair, which she wore long and loose, was the colour of wheat. She was nervous, as he was, at their meeting. They stood rather stiffly on the platform, with Pennycuick, the broker, asking about the house. Frank laughed as he told how Rowbotham the builder had been caught with the glass dome of the library upside down in a thunderstorm. Emily laughed gratefully at his description. Too much was expected of their meeting.

Immediately Frank had bathed and changed they set off to see the farm. It was called Weltevreden.

'I hope it's not too far?' asked Emily as they walked around the old slave quarters.

'Too far. My dear Miss Pennycuick, it is the most beautiful house in the world. After Hilldrop of course. I am, as its name suggests, well pleased.'

Emily, in her pleasure, clutched his arm. For Frank it was shocking and thrilling.

Weltevreden was a long, low, Dutch house with four gables and deep, elegant windows. Behind it, above the oak trees and the straggly vineyards, rose the mountain in all its wild magnificence.

'When can we take possession of it?' asked Frank.

'Soon. Nobody has lived here for a few years. But as you can see it needs a great deal of work.'

'Would you like to be my architect?'

'I am a painter, I believe.'

'And a fine architect.'

'Have you solved your problems in Johannesburg?'

'I believe that I may have. Certainly we are in a position to weather the storm, unless, of course, it engulfs the whole ship.'

He said nothing of the Attorney General's summons.

'It all seems rather far away in this lovely place.'

'Frank, will you forgive me for saying this. You look terribly tired and in need of a rest. Emily and I will show you the beaches and walks we have found. Lady Frere is expecting you to stay whenever you wish. You really must rest.'

'Nonsense. I shall feel perfectly recovered in the morning. It is a long journey.'

Emily was at first disappointed by Frank's appearance. He seemed rather grave and provincial. His clothes, the tight narrow jacket and heavy shoes, gave him an awkward look. But he was suffering from fatigue and worry which added to this slightly grey, uncomfortable appearance. His eyes were dark, wreathed by dark half-moons of exhaustion. They drove with him back to the Mount Nelson.

'Will you excuse us, Miss Pennycuick, for a moment while I talk with your brother?'

'Of course.'

They walked in the gardens of the hotel.

'Forgive me. I do not wish to seem churlish about Lady Frere's invitation. I cannot accept. I may be placed under arrest when I return to Johannesburg. I could not decently be a guest of the Governor in the circumstances. You and Emily would be advised to stay in Cape Town until you hear from me. I don't believe it is likely but it is possible.'

'On what charge, may I ask?'

'As an accessory to murder. My servant, Tshabalala, killed a child and I concealed him from the authorities.'

Pennycuick remembered the strange figure at the site.

'But you must stay here. You must rest.'

'I must go if they want me. I had to come and tell you.'

'There was no need. Why could you not have sent a cable?'

'John, to tell the truth I wanted to catch a sight of your sister in case they put me in gaol. And of course you could not be mixed up in this affair by coming to Johannesburg.'

'What do you think of Emily? Do you like her?'

'Forgive me, John, if I sound crazy. I love her already.'

They hugged each other. Pennycuick thought for a moment that Frank had fainted because he seemed in the embrace to become a dead weight. Out in the bay a ship moaned, like a lover deserted or perhaps – unworthy thought – like a lover in ecstasy.

CHAPTER 11

Frank Thompson was not charged. The only price he had to pay for harbouring a child murderer was a certain reputation for approving of witchcraft and black (in the literal sense) magic. Myths are potent forces; this one clung to him until the day he died, and indeed survived him. Frank knew about this myth; it lent him a certain fascination. And in a sense it was true.

He and Emily were soon married. They spent their honeymoon at Weltevreden, which John Pennycuick had refurbished and furnished with Cape Dutch wagon chests and yellow-wood tables and chairs. On the walls he hung Aubusson tapestries and English and Dutch paintings, of horses and burghers going about their business. Pennycuick's book was published; it was a minor success and contributed greatly to establishing his subsequent reputation. Before he left South Africa he completed the decoration of Hilldrop, lending it a romantic yet very modern look with Morris wallpapers, chintzes and carpets.

The slump in gold mining was over. Chartered emerged as the biggest and strongest single company on the Reef; Frank Thompson was its biggest single shareholder. The farm near Barberton was nelgected, unnamed, never spoken of. Tshabalala lived there, close to the grove of trees Frank and he had planted in memory of Lucy. By the end of the year Emily had fallen pregnant. In Frank's mind Lucy and Emily had begun to merge; he did nothing to discourage the merger. Despite his many preoccupations he was kind and affectionate. She loved Frank as her brother had known she would. When she told him of the pregnancy, he felt that a process, cruelly interrupted, had re-started. The child would be as much Lucy's as Emily's.

Around them, the town of Johannesburg was tumescent. Most people now accepted that the life of the gold mines would be at least ten years. Others, like Frank, believed that gold would be found at deeper levels away from the obvious outcrops. Ludo Stephens recommended to Frank that he buy cheaply further and further away from the line of the Reef. In Scotland two scientists developed a method of using cyanide to extract gold from the crushed ore, which made deep level mining ever more profitable. There seemed to be no end to the Reef. The improbable, which Rhodes had feared, had happened; another vast source of mineral wealth, a treasure trove trodden unheeding by the langoustine-pink soles of aimlessly itinerant kaffirs for hundreds of thousands of years, had been discovered and exploited, by the ingenuity and determination of the restless, questing white man. Frank himself sometimes wondered how it had all happened. It was impossible to escape the conclusion that destiny was manifest here. For the Boers, alas, it seemed that their destiny was equally manifest. There were now in Johannesburg almost as many foreigners as there were Boers in the whole of the Transvaal. They began to think of ways of containing this influx. Nobody, in truth, gave much thought to the blacks.

Frank made a trip to Barberton on the pretext of visiting one of his mines. The town was cheerful despite its eclipse. Frank arrived at the farm on horseback, as in the old days. Tshabalala had built his kraal near the grove above the waterfall. He had taken as his principal wife a minor princess of the royal household, but with the death of his King his position had been perilously exposed. Swaziland was in the grip of uncertainty. The new King, Bhunu, was only fourteen years old, and no match for the bewildering forces that surrounded him. Frank walked through the garden he had planted. It was still tended, the trees dug out around their bases, although many of them were now quite large. Down below in the little valley children played at the pool beneath the waterfall. Each tree was still identified by a little brass plate, thrust into the ground on an iron rod; these plates were polished. Tshabalala was waiting for him, sitting on the ground beneath a spreading native fig tree. He had built his kraal around it. Frank sat down next to him and the women brought beer; children stood at a respectful distance, peering silently at them, until Tshabalala waved for them to go away. Large red ants, busy in the sand, carried morsels of grass and bits of dried porridge to their nests.

'I hear that Ukwhalimanzi has become a very big man,' said Tshabalala.

'You must not believe everything you hear,' said Frank uneasily.

The beer was sour and grainy. Tshabalala's eyes had become yellow since he had last seen him. His kilt of animal skins was shabby and his hair thin, in little tufts.

'What will become of us, Mr Frank?' he asked.

Frank did not answer. He looked at Tshabalala, whose eyes were cast down on the ground in front of him. They talked instead of children. Tshabalala assumed that Frank was hoping for a boy. Frank did not correct him. Tshabalala was more or less the same age as he was, thirty-one years old, but he looked very old. He reminded Frank of another failed necromancer, Sekukuni, all those years ago.

Guiltily, he rode back to Barberton to complete his business. Guiltily, because he could not tell Tshabalala what he suspected, nor could he answer his question: 'What will become of us?'

PART II

CHAPTER 12
1959

Sir Frank Edward Thompson, one of the last of the Randlords – pioneer, humanitarian, soi-disant necromancer – died in 1948. He was eighty-nine years old.

'*My properties in the district of Barberton, I leave to my grandson, James Edward Thompson, in the expectation that....*'

For some reason that sentence in the over-long will was never finished; the lawyers believed that it did not invalidate the bequest, whatever the end of the sentence might have revealed.

It was eleven years before James Edward Thompson, the grandson named in the will, took any notice of his inheritance. He wrote unexpectedly from New York asking about the properties. No one knew much about the farms, except that there was a house on one of them, which had been let for many years but was believed to be vacant. The place was in the hands of a caretaker who was paid a retainer. Certainly there was nothing suitable for occupation.

In the expectation. The great man presiding over the family amiably from the huge, rather whimsical house on the hill, had always seemed to James to be keeping something back, so that this sentence may have been deliberately cryptic, although the will was the longest document of its kind ever seen in Johannesburg, with hundreds of bequests to charities, detailed gifts to distant relatives and provision for retainers meticulously listed with their full tribal names. This last was considered, if not eccentric, certainly rather show-off. Everyone knew that these people had their own names, but, by the same token (a popular phrase in the family) they had chosen to work in the twentieth century in industrial society and had taken European names. And so on. James remembered thinking that perhaps his grandfather had gone to such lengths with all these names out of a sense of mischief. In the few years that he had known him, the old man had always liked to present a puckish picture of himself, of a sage old chap who took the world and its pretensions lightly.

'Are you saying this is it?'

She looked pathetic now, very unlike her self as established by Avedon.

'I'm not saying it. You said it the other day.'

'Everybody has rows, for Chrissakes.'

'We have nothing else.'

'Thanks a bundle, James.'

She lay on the bed, weeping and gulping for air.

'Look, can I be honest with you?'

'Why not, try something new.'

'Very funny. Let's just face it, it was a mistake. I was pissed when I met you. I was taken in by the glamour. I wanted to be hip. I've got any number of excuses. The truth is we should never have been married.'

She did not answer. She began to dab her eyes and fiddle with her make-up determinedly.

'Where is this fucking place?'

He was still disturbed, a sort of fizzing uneasiness, by her swearing. She thought it was because he was basically conventional – square was the word she favoured – but he was disturbed by her swearing because she misjudged its affect. Far from making her seem excitingly unconventional, he thought it made her ridiculous; a girl from the Mid West trying to shape up.

'This fucking place is a farm I was left by my grandfather.'

'Well that's just very convenient now, isn't it? Did you just remember it?'

He looked at her and The Look, with loathing. She was, he was painfully aware, more beautiful each day. A year ago she had been on an assignment to Europe with a photographer. She now looked, some days, like a French girl, a young Juliette Greco, others like a Swede, long straight hair, little obvious make up, demi-vierge. The stilettoes, hairy cashmere jumpers and straight skirts were no more, banished with the bobbed hair. Her sweaters were now thin and provocative.

'I didn't actually just remember it. I never really thought about it, that's all. Since my father's illness I've been thinking more about that sort of thing.'

Her face, so beautiful, so regular, so American really, was to him the more pitiful because of the illusion it presented.

'What about me?'

'You'll be okay.'

'Is that all you can say?'

'No. I could say a lot more. But what's the point? It's the truth. You will be all right. You're young, you're beautiful, I'll support you if you need it.'

'Jesus, you can be a hard bastard.'

'That's not what you were saying the other day. You said I was weak, soft, useless. You said I had never made a decision or a commitment – big deal, a COMMITMENT – in my whole life. Your actual words were that I had as much fucking backbone as a fucking jellyfish.'

'Jimmy, for God's sakes, you know you manoeuvred me into saying those things. I had been working hard all day, while you lay about contemplating your navel.'

'I know how awful it must be. Richard Avedon is such a slave driver. Ooh, gasp, help, how terrible.'

It was true, sadly, that he had manoeuvred her. It surprised him now that she had realised.

'Are you saying that I asked you out of some deep inferiority complex to explore my deficiencies of character for me?'

'Not exactly. No.'

She always tried to tell the truth in her way.

'But you provoked me,' she added.

'Jo-Anne, can you tell me what future you see for this marrige if, after less than two years, we are already wasting our precious youth trying to find out who started the last argument but one? It's about as pointless as asking why the pop-up toaster is on fire after an atom bomb has fallen on Sutton Place.'

'You hate New York. You hate me. You hate America. You would like a bomb to fall on us.'

'Only one of those propositions is correct. Try and figure out which one.'

He walked out of their chic, but untidy loft on 8th Street. It was not a clean break like that. There were weeks of packing and bank accounts and lawyers to deal with. Fortunately he had few assets in America, so she had to be content with the apartment and a promise of maintenance.

He could not explain to her his real reason for leaving her;

primarily it was a fear of his own capacity for petty vindictiveness. In this marriage, perhaps in any marriage, this ability would flourish. Life with Jo-Anne produced exactly the right climate for its spontaneous culture, like some cryptogamous plant. Her lack of any systematic education, her belief in astrology, her vacuous absorption in trashy old movies, her untidiness (which contrasted disastrously with his own), her love of convenience foods, her long and repetitive telephone conversations, the hours of making herself up (whole days passed in this way); all these might just have been annoyances had they not been packaged in her ridiculously beautiful self. While everyone else was envying him his good fortune in having this living doll all to himself (or largely all to himself), he could not lay off; he felt obliged to point out her deficiencies, morally bound even, to point out the fraud she perpetrated by her appearance. The only way he could stop himself was by leaving her.

He caught a plane to London, en route for Johannesburg – home – feeling not sad but guilty, for she had loved him.

London was like a village from another century. Dark, grimy, with a perky Dickensian quality about the people. For two years he had worked in the London office of Chartered in Moorgate. The boardroom held a marvellous portrait of his grandfather painted by his maternal great-uncle, John Pennycuick RA. How lightly it sat next to the pictures of old Dinkelsbühler and Winkelmann, both of whom had obviously taken portraiture rather seriously. Frank Thompson looks keen, his grey suit catching an improbable shaft of light from a window in this very boardroom, greying hair neatly brushed, his expression amused. Pennycuick had inadvertently pointed up the difference between the three founders. Where the other two belonged to a forbidding world of Levantine commerce, of dark suits and darker promissory notes, Frank seemed to be smiling encouragingly. *It's all clean and above board and progressive, chaps; it's all part of a natural process.* In truth, after the Boer War Frank Thompson had made sure that the two older partners could take no active part, by playing on their ignorance of the new techniques of deep level mining. He had out-manoeuvred them. One joke in later days was that he had shafted them. The old man would probably have explained it in terms of

Darwinism; he had been a believer in determinism of all sorts and varieties.

London with its pinched faces and smug quaintnesses, held at least the promise of old friendships from a happy period in his life. He did not want to tell these old friends the true cause of his separation. How could he explain that Esther Williams movies and star signs had broken up his marriage? But he could comfortably slip back into the role he had enjoyed at Oxford, of devil-may-care stylish gadabout, his marriage to a top model in New York an incident, on a par with daubing the Master of Balliol's dog pink, which he had done.

'So you're going back to Bongo Bongo land?'

'Yes, I am. Don't ask me why.'

'Why are you going?'

'Thank you. I am not really sure. I was not a great success in the family business as you know. Please try not to laugh: I am going back to see if I can find out why I am going back.'

'It's difficult not to laugh. Have some more Chablis.'

Wheelers was the perfect choice for this meeting with his old friend Giles Mourville. Mourville was something in the City. He was losing his tendency, so attractive when they had both been there, to make fun of the place. This was presumably because he was doing well in his merchant bank. The cosy, slightly secretive atmosphere of Wheelers (the creaking stairs, the stained-glass windows, the large, no-nonsense plates of large unexotic fish – plaice, sole, turbot, halibut – and all the smaller plates of whitebait, oysters, smoked salmon and fishy pâtés) was from a world he had left forever: Oxford, the City, Belgravia, gambling clubs, deb dances. Once at Wheelers when the two of them had been lunching, a man at a nearby table had fainted, falling head first into his mussel soup, which had been mercifully tepid. As they revived him, slightly disappointed that he had not had a heart attack, he began to apologise:

'Carry on. Hope I haven't spoilt your lunch. Terribly sorry.'

He was still apologising as the ambulance men carried him out.

'I don't have time to find myself any more,' said Mourville. 'Too busy finding the mortgage.'

'You're right, of course. You still think I'm very self-indulgent, don't you?'

'Yes,' said Mourville amiably, between bites of plaice and tartare sauce. 'I envy you.'

'Well, let me tell you, I'm not going to pretend that I would prefer to be poor, but it has been a burden. If you get pissed and fall into the river before the Oxford and Cambridge match...'

'Which I did.'

'Exactly, that's why I mention it. If you do that it's regarded as very amusing. If I do it...'

'Which you did.'

'Yes, yes. Jesus you're getting pedantic. If I do it, it's a case of an over-indulged rich kid behaving like a clown.'

'Hear, hear.'

'How would you like a piece of halibut up your nose?'

'I prefer it up the arse.'

'So I've heard. The City is buzzing with rumours. Men in top hats are running down Throgmorton Street muttering. Listen, if you want to know, which you obviously don't I am beginning to feel the strain of being, if not exactly a failure, a non-starter. I am also, before you point it out to me, only too aware that I can afford – I talk of money – not to start.'

'I understand. It's hard to lose any sleep over your predicament, but I do understand.'

Mourville's face was lit by a stained-glass window, so that the green and amber hexagons gave him an unhealthy look, something like a denizen of the deep himself, with crafty eyes and a submarine glow.

'You think I'm suffering from over-indulgence in the world, don't you?'

'Those weren't exactly the words that were tumbling from my lips, as it happens.'

'The truth is I'm not. I'm actually suffering from a lack of contact with the world, real or otherwise.'

'Because you take no active part. Could that be the reason?'

'In a way, yes, I suppose it could.'

'So you intend to go back home and find yourself.'

'This conversation is cyclical, isn't it?'

'Yes. It may even disappear up its own fundament shortly, which would be a blessed relief. Here, have some more wine. I'm just a simple banker, trying to lend money to people who don't need it, and trying not to lend it to people who do need it.'

'Was it Isaiah Berlin who said that to understand all is to see that nothing could be otherwise?'

'He did, but only to show that this view was pure ignorance. Things can be otherwise. Individuals, to some extent, choose.'

'It must be something in the water. We've become very philosophical.'

'God I like talking to you. You're the only person I know who still has time to think.'

Giles Mourville was mopping his plate with a piece of bread. His hair was receding from his forehead, giving him a jolly look, slightly coarsened, like a baker or a candlestick maker, quite at odds with his sharp intelligence.

'I don't have time to think, as you put it. I simply seem to find myself sitting about a lot, waiting for ordinary people to finish work. I worry. I become anxious. It's a piss-poor form of thinking,' said James.

'Do you really imagine going back will help this existential problem?'

'Are you being sarcastic?'

'Yes and no.'

'Ja. Well I don't really know, but I've got to do something.'

'Why?'

'Why? Because I feel I have to.'

'Is it a case of the genes asserting themselves at last?'

'I doubt it. They've been very recessive until now. No, I've inherited a farm I want to look at. I hope it doesn't sound too trivial, but I would like to try farming for a bit. I also want to learn something about the local darkies. My grandfather was a great linguist, very interested in all their little secrets.'

They drank another bottle of Chablis before stumbling out into Old Compton Street, where the light was as sharp as knives, as it can be on an autumn day. Mourville went back by underground to the City to work and he took a cab to the Connaught, to sleep. But he did not sleep. The flight, the wine, his changed circumstances, all kept him awake so that by seven o'clock when he was due to go out again he was tired and stunned, and missing Jo-Anne, but missing her dishonourably like a personal possession lost.

He stood outside the Connaught, underneath the quaint glass cupola arrangement that protected the patrons from inclement weather, waiting for a cab. The doorman, in his long brown coat waved. He had cornered one. James walked down the steps and into the cab, hoping to find some diversion.

The night was wet and electric. It reminded him of South Africa because of the lightning in the sky. Thunderstorms in the Transvaal usually produced from nowhere toads hopping erratically about in the rain.

He remembered a line he had read:

'The dissection of frogs is more important than poetry, because it leads to truth.'

His grandfather would certainly have approved. But of course his grandfather did not know that there was no truth.

CHAPTER 13

The child was dressed like a tar baby, with a ribbon in its suprisingly long hair. The mother wore a kaftan of the pseudo-ethnic variety now affected by newly independent states. She was a beautiful woman with high cheekbones and high breasts. She wore bulky French jewellery of ivory and coral. The baby looked dazed. It began to cry. The mother produced a blanket, wrapped the child in it, and slung it across her back. This could not have been a comfortable arrangement for the mother, because it meant she had to lean forward so far that she was hunched on top of her airline dinner. The baby went quickly to sleep as the mother ate, her long fingers bunched together to pick up her tinned asparagus, popping them into her mouth eagerly. She looked up at James, watching her eat, and smiled.

'*C'est bon?*' he asked.

'*Oui, tres saporeux, merci, monsieur.*'

She spoke French elegantly with a touch of the jungle. What did *saporeux* mean, for Chrissakes? He remembered: juicy, tasty.

She was licking her fingers to prove the point. Child and mother had a puple sheen, as people from Central Africa do. She would be getting out at Stanleyville. Juicy asparagus from California. Where she was going with her baby (now delicately asleep), the white man had only been known since Stanley. Stanley had crossed Africa at the same time as Frank Thompson had landed in Durban. And here she was eating Armor asparagus and wearing expensive jewellery from the Faubourg. What had she absorbed of European culture and society? Did she, like Jo-Anne, love all the detritus of fast foods and TV quiz games, or did she retain in the deepest recesses of her soul a reassuring pantheism, which told her that trees and rivers and stones contained the spirits or the one spirit in many manifestations. If so this would probably exclude star signs and Esther Williams from serious consideration. Or perhaps she had read Valéry and Rimbaud and got her bac at a smart school in Fontainebleau.

Très saporeux. Now she was eating the *côtelettes d'agneau au rosmarin* with equal enjoyment, sucking the juicy bones so that little rivulets ran down her chin, which she wiped casually away. All planes are full of people travelling at some unknown behest or urge, paying for the flight with illegal bank accounts in Zurich, or company stipends, or little nest eggs, bent on adultery or escape from marrige or images of love or the illusory notion of duty, like leaves blown in front of a sharp autumn breeze. Where she came from there were no seasons, only long steady, steamy days with great gravid drops of water bouncing off waxy green foliage in the intermittent showers.

She got off at Stanleyville, carrying the baby on her back. The baby was bewildered by being disturbed in the middle of the night, its little face as frightened as a forest creature's caught in a car's headlights. He wanted to comfort it in some way.

The plane climbed into the warm African night. Below he could see a few lights winking uneasily on the banks of the Congo. In Katanga missionaries had been killed savagely only a few weeks before. The new Africa would be as bloody as the old. Down there below (he hoped they were out of rocket range) was a world of darkness, of strange tribes, of eccentric doctors, of outcast mercenaries, of psychotic pygmies, of witch doctors and shamans, of close jungle paths and arcane rituals. His grandfather had believed in the inevitability of progress. All human activity was leading inexorably down the road of progress through – if he understood the old man correctly – the resources that science had placed at the disposal of the nations of Europe and America. What fulfilment was there at the end of this road? And was this belief not merely another superstition, another form of animism? He ordered a drink although he had already had five or six glasses of champagne. He was, now that the beautiful woman had got out, one of only three passengers in first class.

'Are you going home?'

'Yes, I am. I suppose so.'

She, being French, looked disdainful.

'Where do you come from?' he asked.

'*Paris. Je suis Parisienne.*'

It was his experience that all French people claimed to come from Paris, unless they were intellectuals, when they explained that they were merely forced to live there.

'Yes. I am separated from my wife. I am looking for a nice

French girl to shack up with.'

'*Pardon?*'

'*Je veux faire l'amour avec vous.*'

'*Excusez-moi, monsieur.*'

She left him to busy herself with some form-filling, but he was sure he had not offended her. She had that peculiarly French look, slim hips, dark hair bleached to the colour of a setter's coat, small firm breasts and strong thin legs. Her upper lip had the merest suggestion of a moustache; the canine hair was swept back and tied severely.

Going home. The champagne and the low scream of the engines combined to give him a headache. He slept for a while and woke again feeling dry in the mouth and profoundly unhappy. Going home. Home had always seemed to him the end of the line. Here he was, thirty-one years old, going home with nothing but the burden of twelve years since he had last lived in his own country. Who are these lucky people who have a sense of country? The stewardess with her delight in being French, one of De Gaulle's children, was one.

The passport officer at Jan Smuts Airport was certainly another. And who could blame him? James's passport told a tale of aimless and selfish peregrination.

'Welcome home, Mr Thompson,' he said.

'Thank you.'

'I hope you're staying a bit this time.'

'I think so.'

'That would be nice.'

'Can I go now?'

'Of course.'

He sees my freedom as an affront, thought James. The chauffeur was new, but he came with the estate manager, Mr Voss, who had looked after Hilldrop for thirty years.

'How are you, Jimmy my boy?' asked Mr Voss.

'I'm very well, Mr Voss; how are you?'

'I can't complain. Except that your mother keeps me on the hop from morning to night.'

Mr Voss loved his mother. He followed her around the huge gardens on a daily tour of inspection. He bowed to her every whim in matters of planting; he believed her taste to be absolute.

'She couldn't come to meet you,' he said as if he were protecting her.

'Don't worry about that, Mr Voss. And the old man?'
'Your father is not getting any better, Jimmy.'
'No change?'
'No.'

Mr Voss had grown old in the few years since his last visit. Mr Voss was a failed farmer when his mother had taken him on. As a boy he had ridden with Mr Voss on the small tractor that trundled around the garden. Mr Voss had taught him how to whistle and how to make catapults out of a forked stick and two bits of inner tube. In fact Mr Voss had been a source of a lot of rural lore, which he had brought to town with him during the Depression. He had always made James welcome, with sweet tea and Marie biscuits in his store-room at the end of the old stable block. Here Mr Voss had established a little corner for himself, with an old leather chair, a wooden table whose drawers was stuffed with useful articles, a racing calendar and innumerable nursery and seed catalogues. One day Mr Voss had killed a large snake, a Cape Cobra he said, in the garden, and he had skinned it and pegged out the virulent skin. That, too, found a home in the store-room. For James as a small boy, Mr Voss's store-room was a place of magic and Mr Voss a magician. And now he was an old man, wearing khaki shorts, a white short-sleeved shirt and new shoes. His face was a mass of sunspots and tiny burst blood-vessels. His large body had remained as stout as a barrel, but his legs and arms had shrunk, so that he appeared unsteady and unbalanced, all his weight and strength in the wrong places as he climbed into the car.

Mr Voss seemed genuinely happy to see him and curiously deferential. James was touched and guilty. He had hardly given Mr Voss a thought for years.

'Do you mind if I smoke?' asked the old man, already lighting a Springbok from its flat green box which he carried in the pocket of his shirt.

'No, no.'
'That's my boy, Jimmy.'

He could see the hills of Johannesburg proper, where his grandfather had so quickly found himself. They turned off the main road before they got to the city itself and swung through the leafy suburbs.

'There she is.'

Honey-coloured in the morning light, Hilldrop could be seen from miles away. Mr Voss called many things 'she': horses, cows, cars, dogs, tractors and the house.

'What do you think of that?'

'Wonderful, Mr Voss.'

'Do you know what your mother has got me doing now?'

'I give up.'

'What? Oh she's got me installing a sprinkler system. The whole garden, the whole fourteen acres, can be watered by turning on a few valves. That's the idea, anyway.'

Mr Voss, survivor of many such whims, laughed.

They drove through the gates, James's feelings as always at arrivals or departures, ambiguous. The garden, which his grandfather and grandmother had started, was now in its maturity, huge jacaranda trees lining the drive-way, the steep hillside a series of glades and glens and secret gardens. His father had collected sculpture, so through the trees – lying, reclining, embracing, running – were glimpses of his eclecticism. The house itself, although huge, had a human scale; it had been designed by his maternal great-uncle, a disciple of William Morris; later, in his thirties, a well-known painter.

His mother was not really waiting for him. She was going about her normal business, gardening, with one ear cocked for his arrival. He walked down to what Mr Voss said was a new Japanese garden, where his mother was standing, wearing a broad-brimmed straw hat, a basket over her arm and a pair of secateurs at the ready. She was watching the release of some nobbly fish into the pond. Above the pond was a stone bowl from which water trickled with Zen spareness into the pond.

'Hello, my boy, how are you?'

She turned her sad eyes, her intelligent sad eyes, upon him.

'I'm all right, Ma, how about you?'

They kissed, briefly, his stubble upon her parchment.

'Japanese carp. Aren't they beautiful? Laurens suggested it.'

'The garden looks wonderful as always.'

'Why do I bother?'

'Because you love it.'

'For what? For whom?'

'Let's not be philosophical so soon.'

'You always were a tough little nut, weren't you?'

She said this without malice, but with the air of one who has borne many things with fortitude.

'Show me around the place.'

He took her arm. Between them there was a residual affection, surviving from his childhood, that could never be lost completely. It had survived her many disappointments in him.

'That poor girl,' she said after a few minutes.

'You heard?'

'Of course I heard. We have a telephone in the house, you know. Her mother rang from Minnesota.'

'Michigan, I should think. Is she upset?'

'Of course she is.'

'I suppose it would be useless to remind you that you said she was not right for me? I should have taken your advice.'

'Why are you always off and running? School, Oxford, the firm and so on? Can't you stick?'

'You know it's not that simple.'

'To be honest I don't know anything.'

They strolled through a walk of pleached avocado trees, not a success.

'How's Father?' he asked.

'Oh God. Sometimes I hate him for his disabilities. Except when I wake at four a.m. when naturally I feel guilty.'

His father had suffered a stroke, which left him highly irritable and virtually incapable of speech or movement. He was looked after by a black man who had been his chauffeur, a man called Solomon. They never went out. The two of them had a symbiotic relationship, Solomon deliberately shutting out his past glories chauffeuring the Master's Rolls Royce from the Rand Club to The Chartered Company in Main Street, a few significant blocks, and James's father preferring in his helplessness the unblinking devotion of Solomon to all the members of his family. He had come late into his full inheritance, only to be punished for his presumption in trying to fill Frank Thompson's shoes.

'I love those trees. What are they?'

'Ah, that's a section of the garden you haven't seen. We planted it three years ago entirely with shrubs and trees from the Eastern Transvaal. Do you remember Lucy Thompson, who died so tragically?'

'I've heard of her.'

'Well, she was writing a monograph; you know how keen the Victorians were on natural history and little studies of this and that. I have planted every single plant she listed. Many of her drawings were charming, though she got most of the names wrong.

Look, this is extraordinary, it's the rock-splitting fig, *ficus sonderi*. Nobody else has been able to grow one. I'm putting in a sprinkler system.'

'So Mr Voss tells me.'

'God, he's a horse's arse. I don't know why I put up with him.'

They wandered around the garden for half an hour. She asked him no questions about how he had spent the last two years in New York. She was no longer curious about anything that happened outside the gates of Hilldrop and Weltevreden. Except for her charity.

'How is the feeding scheme?' he asked, of this charity.

'They all have a plan to rise up and murder us one night. The only problem holding things up seems to be that no one agrees which night.'

'You can't blame them.'

'I don't. I just wish they would get on with it.'

He laughed. After his last visit, he had not expected to see his mother again. She had said as much as he left, early as usual. And yet here they were. Her face had a slightly demented look about it, which overlaid the beauty he remembered from his childhood; a painful anxiety as though she had pulled on a translucent latex rubber mask from Carnival Novelties.

'Are you going to stay here?'

'Not for long, Ma; I'm going down to the farm Grandpa left me.'

She showed no interest in this proposal.

'Would you like some tea?'

'Yes, please.'

She walked gracefully, her hair grey now but still simply and youthfully arranged. Her legs were brown. She rang a bell on the wall of the verandah.

'You need a shave,' she said suddenly in response to his scrutiny.

'I know. I've been on a flight.'

'And you've been drinking.'

'Only a little champagne.'

'I'm glad you can afford it, without working.'

'Don't do this. There's no need.'

The verandah faced north. It was draped in bougainvillaea, in full flower in tones of chalky pink. Away out there were the blue hazy mountains which must once have spoken of the wilderness.

A fresh walnut cake had been baked. He ate as she picked distractedly, staring down at the garden. Suddenly she stood up and strode back into her bosky world.

He went upstairs to his room and ran a bath in the huge tub, the brass taps gleaming as ever. Brass presents an irresistible challenge to the servant class. The house smelt of his childhood, a mingling of the scents that his grandfather and grandmother had harboured and those his parents had imported when they took over. How haunting, and yet how trite.

The family aroused in him a deep unease; existential unease, as the French would have put it. Family makes a person again what he was, or tried to escape, or never was.

He fell asleep in the bath and awoke perhaps twenty minutes later, tepid water lapping his mouth and nose. *I might have drowned in this ludicrous fashion on the return to the heimat.* He lay on the bed and covered himself with the rough candlewick bed-spread.

Someone knocked on his door. God knows what time it was.

'Come in.'

He could not make the figure out, standing against the dark panels of the doorway.

'Who is it?'

'It's Solomon, Master James.'

'Oh, hello, Solomon, how are you? For a moment I thought you had come to cut my throat.'

Solomon did not get this little joke.

'Master want to see you, Master James.'

'What is the time?'

'Half past four, sir.'

'All right. I'm coming. How is the Master?'

'He's okay, sir.'

'Fine. I'll be a few minutes.'

Solomon left the room he had never fully entered.

James stirred himself slowly. He dreaded seeing his father. His father had gone straight from being an attractive and energetic playboy – polo player, proprietor of several Ferraris, houses in Antibes and London and so on – to being an invalid. To James his father had always been an insubstantial figure, as ephemeral as his grandfather had been real. Of course it was obvious now that he had suffered by Grandpa's longevity and exceptional vitality. Perhaps they had all suffered.

He dressed himself in jeans and a short-sleeved shirt. His things had all been neatly unpacked by unseen hands in the dressing room, but he did not put on shoes.

His father's face seemed to have been dragged down on the right so that James could see the inside of his eye socket. An oxygen cylinder, grotesquely big, big enough to blow up balloons at Boswell's Circus, stood beside the bed. His father, however, was sitting in a wheelchair, dressed in a blazer with a navy blue shirt, blue trousers and rope-soled blue yachting shoes. His hair was brushed back in the way he had always favoured, Clark Gable raffish, yet now it looked like the toupee on a shop dummy. Solomon libated him every morning with Trumper's West Indian Extract of Limes. This familiar smell, obviously overdone, struck him heavily as he stood in the doorway waiting for a clue as to what was expected.

The face, half-frozen along with his right side, struggled to say something.

'The Master says you must sit down,' Solomon interpolated in the awful quivering and muttering.

James sat in a leather chair, which drew him backwards into a position which would be suitable for reading back copies of *Punch*, but which put him at a disadvantage in his role as prodigal son.

'How are you, Pa?' he asked with desperate banality.

Again the muttering and twitching.

'Master says he's feeling better today.'

'I'm glad. Pa, I'm separated from Jo-Anne and I'm going down to the farm Grandpa left me to live for a while. I may come into the office from time to time if that's what you want, although I'm sure they don't need me.'

His father's good hand clutched the side of the wheelchair. They were equally impotent as they sat here facing each other.

'Mother seems to be well. Her garden is beautiful. Would you like me to read something to you?'

He felt ridiculous as he asked this question, but surprisingly his father, through the medium of Solomon who stood at a distance but close enough to scan his father's face, asked him to read from the evening newspaper, which lay folded on a desk.

He read the racing results first, from Turffontein and then the National Hunt meetings in England, carefully going through the breeding, the trainer and the jockey.

'Alcazar by El Cid out of Salazar, by a short head. Going Good. Trained by T. de Klerk.'

'Bay gelding by Prince Charming out of Hay Loft, ridden by S. Mellor, trained by Nicholson at Highclere. Two lengths.'

All these horses and their breeding meant something to his father because if he skipped a detail he was admonished by Solomon.

'The Master says the young Master must to read properly.'

A children's meal was brought to his father, which Solomon fed to him as James read through the papers. There were serious disturbances amongst the natives in Langa, in Durban, in Johnnesburg. He looked at Solomon's face as he read, but he could catch no reaction. The Prime Minister, Dr Verwoerd, was explaining his invention of separate development to an appreciative audience of schoolteachers in Bloemfontein. Cliff Richard and the Shadows were to visit Johannesburg. Gary Player expected to win the Masters. Gold shares were falling because of the riots. A novel fish had been discovered in the Mozambique Channel, which appeared to be teeming with finny creatures previously believed to be extinct.

His father dozed off. Relieved, James left the room as Solomon tucked a rug around the jaunty blue knees of the invalid.

The air was heavy with an impending thunderstorm. It flashed and crackled over the mountains to the north and the sky there became Wagnerian.

As dinner was served, the storm struck with a savagery he had forgotten was possible. The cracks of thunder were like whiplashes close to the ear.

'You used to be so frightened as a boy. You used to hide under your blankets,' said his mother gaily.

'I'm still frightened. What a racket.'

'I love it. It's cathartic. How was your father?'

'God knows. I couldn't make much sense of him, but then I never could, even when he was allegedly all there.'

'He's getting worse. Do you know that I don't even go in and see him some days.'

'That's not very nice.'

'No, it isn't,' she said. 'But I'm afraid I like to believe it's an honest policy. I really can't stand trying to talk to him through Solomon.'

'Yes. He is a bit creepy standing there.'

'It reminds me of your grandfather's dark secret.'

'What are you talking about? The business about the ritual murder?'

'Yes.'

'What was the truth of that really?'

'I'll digress for a moment. Laurens, you know how he likes to think he knows everything, told me something interesting. He said that ritual murder is on the increase because more people in Africa can afford it. Along with the new Mercedes comes this new buying power.'

'And what about Grandpa?'

'Ah. I think he liked the whiff of notoriety, that's all. He didn't like to be thought too regular a fellow you know. He never talked about it, not even to deny it.'

The lights flickered, and then recovered and then flickered again under the assault of the electric storm. His mother got up and left the table as if in response to this signal, a personal semaphore, and he ate on alone. The potatoes were cooked exactly as they had always been, whole and crisp. *What is the significance of our childhood memories? Why are they so acutely evocative?* A smart looking servant, white suited with a red sash, took his plate.

'Who are you?' he asked.

'I am Cephos, sir.'

'Where are you from, Cephos?'

'I am from Rhodesia, sir.'

'Is Elliott still here?'

'No, sir, he's gone home.'

'No pudding, thank you. Just some coffee in the living room.'

He drew back the curtains to watch the storm. These storms passed overhead very quickly. Now there was, on the distant hills, only the flash of spent lightning, just as he imagined artillery seen from the trenches might have looked.

CHAPTER 14

Mr Voss assumed that James had done the honourable thing and come home to take care of matters. He had never doubted James, through all the ups and downs. But Mr Voss had an unquestioning loyalty to the family.

'Ja, Jimmy, it's not been so good around here for a few years, you know what I mean?'

Mr Voss stood with a set of Champion spark plugs in one hand and an enamel cup in the other.

'It's a shame to let it all go,' he went on, 'that's why I was very pleased you've come back.'

'I hope you're not expecting too much of me, Mr Voss. You know I'm going down to the Eastern Transvaal.'

'Ja, I do. Listen, if you want any help there getting the place going and so on, I'm sure your mother would let me come down and spend a few days.'

'Thanks. I'll keep that in mind. I know nothing about farming. Bugger-all.'

'And I have probably forgotten everything. But we'll get things going, hey, Jimmy.'

'Thanks for the offer, I'll remember it.'

Mr Voss wanted to talk some more. He wanted to tell James what was on his mind. He wanted to talk about the decline in morale, but James would not be drawn in.

'Anyway, I'd better go, okay, Jimmy?'

'Sure. See you later.'

Mr Voss swallowed his tea, mounted his little tractor and chuffed out of the stableyard. He left James with a heavy sense of other people's expectations of him. Despite this he walked eagerly out into the garden. The sun was warm and the garden enchanted. Birds whose names he had forgotten fluttered, preened and called; cicadas warmed to their tune as the day grew hotter; there was a pleasant snap of grass clippers. The mad world his mother was creating, her own Tivoli, had this morning a beauty and permanence that he could well understand and appreciate. If anything had permanence it was gardening. The Medici, or even the Hanbury family of La Mortola (with whom his mother exchanged plants) never took a long view. One day they would all rise up and turn this garden into a people's socialist educational park. Who cared? Gardening was an abstract, profitless occupation, the pursuit of beauty. In this tolerant frame of mind he walked about. He recognised a black collared barbet, sitting in a tree and singing an intricate duet with its invisible mate, somewhere in another tree. As a child he had wondered how these birds subsisted, spending most of their lives ululating at one another. He watched a pair of lizards chasing with reptilian viciousness round and round a rock. At the Japanese pond he found one of his mother's fish floating near the surface, its silver-scaled belly sometimes uppermost and its swimming movements weak and irregular. His father's sculpture, with its massive, oppressively poor craftsmanship, littered the garden like obsolescent machinery, as out of place and obtrusive as a rusting car or a heap of beer-cans in this arcadian world. Where his grandfather had believed that the new order was really God made manifest to rational people, his father believed in conspicuous acquisition to stave off the darkness. These dreadful sculptures by sculptors whose names were mostly already forgotten, were totems. And he, the son and grandson, believed in – well – nothing much, except at this moment in the creation of that beauty which his mother followed with an inexpressible, atavistic urge. The rock-splitting fig, planted artfully in a crack beneath two granite boulders, was labelled with a little brass plate: *ficus sonderi, mountain rock fig*. Most of the trees and shrubs in the garden were labelled, a practice his grandfather had started.

'Hello, my boy.'

'Hello, Ma. What mightly enterprise are you and Mr Voss on to today?'

'Mr Voss is a nincompoop. He may soon find himself planting mealies again.'

She was wearing a hat tied with what looked like a beekeeper's veil, although they did not keep bees as far as he knew. She was carrying her gardening basket and notebook. Behind her stood a bed of iceberg roses, the sharp sun producing a halation around them.

'Poor Mr Voss. He loves you.'

'If he loves me so, he should learn not to use DDT near water gardens.'

'Yes, I noticed a fish which had gone to meet its maker. I assumed it had commited hara kiri.'

'I'm surprised you saw only one. At least ten are dead and the rest will follow.'

'That's the Orient for you,' he said, but she was off again, as mercurial as a character in a film by Fellini. Or Kurosawa.

A group of four black gardeners, pushing wheelbarrows, appeared. They replied shyly to his greeting. What did they think about all this? Of all the white man's stupidities, a huge garden, as big as a small farm, with barely an edible article in it, must have seemed one of the least explicable. Still, it was probably a relatively pleasant life here, safe from many of the hazards of the outside world. All this was repeated at Weltevreden, where his mother kept another small army of gardeners busy.

He settled down in an arbour with a new book. *Lolita* by Vladimir Nabokov, which he had brought into the country hidden inside his dirty washing. The corruption of the old world by the new and so on. Here the new world took no account of the old African world it had found. There was not even the amusing diversion, enjoyed by Nabokov, of toying with the pretensions and affectations and pre-conceptions of the old, because no one, except perhaps Frank Thompson, had enquired what these might be. The blacks were a mystery, as blank as a stone. Was this because they had nothing worth the effort of enquiry? More probably the answer was that what they had was so insubstantial that no one could be bothered. It was only when they started wanting what white folk wanted, that anyone took any notice of them. Then it was assumed that they had been corrupted; woken up from an enchanted sleep; got above themselves; lost their way; embarked (ironically by taking up the white man's culture) upon a doomed journey. A no-win situation for the benighted black. All metaphors.

His father's condition was said by his doctor to have improved that very day. James could not accept the premise that this was the result of his arrival. In fact he was not keen to go in and see his father on a sort of congratulatory visit, expected by Dr Applethwaite, a tall man with a hugely protuberant Adam's apple; he did and could see no improvement.

'The brain compensates by gradually applying other parts of

itself to the motor and cerebral functions. In plain words ...'

'Yes, I know what that means,' said James sharply. 'But I am not sure you aren't just whistling in the dark.'

Why was he so sharp with Dr Applethwaite? His smug professional manner, his measured omniscience and his well-ordered appearance irritated James, because they suggested a kind of parochial quackery. But he tried to make up for his rudeness.

'Do you think he will have another stroke or continue this improvement?'

'I can't say. In some cases the improvement can be good and permanent, in others a stroke follows after a few years.'

'You can't say which? Are there no tests?'

'We've done all of them.'

'Would there be any advantage in sending him to London or New York?'

'I don't think so.'

He gave the doctor a glass of sherry in the hallway, beneath a portrait of Emily Thompson, girlishly eager, the harsh African setting made pastoral and mysterious by her brother, the painter. He sipped the sherry carefully.

'Well, I'll be going now, James. Jolly nice to see you again after all these years.'

'Thank you.'

His mother appeared in the doorway just as he was opening it, saw Dr Applethwaite, said 'Oh' and moved on.

James did not leave the grounds of Hilldrop for a few days. Lawyers came to see him. Old friends rang. A former girlfriend hinted that they should renew their liaison; her husband was away as usual. But he did not move out once. The newspapers reported his arrival. The gossip was that he was recovering from his broken marriage, but the truth was that he hardly gave Jo-Anne a thought. All the bitter sarcasms, the terrible inquisitions, the constant irritations and suspicions and above all the sense that he was, in all ways, responsible for their unhappiness, all this had receded rapidly into the past. Jo-Anne's demands, transmitted from America by lawyers, were to him as real as satellite bleeps from space. A large sum of his money was suggested as a settlement by his lawyers. He agreed, with mild surprise that she should want anything of him at all. In this haphazard fashion his marriage dragged its feet to a formal end. The past is truly another country.

Finally he went into the grey office on Main Street to see the acting-chairman and sign some papers. The place was so much his grandfather's monument that he wondered how anybody could have expected his father to assert himself here. It would have been dancing on his grave. That night he rang Mrs Kathy Greenhalgh, the concupiscent wife of Gerald Greenhalgh. They were usually known as 'Kathy and Gerald', a unit. A maid answered the telephone.

'Mr and Mrs Greenhalgh's residence.'

'Is Mrs Greenhalgh there?'

'No, Madam is at a meeting.'

'Oh, could you tell her to ring Mr James Thompson.'

'Yes, sir.'

Did the maid know her madam's susceptibilities? Kathy rang back promptly.

'Is Gerald about?'

'Oh God no, he's flying around the country somewhere looking for something.'

'Shall we do it tonight then?'

'What exactly?'

She enjoyed the insinuation.

'Have dinner.'

'Okay, where shall I meet you?'

'Come to Hilldrop.'

'Isn't your mum there?'

'No, she's gone to Weltevreden. At least I think so. Anyway she would love to see you again. She's not a prude.'

'James, we're just having dinner, perfectly natural for two childhood friends.'

'Did you ever tell Gerald what we used to do in my tree house?'

'No, but knowing Gerald he's probably got this phone tapped. I'll see you about eight after I've got the children off.'

'Okay.'

It had not occurred to him that she had children. He wondered if this would make her more ardent or more vulnerable. She had been a near perfect girl, bronzed and made luscious by the sun. He remembered her vagina as though it were yesterday when they had been lovers. And this after all the women he had made love to in the intervening twelve years. He began to feel nervous and excited. He undressed and found a pair of shorts so that he could swim and lie in the sun to lose some of his unhealthy northern pallor. Although it was never used, the swimming pool was kept so clear that the water appeared to have an unnatural vivacity, like Perrier. The gardener whose job it was to perform the ritual of vacuuming, scooping and dosing the pool with chemicals seemed bemused by the sight of a swimmer disturbing his harmless labours. He stood for a while, scoop in hand, and then wandered off, muttering.

The water tasted of childhood; the slight sting in the eyes and the chemical cleanness. He swam a few lengths and then lay on a towel on the flagstones near the diving board (where he had mastered the back flip) and wondered if all lovers remembered each other's genitals with the exactitude that he did. He could remember them all. 'Sorry, I can't remember your name but I never forget a cunt.' He dozed happily in the sun.

'Jimmy, wake up, there's my boy, you'll burn all the skin off your back.'

It was Mr Voss, fatherly.

'Thanks, Mr Voss. What time is it?'

His back was burnt red, but his stomach and thighs were still pale.

'It's four. Your mother's gone down to the Cape.'

'Yes, she said she was off.'

'She's got lots of meetings and things there.'

'When is she back?'

'I'm not sure, you know what she's like.'

'I do.'

A servant brought tea and cakes, unbidden.

'Have a cup of tea, Mr Voss.'

'Oh, that would be nice. Tip top, Jimmy.'

Mr Voss sat on a swing bench with a fringe around the canvas roof, uneasily as a girl at her first party. He handled the Limoges china gingerly as though he was afraid his horny hands would break it. From where he was lying, James could see Mr Voss's thin, venous legs all too clearly. Mr Voss wanted to talk about the sad decline. He had a sense that the whole enterprise – the houses, Chartered, the family – was spinning out of control. No use explaining to Mr Voss about trusts and boards of directors and so on. He believed that without a member of the family directly involved everything would go to pieces.

'And you know, Jimmy, things aren't so good in the country

either. The natives are really stirred up. In all my times I've never seen anything like this.'

Mr Voss spent a lot of time with his black gardeners, so he probably knew what was going on. Or perhaps, like many elderly people, he was simply prey to more and greater anxieties.

'Look, as you know I've been out of it myself, Mr Voss. Since Bill left a lot has been expected of me, but really I don't think I'm in a position to do much.'

Bill, his brother, had been trained to take over but his homosexuality had disqualified him; it was thought best that he go and live in Antibes where he was now a partner in a restaurant and antique business. James had pointed out to him that there was something rather predictable about going into this kind of business in his situation. He had visited him on his way to Johannesburg. Their meeting had been curiously inconclusive. Bill, too, was happier to forget his past and his family. He talked English with a French accent and had become lispingly camp in both languages. His domestic and social arrangements were delicately poised. Bill's defection, his change from pin stripes to sailor stripes, had come a few years after Grandpa's death.

'It's too late for me to try and take over. For a start I wasn't a great success in London. They all remember.'

'You were very young then, Jimmy. And your dad was the boss.'

'Let's see how I get on farming for a bit, okay?'

'But will you promise to give it a try?'

'Maybe.'

Mr Voss was happy. He ate the Victoria sponge with greedy gusto.

'This is good cake,' he said, wiping invisible cumbs from his khaki shorts.

'Have some more, help yourself.'

James lay on his back to try and even off his tan. He had grown slightly flabby. On his farm he would lead an ascetic, hard-working life. The idea of this Thoreau-like existence appealed to him. He was tolerant of Mr Voss's bonhomie; it was comforting.

Mrs Greenhalgh, the same person who used to touch his trousers in his tree house when he was fifteen and she fourteen, arrived at the front door in a Porsche. He kissed her lightly, but she hugged him to her for a moment.

'You look well,' he said.

'So do you. Your hair is a bit thinner, otherwise you look just the same.'

'No wiser?'

'I hope not. Shall I come in now?'

'Oh yes, come on.'

She was slightly thicker around the waist, he noticed, and her once free hair was shorter and waved. Her eyes, heavily made up, were minutely lined.

'It's having children that does it,' she said, seeing him studying her.

'You look fabulous, really. I'm admiring you.'

'I thought it was my mind you were after?'

She had always had a good line in banter.

'I am; that too. Come, let's have a drink.'

'God, this house. I used to think it was a terrible old dump when we were kids, you remember your grandfather's birthday parties? Only now I realise what a wonderful house it really is. Look at this panelling. How's your father, by the way?'

The silent guest upstairs.

'He's not well, obviously, but the doctor thinks there is some improvement since I got back.'

'Kiss me once, James.'

He kissed her and their bodies pressed close together. Her mouth was no longer sweet and girlish but musky and warm.

'Oh, Jimmy, what has happened to us?'

'Christ, I thought you were coming round for a screw, not a canter down memory lane.'

'Oh well. I used to love you because you were dangerous and intelligent. I hope you're not just a failure as everybody says.'

'You've become very candid these days.'

'Well, you know how it is. I married a solid but boring dum-dum and now I have kids and now I am harking back to when everything was rosy. That's why I called you. You are an anarchist.'

'Thanks a whole lot. I'm not an anarchist at all. I'm actually looking for order.'

'You've come home at the wrong time in that case. The whole place is falling apart. The natives are revolting.'

They sat on the verandah, bathed in the rich and exotic scents from his mother's garden.

'It's so good to see you, Kathy.'

They were not really equipped to tell how they felt; nothing in their upbringing had given them the capacity. James wanted to tell her that the youth, hope and innocence which they had had in those few over-charged years were what he was desperate to glimpse again. He wanted to tell her that he was not interested in her as she was now: society lady, two children, rich husband and Porsche, but as she had been: eager, lithe, sensual as an animal, with girlish whims which had left him breathless.

'It's no use trying to go back, is it?' she asked almost ingenuously.

'No. I'm afraid not. Let's have dinner.'

'Okay.'

He rang a bell.

'We'll have dinner now.'

'Yes, Master.'

'You were against all this sort of thing, I thought,' she said gesturing at the back of the servant.

'Well, I was, but I'm sort of neutral about so many things now.'

'Are you upset about Jo-Anne?'

'I'm upset by the fact that I am so fucking pleased to be rid of her. For two years I struggled with myself.'

A gong sounded.

'Help, what's that?'

'That's dinner. My grandfather's custom.'

'What are we having, Bengal Tiger?'

'No, just Knysna oysters and champagne.'

'Aren't oysters supposed to be aphrodisiacal?'

'Are they? Good heavens.'

In bed she was less sure, perhaps worried that he would look for stretch marks or leathery nipples and all the little things that women fear. She was frantic to please. This was a reversal of roles, because as children he had always been desperate to please her. They clung together and made love furiously, like two drowning swimmers. It was false, but afterwards they found some of the intimacy they had both been seeking.

'Shall we meet again?' he asked.

'I hope so. But not too regularly. Gerald's a pompous old tosspot but he is instinctive.'

Along the corridor they heard a muffled crash and subdued bumps.

'Nothing to worry about, just my father doing his press-ups.'

CHAPTER 15

He did not see Kathy before he left, nor did his mother call from Cape Town. But he paid a long visit to his father and his amanuensis, Solomon, to read to him from the sporting pages again. They read *The Star, The Rand Daily Mail, The Times* and *The Sporting Life*.

'I'm going off first thing tomorrow, Pa, down to the farm. I'll be back. Is there anything you need?'

Solomon interpreted the shakes and splutters.

'Master say you must have too many children, sir,' he said gravely.

Could this be real? Did his father truly want him to produce grandchildren?

'Tell the Master I will try. I've been practising. Goodbye, Pa, goodbye, Solomon.'

He left his father sitting, stricken, his half-frozen face with its mute plea for relief apparently unable to change its expression, like the Sirens in a nineteenth-century German painting, forever leering at the Rhine.

He had loaded the car with useful items, chosen in a haphazard fashion with a little advice from Mr Voss, who would have liked to come along in his pick-up. Mr Voss hooked a water bottle of leaking canvas on to the front of the car to keep cool. This, he said, was indispensable for long journeys. James took a gas cylinder for cooking purposes, matches, a few pots and pans and a sleeping bag. He had wanted to buy some seeds and plants, but the range offered and the demands of season obviously needed careful study. Mr Voss gave him a present of a Canadian axe in a neat leather pouch. At the last minute James ran into the house and filched some wine and a case of beer. Mr Voss waved goodbye, and he set off lightly.

'*I Robinson Crusoe was born in York of a good family in the year* ...' he paraphrased as he turned out of the huge armorial gates. He was only vaguely aware of the route to his property, but he preferred it that way.

The veldt was green and tall; the first evidence that the natives actually lived somewhere came to light, in the form of very simple mud huts with sheets of galvanised iron on the rooves, not nailed, but weighted down with brown rocks and white pumpkins. These huts were mostly adjuncts to the tumbledown farms that clung to the fringes of the city, waiting for the suburbs to engulf them. The sky was as big as in a John Ford western. Rolling hills, all clad in this unlikely green, stretched away into the distance. Clumps of blue gum trees, natives of Australia, stuck up into the sky to break what would otherwise have been a landscape of low, rounded hills only. The road became dead straight, shimmering in the hollows with heat haze like patches of water; little towns with catholic names – Devon, Kinross, Evander, Olifantsfontein – passed by quickly, each one with its church, garage, butcher, café and rugby field. The canine mortality rate in these places was high; he saw at least five dead dogs. The towns became less frequent, the sky now dull and metallic as the heat of the day asserted itself. He ran parallel with a railway line and eventually caught up a freight train, the locomotive puffing and blowing fiercely, sending out behind it, flat over the brown trucks, a bag of white smoke that contracted and expanded as though there were restive animals inside. He waved at the driver, who waved back. Over the past few years he had had difficulty in understanding what made ordinary people do what they did. How was it that they got willingly out of bed, went to work, did the shopping, got married, had children and so on? It was to him a mystery as inexplicable as the omnipresence of religion. And yet the train driver, waving cheerily, had the best job in the world this morning, a job James might have liked himself, racing across the empty landscape. *Freedom may well be the recognition of necessity. I have never had to do anything. I am so free I am incapable.* But these thoughts did not depress him. On the contrary he felt an exhilaration. He turned up the radio; it was playing a song called 'Oh Boy', perfectly attuned to his mood. He passed a donkey cart, miles from anywhere, pulling at least six women along the side of the road at a pace so slow it must surely have been quicker to leave the two dispirited donkeys at home and walk. He passed a muddy stream, called the Olifantsspruit, and imagined the herds of elephants that must once have rumbled and trumpeted down there in the ash grey water. His grandfather might have seen elephant here, but they had long since vanished, pushed aside by the new order he had been so eager to establish, the regime which would inevitably make all men free; free from hunger; free from anxiety; free from want; free from oppression.

'*Oh boy! Stars appear and the shadows a-falling, you can hear my heart a-calling. Little bit of loving makes everything all right. Oh boy. I'm gonna be with my baby tonight.*'

It was hot in the car. He stopped under some gum trees and had a swig from Mr Voss's bottle; the water, just as Mr Voss had predicted, was wonderfully cool. Huge glossy brown cattle stood in a field looking at him suspiciously. A small boy, wearing only a pair of tattered shorts and a vest, appeared whistling sharply at the huge beasts and waving a stick. He was attacked by timidity on seeing James. James beckoned to him to come over. The little boy, his brown skin dusty, and his legs scratched, came over nervously. He showed very pink gums.

'Baas?'

James gave him a five-pound note. The little boy looked at the money uncomprehendingly. James gave him sixpence. His eyes became bright. He ran off towards a group of huts with his booty.

James drove on cheerily. *I'm disrupting the local economy. I'm spoiling them.* The country became more mountainous; the rifts and folds in the hills were thickly wooded. There were plantations of trees and sawmills. The land seemed to be falling off, down into a deep rift. Far in the distance a range of hills was burgeoning into massive mountains as he sped along. He stopped at a small town for a Coke and a pie, served piping hot from a glass oven. In the other half of the oven a few chickens rotated languidly, being grilled by a curious blue light that looked exactly like the insect electrocutor hanging in the window above the displays of dried sausages and true confessions magazines. He had always loved these pies, made with god-knows-what bits of leftover beef and kidney; he took another along for later. The little town marked the end of the tarred road. He closed the window against the dust and took off his shirt; it was so hot that his back stuck firmly to the seatcovers with the suction of a child's rubber-tipped arrow. The road now began to tumble downhill towards a more interesting landscape of hills and valleys and streams clad in bush. It was down here somewhere that his grandfather had first started work in the gold mining business. It was down here that the gold rush had begun and his grandmother who never was, had written her monograph. He felt curiously at home.

I haven't been alone for four years.

It was stimulating. His mind raced with schemes involving writing, planting trees, conservation, perhaps a school for African children, growing an exotic crop like saffron or cepes; all manner of good ideas welled up, released by this douche of solitariness. He munched his pie, better still now that it was cold. The radio played Johnny Mathis's 'Misty'. He passed a farm sporting a clump of bananas and a huge poinsettia, its powder-red flowers a promise of more tropical things to come. He stopped at a store sited on a bare patch of red earth beside the road to ask the way. The store was stuffed with bathtubs, blue soap, sacks of meal, work clothes and crates of drinks: American Cream Soda, Coke, Pepsi, Fanta Orange and Fanta Grape. He could remember their tastes as if he had never been away: American Cream Soda, slightly perfumed and all too ready to erupt into the nose; Fanta Grape with its purple sweetness which he had always thought of when reading *Ode to a Nightingale*, not exactly Provençal as in the original, but a contemporary version. Coke and Pepsi were quite different; Pepsi was more racy.

The owner of the store, a tall elegant Indian, took so much time explaining to him the way, while a group of adolescent children stood, ignored, by the counter, picking their noses and clutching empty bottles, that he felt obliged to buy something. He bought a case of candles, a spade and some paraffin.

The proprietor stepped outside to bid him farewell, having conscripted two boys to carry the goods. His son was carefully dusting the red Maserati.

'I have a brother who lives in Johannesburg. Do you know Patel's Supply Store? What a pity. He's doing very well. Have a safe journey.'

'Thank you. You've been very kind.'

The Indian turned sadly to the task of exchanging empty bottles. James had forgotten all his directions by the time he had gone a few minutes, except the instruction to take the first left, which he did, but something was clearly wrong because it proved to be a forestry road leading only to more rows of trees. Quickly the forest closed in all around and the road dwindled, becoming a track. He reversed the car. He decided to return by the same route, but made a wrong turning; he came to a bald cranium of rock rising out of the alien pine forests. A stream flowed over this rock and became a small waterfall on the other side. He filled his canvas bottle, the gift of Mr Voss, and lay down on the grass beside the stream trying to control the ferment of ideas and inspiration that tumbled and rushed within him.

He put some beers in the stream and watched an eagle (or hawk) float about in the thermals that held it effortlessly aloft. He unpacked Roberts's bird book, but by the time he had found the page which demonstrated the wing configurations from below, which of course was where he was, the bird had flown off to fall on little rodents over the next hill. All he saw was a streak of brown as it plunged. Perhaps it was a bateleur eagle. He drank the Lion Lager almost at a gulp. He thought of his grandfather unsaddling his horse here on his way to the goldfields. The horse had lived to the age of twenty-seven, almost unheard-of antiquity, living to see the Boer War break out, the consequence of the discovery of gold. His grandfather was one of the few men who had pointed out to Milner and Co. that a settlement of the war which took no account of the blacks was merely laying up trouble for the future. The future, judging by Springbok Radio, appeared to have arrived.

He lay on his back, naked. He gazed at the inscrutable, gunmetal sky. He heard a horse; quickly he pulled on his trousers and turned to see a martial figure, an elderly black man on a grey horse. The animal was so old it might have materialised to give flesh to his thoughts about Grandpa's horse. The old man was dressed in a khaki greatcoat, despite the heat, and wore a slouch hat and brown lace-up riding boots. He reined in the horse, which was no great achievement.

'Good afternoon, sir.'

'Good afternoon. Do you know the way to Trichardt's Rest?'

'Good afternoon, sir,' he repeated.

James offered him a cold beer from the stream, which he took calmly, thrusting it into the pocket of his greatcoat. He saluted smartly and urged the old horse on. James saw a red flash with the word 'Forest Ranger' on his shoulder.

He jumped into the car. The curious thing about the old man on the horse, he realised, was that he had a goatee beard and moustache, carefully shaped in the Edwardian manner, like the picture on the cigar box. And like Jan Smuts's picture, taken after congratulating his grandfather on his knighthood from the Edward in question. The grey beard and moustache reminded him of a black Santa he had seen outside Macy's ringing a bell for laughs.

Or perhaps it was a cartoon in the *New Yorker*, he could not be sure.

New York and Jo-Anne were far further away than their geographical distance. New York with its rushing, howling, violent energy, its jumble of buildings, its pools of greed and skill and anxiety, its naïve art bridges, its whole chaotic order, must have been a dream he had dreamt and not fully believed in when he woke. As a child he had dreamed of a celestial city (actually a nightmare version of a favourite book called *Pookie the Rabbit*) where nothing responded as expected. This dream became so familiar and so palpably a dream that even as he dreamt it he was able to make mental adjustments and wake up sensibly to restore order to the clamour going on in the cortex. So New York. He could half believe that he had never even been there. Poor Jo-Anne was as illusory as Pookie, flown off on those silken, unreliable wings. He was happy to have woken in this distant place. *Perhaps the human condition is naturally solitary. Or more likely the whole notion of the human condition is a poor cosmic joke.* Whatever the answer to this old chestnut, he was happy, as he drove blindly along until he found a sign for Trichardt's Rest. Trichardt was, according to his rough calculation, six miles from the farm.

The town of Trichardt's Rest was named after a quixotic Boer leader who had led his followers to their death in Mozambique. It was set in mountainous country but sited rather prosaically (it appeared from the road above) on the floor of a low valley. In the centre of the town was a small hill formed from a huge pile of boulders. These boulders were the centre-piece of the town's park. An attempt at a subtropical garden had once been made around this curious little hill. Inspiration – or will – had failed and it was now mostly a garden of aloes and thorn bushes with a clump of erythrina and banana trees testimony to a more ambitious plan. As he came closer he saw that the town, really no more than a small village, was gripped in the embrace of afternoon lethargy. A few timid black boys hung about the Indian store and café, hoping to negotiate empty bottles for coins; a farmer passed through town, the back of his truck loaded with bags of mealies and black workers all equally dusty. In the middle of the main road, on a traffic island, was the only sign of activity, a black man standing with a hose watering some leguminous cannas.

But in the café there was activity of a subdued sort. Grain was being weighed and bottles stacked. The proprietor was interested to hear that he was going out to the farm, which he said was known as Thompson's. Nobody had lived there for years, although just before the war some squatters had been evicted. One of the farms had been let for grazing but this arrangement had ceased five years before, after a dispute.

'May I ask you, sir, if you have bought the place?'
'No. I've inherited it.'
'Is your name Thompson, sir?'
'Yes, it is. The old man, Frank, was my grandfather.'
'Well, welcome to Trichardt. Your grandfather, Sir Frank, is really a legend here.'
'Is he? Well I'm not going to be doing much of that sort of thing,' he said foolishly.
'I quite understand, sir. My name is Pahad by the way. If there is anything I can do to supply you please let me know.'
James picked up some shorts.
'No, no, sir, these will never do for you. I have a much more modern line from America.'
'I like them.'
'Well, if you insist. Would you like to try them on?'
'No thanks.'
'You may have an account here if you wish.'
'Thank you, Mr Pahad. I should think I'll be in quite a lot.'
'Lovely spot, your farm, sir, lovely spot.'

What brings them here, to these dusty corners of the country, to trade in pennies, to live behind the store and work all hours, in a land which doesn't give a toss for their culture or beliefs? Perhaps they enjoy being outsiders and therefore morally neutral.

He had no idea what to expect from Pahad's cryptic description of the farm. Now that he was about to arrive he half agreed with the old adage about travelling hopefully. It might be a grave disappointment. He turned left past the grain silos and right past the location where the blacks lived incognito.

The road, evenly rutted like corrugated iron, led upwards towards another range of hills with some steep, wild mountains beyond. It was stiflingly hot in the car, even with all the windows open. The Maserati was not suited to this sort of work.

He had given no warning of his arrival. The lawyers were sure to have told somebody; they had always felt obliged to smooth his way wherever he went. He passed a small group of women walking with tiny children towards town. The women stood aside. The little children ran to catch them up and stood, nervously clutching their skirts as he passed. The blacks in these parts were cast in minor roles only. At a cairn of stones, recently whitewashed, he turned off the road and crossed a cattle grid. On a board, only just legible, he read 'F. E. Thompson'. The track ahead was overgrown and rocky. The house was not visible, but he could see a deep valley tumbling below the road; it was richly wooded with lovely trees. High up at the head of the valley he glimpsed a waterfall, flaring like a mirror through the trees and bush as he drove slowly along. The farm appeared to take in the whole valley and the mountains behind. His heart swelled and he blessed his grandfather.

Half way up the valley he passed a simple village of huts, grouped around a small open area and a cattle byre. Here, too, there were pumpkins drying on the rooves. A few grey hens scratched underneath the tall stalks of a patch of mealies. There was nobody about.

Further up the valley, on a little rounded hill, stood a clump of old gum and jacaranda trees. He guessed correctly that the house would be there behind the trees. It was a low building, its four gables edged in decaying wooden lace with little sharp peaks like Kaiser Bill's hat. On three sides, but not where the track approached the back door, was a verandah. The roof was of red corrugated iron, but so faded as to be ochre in colour. Outside the door stood a huge erythrina. There were also a few broken-down farm implements nearby, overgrown by khaki weed. A water tank, rusting, rested on a tower which looked dangerously dilapidated. James began immediately to make mental notes as a good proprietor should.

The house was locked at the back. He walked right round. There was a marvellous view of the mountains and the wooded valley below. Down at the bottom of the valley the river glistened like running mercury. Up above at the head of the valley, falling from a flat ledge of rock, was the waterfall he had seen from below. He found a side door which pushed open easily. The room was shuttered. He unlatched the shutters and pushed them open. Heat flooded into the cool room with the light. It was a huge room with a small dog-grate in a simple fireplace. The ceilings were pressed into a pattern of flowers and leaves and the floor was covered with faded duck-egg coloured linoleum. The linoleum was carried through to the kitchen, which was also huge. There was a wood stove, above which hung a clothes horse on a pulley arrangement. The place had obviously been cared for in a desultory sort of way. The rest of the rooms were spacious, all with pressed ceilings and closed shutters. The corridors were long and narrow, purely functional. There were seven rooms in all. He tried the water in the kitchen. None had flowed here for years. Thank God for Mr Voss's water bottle. He began to unpack, no longer filled with euphoria but a serious man with plenty to do.

As he was unloading the car, he saw coming towards the house up the dusty road, a bicycle. Its rider was silhouetted against the molten lead sky. James carried into the house an air mattress and the candles. When he came out again the cyclist was free-wheeling down the last few yards from the crown of the track. He was an elderly black man, with a beard of tightly wound clumps of hair, greyish. His face was oriental, the skin stretched over his cheekbones. He dismounted from his bicycle, a Hercules, and placed it carefully against a rusty barrow. (There was once an ad showing a lion chasing a man on a bicycle such as this. The pictograms showed him easily outpacing it, an unlikely outcome on this square, solid machine with its huge balloon tyres.) When he withdrew his felt hat from his head James saw that his hair was not as grey as his beard, but more closely growing. He held his hat in two hands in front of him.

'Hello,' said James.

'Good afternoon, sir.'

In the heights of the gum trees the turtle doves were simpering gently; the evening insect life was tuning up and the air was charged with these simple sounds.

'Can I help you?' asked James after a while.

'I'm Ephraim, sir.'

'I'm James Thompson.'

'You Mr Frank's little son.'

'Yes, I'm his grandson. How did you know?'

'Some man told me, sir.'

'And what do you do?'

'I live here, sir. I'm the boss boy of this place.'

'How many years have you lived here?'

'Since too long, sir, my father work for Mister Frank before time.'

'What's your second name?'

'Beg yours?'

'Ephraim who?'

'Tshabalala, sir.'

Here he was, on his own at last, but entering Grandpa's world.

CHAPTER 16

Ephraim Tshabalala – the child murderer's son – soon made himself indispensable. It was not a case of working himself, but of providing the necessary hands. He supplied a gardener, a cowman and a handyman, and he conscripted his daughter Daisy to work in the house.

The water was fixed, a makeshift chicken run and some listless fowl instituted and the fences were mended. Daisy began a ceaseless round of polishing and sweeping the house although there was no furniture, no carpet and very few utensils.

The first cow died in transit; at least by the time it reached the farm it was *in extremis*. Tshabalala took it away. A routine was quickly established. Tshabalala would come up to the house and wait for James to get up. Then he would gravely write notes in his little exercise book and move off to disseminate James's instructions. He became James's mouthpiece. Tshabalala's father had been a substantial man in the district, when the country was wild and uncharted and farms could be had for a few pounds. Gradually the white man had bought, sold, enclosed and regulated so that local chieftains, like Tshabalala père, became merely dependants living on little patches of land. Most of the young men went off to the mines or tried to get jobs in the city, leaving the headmen ever more isolated and impotent. So Tshabalala enjoyed his return to authority. The grandson of Sir Frank conveyed upon him some standing; he was able to chivvy and organise the few remaining old men and boys into a ragged labour force. The problem was that James did not really know how to begin. He decided on a cautious approach to farming; he would plant a few trees and some vegetables, try to produce his own eggs and milk and tidy up the house and garden bit by bit. The workers Tshabalala had conscripted were not well equipped for their tasks and had obviously had no recent experience of work. Tshabalala requested a set of gum boots for each of them, which James bought at Pahad's store.

Daisy, however, appeared to have had some coaching in her duties. She arrived at the house at dawn and brought him tea in bed at five o'clock. It was difficult to discourage her. She laid out breakfast like an obscure Japanese tea ceremony. He wondered how old she was. She was always busy, smiling shyly when he spoke to her. He thought about sleeping with her. She was tall and thin with skinny legs. He watched her watering the little succulents on the verandah; she used a jam tin with holes punctured in the bottom to make a watering can. She turned and smiled at him, and he looked away.

James explored his property. It stretched right up into the mountains. There were two valleys which could not be seen from the house before the mountains were reached. These secret valleys gave him a sense of what the country had once been. A mile upstream, above the waterfall he could see from his verandah, he found the site of his grandfather's retreat, with its arboretum, now overgrown. The cottage his grandfather had built had fallen down leaving only a wall standing out above the undergrowth. Tshabalala's father's kraal was nearby, returned to fairy rings in a clearing. It was overlooked by a huge fig tree. Nothing was standing, yet the bare earth of the cattle byre was still clearly visible. From his grandfather's garden there was a stirring view of the misty, purple mountains of Swaziland. He found some little brass plates near the trees and shrubs, recording their names and date of planting. He could imagine his grandfather's pleasure in this beautiful place; with his passion for order and regimentation, the sight of the abandoned grove would have saddened him. James set the gardener to work clearing the place. The gardener was reluctant to work there, Tshabalala said, because it was now consecrated ground; when a great man died his kraal was abandoned.

His grandfather's drive to establish order and permanency in the shifting (and shiftless) wilderness had found expression in these mountains. Had the order he sought, the organisation and regimentation of daily life, the imposition of logic on the illogical, produced happiness? The burning of a kraal and the destruction of a man's visible remains on this earth, surely proclaimed that no one should expect to endure except in the memory. Buildings, roads, mines, dams, fences, all these things trammelled the flow of nature and life. Furthermore, they were all vanity. Happiness was the absence of constraint: the constraint of property, of fixed location, of accumulated wealth, of artefacts, of buildings. Happiness, or more properly a sense of fitness – was the acceptance of transience. This was why the blacks burnt kraals and moved on. But that era was now over. There was nowhere to move. The freedom his grandfather had foreseen had not turned out as he had planned; it was the freedom of the wolf, which is the death of the sheep.

The waterfall plunged down about two hundred feet from his grandfather's garden. It fell into a deep pool, overhung by a mountain rock fig, of the sort his mother was fostering. Loeries with wings dipped in rich episcopal crimson sailed into this tree. Monkeys played and squabbled in the bush. Every time James came to swim, an iguana would scuttle from the rocks where it had been sunning itself and plunge into the cold water. He hoped the creatures did not bite. This one was as big as a small crocodile. The water fizzed with oxygen after its long fall. This overcharged water produced a great sense of well-being.

I must rid myself of this feeling that there is a central mystery that can be discovered, or be shown not to exist at all. I must learn to live just like the black people, without questioning. I must find my essence by trying not to look for it.

Perhaps it was the bracing water or the beautiful loneliness of his grandfather's garden that gave him this appetite for harmless abstract thought. But banal his every thought was. He wanted a sense of place to anchor him. like the technique of plant propagation that involves weighing down springy branches of trees with a stone so that they take root. He wanted a feeling of belonging somewhere; not somewhere grandiose like time or space or history, but merely – unconsciously – the right place. To have to wish it was to acknowledge its impossibility. Once you were a wolf you could never become a sheep. Despite these evident obstacles to serenity, he found in those first weeks at the farm a great sense of satisfaction in simple things. He postponed getting Mr Voss down. He postponed getting Kathy down. In fact he postponed almost everything on the grounds that he was trying to take root. He learnt to speak a few words of Swazi with his workers. They encouraged him cheerfully.

'Hello, how are you?'
'I am fine, sir. How are you?'
'I find myself alive.'
'That's good.'

He had visions of learning the langauge and customs of these people properly. He asked Tshabalala about his King, who was Sobhuza. Tshabalala told him very little. He seemed to suggest that his ties with Sobhuza were not a subject that would interest a white man. He asked about Tshabalala's father's duties towards previous kings.

'Too much trouble, sir.'
'When did you last see my grandfather, Mr Frank?'
'Too long ago. I was a little boy, sir.'

He cupped his hands to show how small he was at that time, about the size of a mushroom. It was hard to fix any dates, but clearly Grandpa had not come down here much after the Boer War.

'Did he give your father anything?'
'What, sir?'
'Did Mr Frank give your father any pictures or books?'
'No, sir. Just a cup.'
'May I see it one day?'
'Yes, sir. I bring it tomorrow, Daisy must clean it.'
'Okay.'
'Daisy, she's working nicely?'
'Very good, thank you.'

Daisy's shy smile and her large eyes (which had the look of bone china against her hessian-coloured skin) flashed in the corner of the kitchen where she was busying herself.

'Daisy, she wants to learn the house.'
'She's doing very well already. I'm sorry that I don't have more interesting things for her to do.'
'She wants to learn the cooking.'
'I can cook a few things. I'll teach her.'

The hens were laying well; he ate a lot of eggs. He showed Daisy how to make omelettes, at which she soon became very deft. She proved very good at almost anything he suggested around the house. She wanted a uniform and he bought her a nylon housecoat in blue with white cuffs from Pahad. She wore it proudly. They were slipping into a comfortable relationship.

She came in with the cup her father had spoken of. It was a silver-plated chalice, the sort of thing communion wine might have been put in. On it was an inscription which read: 'For Mndeni Tshabalala to mark the birth of a son, November 1892, F. E. Thompson'. Queen Victoria had given a similar vessel to Cetewayo and Rider Haggard had presented his old retainer, the model for Umslopogaas, with an engraved knife. The Victorians liked giving these solid mementoes. Daisy polished it with Silvo. This clue to his grandfather's past puzzled James. It was intriguing to think that there may have been some link between the birth of Ephraim Tshabalala and the ritual murder a few years before. But questioning Tshabalala produced no answers; history was in no sense a continuous stream of events for Tshabalala. As far as James could make out, history was a mixture of seasons, ritual, luck and misfortune. Frequently malice intruded itself. In the field of necromancy at least the white man was blameless. Many people in the area, James discovered, were languishing under the effects of evil wishes. This unlit world was as real to Tshabalala as the substantial world of everyday objects.

He gave up these conversations with Tshabalala after a few weeks.

'Daisy, I'm going into town. Do you want something?'

She gave him a list written in her painstakingly childish hand. He touched her wrist as he took the list.

'I'll get something for you.'

He was wearing his khaki shorts from Pahad's store; his legs, which had always seemed rather pale and formless from his vantage point above them, were now pleasingly brown and knotty.

'Thank you, sir.'

She followed him outside. A flock of guinea-fowl, once domesticated or at least with ancestral memories of being cared for, was hovering near the chicken run, hoping to join in the dole. He fetched the chicken feed and threw them some mealies. They scattered, but re-grouped in their neurotic, anxious fashion. He climbed into the car. He would have to get something more suitable for the roads: the drive into Trichardt was playing hell with the Maserati. It was difficult enough for the local farmers to take him seriously, but now with his cheap khaki shorts, his red roaring Maserati (the exhaust system was punctured) and his outlandish accent, he was all too aware that he was becoming a conspicuous figure.

Daisy waved goodbye as he thundered and bounced away in a cloud of raw sienna. He did most of his shopping at Pahad's. Today he was meeting a man who had antelope to sell, impala and blesbuck, little graceful creatures which would, he said, do well anywhere. There were lots of monkeys and baboons and small deer on the farm, but he had a vision of peaceful co-existence between himself and herds of contented ungulates. Down in the valley he could introduce hippo and crocodile at a later date.

They met at the Grand Hotel, which was a single-storey, tin roofed building, with a verandah on to the street, a bar, a few rooms at the back for commercial travellers and a dining room where waiters in red jackets spent hours perfecting the art of rolling napkins into starched fans (lunch) or coronets (dinner).

Mr Van Rensburg, who dealt in almost every commodity for the farmer, was a large man, but comfortable in his bulk. He wore khakis and blue socks, neatly folded under his knees. He ordered a Lion for both of them. James tried to show some interest in the price per head, but he had no idea what an antelope should cost, and agreed too quickly too the suggested price.

'Okay, and I'll throw in the delivery. But you must have a holding camp for them so that they can get used to the place.'

'All right.'

There was no likelihood of getting this holding camp made by tomorrow, or ever. They had no tools and no expertise. His workforce was capable of a little digging and carrying, but nothing tricky.

'If you don't mind me asking, Mr Thompson, what are you doing here?'

'I'm farming. In a way. I'm just really getting to know the property and so on.'

'Are you Sir Frank's grandson?'

'Yes, I am.'

'People round here, you can understand, are interested.'

'Sure. I do.'

'It's funny that he never did anything with that place for so many years. It's a lovely place.'

'Do you know it?'

'Ja, sort of. Is there anything else I can get you? We sell cattle, farm machinery, anything you want.'

'I want to buy a pick-up.' He gestured towards the Maserati which stood uncomfortably in the street. 'That's not too good for the roads.'

'How much costs a car like that, if you don't mind me asking?'

'I don't know, to be honest. I didn't get it new. I borrowed it.'

'You borrowed it. That's great. You borrowed an eight-thousand-pound car. Jesus.'

He found this very funny.

'I suppose your dad's got a lot of Maseratis lying around?

Anyway, I've got a nice Chev V-8 you can have, do you want to see it?'

'Please.'

'Okay, let's go. No time like today. Kom hierso,' he shouted at a waiter standing nervously further along the verandah. Van Rensburg paid and they clambered into his truck. Sitting mutely in the back were two black men. They sped off towards Van Rensburg's place; the truck was not there. He shouted at someone.

Van Rensburg was already driving off.

'He says I told them to take the Chev out to my farm. They say any fucking nonsense. Come on.'

They took the road towards Barberton. Van Rensburg talked the whole way, racing along the rutted road, leaving the blacks who walked, cycled or plodded in donkey carts, coated in dust. He hooted to give them warning of his approach, but no matter how much room there might be on the road, they were expected to pull over to the side into the deep sand, which caused bicycles to wobble, cyclists to dismount and donkeys to grind wearily to a standstill, like a desert expedition in trouble. This ritual, an assertion of dominance over the roads, was designed to make it apparent to the blacks that they were lucky to be allowed on to the road at all. After all, they had lived in Africa for thousands of years without building a single road, so they could hardly complain.

Van Rensburg's farm was a shabby place. It consisted of a small, pre-fabricated house set in a patch of bare earth and some sheds filled with machinery and vehicles. There were rolls of barbed wire, piles of mealie husks, parts of ploughs, sheets of galvanised iron, pumps, milk churns, sacks, feed and broken-down tractors in profusion.

'Come, let's go and see your buck first. The blesbuck make the best meat. Come.'

They strode off down a path towards a gate made entirely of bits of wire and lengths of gum poles. A few small boys were wrestling with this intractable object, trying to open it. They walked on past a dam, simply scooped out of the red earth.

Van Rensburg gestured towards some ill-tempered ducks plumping themselves up in the sun, by the dam.

'Nice Muscovies. Do you want some?'

'No thanks.'

'Look, there your buck.'

A group of enervated antelope, as skinny as greyhounds, stood under the shade of the one remaining tree in the camp. There were about fifty of each species.

'I'll take them all.'

'Okay. You'll have to give them some teff until they get used to looking after themselves again. I got them from that sugar plantation about six weeks ago. The little bastards are almost tame. Do you need some feed? Okay. I'll deliver. Come, let's go and see the pick-up.'

The pick-up was huge, with a green plastic interior.

'How many miles?' asked James briskly.

'About seven thousand. Goes like a bird. Do you want to give it a run?'

'No. I'll believe you.'

'Come, I'll get one of my boys to drive it to your place with the buck tomorrow.'

'Okay.'

The next day his place looked like a caravanserai. Van Rensburg brought the pick-up, a feed lorry and two huge trucks with the antelope.

'Where's the camp?'

'Here. It's all fenced down to the river,' he lied. He was simply going to release them and allow them to wander, on the principle of sauve qui peut.

'Where's the fence end?' asked Van Rensburg.

'Down there.'

'It's too big.'

'Never mind.'

They undid the ramp and the blacks chased the animals down towards their new home. They appeared bemused and ill. Three had broken legs sustained on the journey. Van Rensburg cut their throats with a penknife.

'Get your boys to skin them and cut them up. You can have the meat and I won't charge you for those.'

Van Rensburg's men threw a few bales of hay over the fence and the business was concluded. James had explained to Tshabalala that the antelope were to be left unmolested and that there would be a cull once in a while for the benefit of all.

James followed the animals as they began to fan out. He stood and watched them cautiously taking stock of their new surroundings. The impala began to nibble some bushes which he interpreted as a hopeful sign. They were said to be as hardy as goats, despite their delicate, stick-like legs and the tracery camouflage of their coats. The blesbuck were more sturdy, but intricately marked in black, white and ochre.

James walked down to the river. The antelope were indifferent to his presence. Three or four groups had formed. The more lively of these was making its way into the thicker bush on the lower slopes of the hill, but the others stood around with their heads held low, clearly ill. He hoped it was only the effect of the journey and not something more serious. He sat on a rock and watched a few animals sniff the water and drink. Two of the impala butted each other in amiable fashion. This was better; once they started to fight and fornicate, there was hope. A troop of black faced vervet monkeys jostled in the trees near the water and turtle doves swallowed their liquid, seductive call. The rock he was sitting on was still warm to the touch although the sun had gone off it some time before.

It was all his.

Daisy had been so happy with the little present he had given her, a Timex watch with bold fluorescent numerals. He had helped her to fix it on her wrist which was thin but strong, like her legs. From close up she gave off a warmth and a slight odour, not at all unpleasant, of Lifebuoy Soap and sweat.

He walked slowly back up to the house along the course of the river, scrambling through thickets and over rocks, disturbing lizards storing up the last warmth of the sun and rock rabbits (more like giant, bloated guinea pigs than rabbits and improbably said to be related to the elephant), basking in their rocky accommodation. He had not spoken to any member of his family for weeks. He had applied to have the telephone connected to the party line, as it was called. In an age when he could fly from London to New York in no time at all, he was here tangibly cut off. The barriers between this place and the outside world were not all physical. That was something his grandfather's generation had failed to see. It had placed too much reliance on the material; determinism was a comforting philosophy, because it absolved the individual of all responsibility for what happened in history. If we remove the barriers of ignorance, of communication, of wealth ... if we wrest control of the means of production ... if we once establish democracy ... if we bind all people in a social contract ... if we ...

Then there will be inevitable consequences. Many people believed that certain things would happen anyway without any conscious human agency, that history was a continuum determined by physical, or call them scientific, facts. Freedom, courage, free will, anxiety and so on were mere P.T. of the human mind, caused involuntarily by an amalgam of chemicals.

Yet here, down on the farm, none of this was worth a toss. His sense of isolation from the outside world with its hopeless obsessions was liberating.

By the time he reached the house, the sun had gone, leaving only a red rib of cloud above the mountains. Daisy had lit the hurricane lamps and the gas lamp he used to read by. She brought him a beer.

'What's for supper, Daisy?'

'Roast chicken, sir.'

The living room in its rough state was softened by lamplight. He had placed an old door on two petrol drums as a table and bought a plastic table cloth to cover the lot, so that apart from a slight smell of petrol there was no trace of the table's humble origins. Once he had picked a rose which had pluckily survived the years of neglect in the garden and now every day Daisy picked a flower or a sprig of a flowering tree and placed it in a vase on the table.

The radio was telling of unrest and riots all of which, naturally, the government had well under control and all of which were the work of agitators.

They come from afar to Truck and Car. Brush your teeth with Pepsodent. That was a catchy jingle. He listened to 'Pick a Box'.

Daisy put the chicken on the table. He had another beer.

'The box, take the box. The money, take the money,' the studio audience screamed. 'Your last chance, are you sure you won't take the money. I'm offering twenty-five pounds.'

'Take the box, you stupid sod,' shouted James happily.

'Okay, Bob, I'll take the money.'

'Right, he's taking the money, let's open the box and see what you would have won. Open the box.'

'A clothes peg.'

'Bet you're glad you took the box.'

'Silly prick,' said James.

He tuned in to Lourenço Marques Radio. Elvis Presley was singing 'Love Me Tender'.

'Sit down, Daisy. Have a beer with me.'

She sat for a moment, so uncomfortably that he was glad when she got up again quickly to go to the kitchen for something.

What do I look like to her with my fair, thin hair, my sunburnt, peeling nose and my long, downy legs? Grotesque probably.

She did not sit down again when she came back, but hovered between him and the kitchen, her lovely face alert, quick to smile, eager to please.

She said 'Ee' (pronounced as in the first syllable of egg) when he praised her or thanked her. He wanted to make love to her. Perhaps he could achieve the sense of belonging that he sought. There was also, of course, the less worthy motive: a tremulous despoliation; the dropping of a stone into a still pond; the sniff of violation. He watched her tidy the room, her nylon housecoat shapeless except when she leant forward, causing it to catch on her hard thin buttocks. He had never seen her hair, she always wore a head cloth, a doek. It was the African chador.

'Daisy, come here.'

She walked slowly towards him.

'Take off your doek. I want to see you.'

'Take a look at her hair, it's real, if you don't believe what I say, just feel,' sang Lourenço Marques Radio in one of those absurd million-to-one concurrences which happen all the time.

CHAPTER 17

James left the farm for the first time just before Christmas, because his father's health had taken a sharp turn for the worse.

The approach of Christmas was signalled by Tshabalala, who suggested a Christmas party with the carcase of an ox (or at a pinch a sheep) as a centrepiece. James was beginning to get the uncomfortable feeling that his staff regarded him as a soft touch. He bought a modest animal from Van Rensburg and loaded this and ten cases of beer into his truck. On the day of his departure, there was to be a presentation of Christmas boxes at noon, to be followed by feasting and drunkenness. Tshabalala's sense of the proprieties of Christmas was undimmed by the gap of the years. He gathered in his best suit with the ragged collection of children, workers and womenfolk, many of whom James had never before seen, on the bare patch of earth outside the kitchen door. From within James watched as Tshabalala marshalled them. He set a chair out for James to sit on and then knocked on the door. James walked out and took his position, facing the small, shy crowd. The children were in their best: little black gym slips for the girls and white shirts with grey trousers for the boys, which they had no doubt acquired in hopes of going to school one day. The women began, on a signal from Tshabalala, a pleasant, swaying, Polynesian dance, clutching torches and flywhisks and even a multi-coloured featherduster. Tshabalala stood beside James, glancing at him once in a while solicitously. Daisy – his Daisy – danced along with the rest of the women, wearing her nylon housecoat and new shoes.

After at least half an hour of this, the ox was driven forward, money, beer and presents for the children were handed out and the party started. James went back into the house to pack a few clothes. Daisy followed him and they embraced briefly in the bedroom, as the shouts and laughs of revelry floated in to them.

'You coming back, sir?'

'Of course, Daisy. Of course I am. My father is sick.'

'Shame.'

He kissed her quickly and her pink mouth opened sharply, as if she had been hurt.

'You must go now.'

On the fence, near the chicken-run, the skin of the animal he had presented hung like a discarded overcoat. He put his canvas hold-all into the car. Tshabalala came over to bid him goodbye.

'Look after the place, Ephraim.'

'Sure, baas.'

'I will be back soon.'

'You are Mr Frank's child.'

Tshabalala was drunk. His yellow eyes were cloudy, and he looked pathetically vulnerable, elderly and tipsy, in his best suit of at least forty years old.

'No, no. I'm Mr Frank's grandson.'

'You his child.'

He climbed into the car. This was not the time for a genealogical discussion.

'Goodbye, Ephraim. Stay well.'

'Go well, sir,' said Tshabalala in Swazi. They sounded like characters from *Cry the Beloved Country*.

Daisy was standing, unobstrusively, around the side of the house to watch him go. He waved to her. She waved back, her smile, it seemed to him, blighted, although to the eye as clear and innocent as ever.

He drove off, leaving the age-old scents of Africa – woodsmoke and roasting meat – swirling about with the gathering drunkenness and magic of Christmas.

The town of Trichardt's Rest was asleep; outside the Indian store small boys hung about listlessly as usual. The proprietor, Mr Pahad, had hung tinsel and cut out Christmas bells and trees in the windows and sprayed 'Happy Xmas to all our customers' on the outside in silver glitter, a tricky job it must have been writing backwards; only one 'ess' was facing backwards. The agitators who, so the radio said, had been shown by a judicial enquiry to have been behind the recent unrest in the country were certainly not active in Trichardt. Nothing was active here except Mr Pahad. It was hot, with a promise of thunder in the clouds massing over the mountains to the east. Outside the police station a group of convicts was having lunch, sitting down with chunks of white bread and mealie meal porridge and mugs of tea. Their guard, armed with an assegai and some sticks, looked on from the shade of a palm tree. James wondered how he regarded these prisoners in their canvas shorts and shirts. Probably with tolerance for the weakness which had landed them here. The white man's rules were very arbitrary; a toss of the coin and their positions could easily have been changed. *Totem und Tabu* in the white man's world were hard to get to grips with.

When he came back he intended to go into Barberton and see where his grandfather had lived. Barberton was not much bigger than Trichardt, but it had a history. It had had a stock exchange, a brothel or two, fabulously rich gold mines and, briefly, a cast of colourful characters, a town visited for a limited season by a touring theatre company with his grandfather as the juvenile lead.

Totem und Tabu. Sleeping with black women was taboo. Daisy's body was muscular, her hands hard from manual work, her buttocks thin and firm. She thought she was nineteen or twenty. Her mouth was large and sensual and took so avidly to the lessons he taught her that he soon got over his sense of guilt. It was the predictability that nagged at him. It was ever thus: servant girls in Victorian households, slaves on plantations, rich employers and secretaries. Determinists in this sense had some justification. Human relationships can be seen merely as the re-arranging of familiar pieces. What did Daisy expect of him? Nothing, it seemed. He had tried to ask her. Nothing except a dress and a wig from Johannesburg, which she had shyly shown him in *Drum Magazine.* They did not talk much; profound conversation was not easy. But he felt happiest when she was in the house.

He sped through little towns and up the long road on to the high plateau where gold – the real McCoy – had been found, locked in the rocks far underground. Alluvial gold had proved to be a mere flash in the pan. Barberton and Pilgrim's Rest had returned to their dusty slumber. He pulled into the gates of Hilldrop as the seven o'clock news, sponsored by Old Dutch Lager, came on the radio. His mother had returned from the Cape, so Mr Voss told him as he offered to park the Maserati for James. Weltevreden was her second home, another of his grandfather's creations. James's father had rarely gone there and James had been only twice since his schooldays. But his mother cared for it and collected the rich flora of the Cape there, some thousand species, in the ten acres of garden.

Mr Voss led him to the garden, where she was wandering about in a determined fashion.

'Hello, my boy. Your father's dying,' she said.

'This minute? Shouldn't we be doing something?'

'No, no, Jimmy. Dr Applethwaite's been. He says there's no point in moving him now,' Mr Voss interposed.

His mother snipped at some camellias.

'How long now?' James asked her.

'I'm afraid it's any day now, Jimmy,' said Mr Voss.

'Why didn't you tell me sooner that it was so serious?'

'Well, your mother thought she should leave you to what you were doing down there,' said Mr Voss in a whisper.

'I'm not deaf you know,' said his mother who was walking off.

Mr Voss smiled indulgently.

'How's it going down there by the way, Jimmy?'

'Fine, thanks. I think I'm going to need your help soon.'

'I'm ready. You've only got to say the word.'

That's what Mr Voss was waiting to hear. James did not like to tell him that he was not talking of agricultural advice, but his presentiment of more serious matters. *Totem und Tabu*. His mother was lost from sight in the direction of the azalea garden.

'Okay. I'd better see Pa and call the lawyers.'

'You'd better.'

He spent the best part of the next day with the lawyers. There were immense problems with his father dying now a mere twelve years after his grandfather. As little as he wanted to be involved, the sheer mechanics of extracting himself and settling matters would take years. Reluctantly, he went to the grey granite building in Main Street to see the acting chairman of Chartered. The sober suited porter showed him into the lift and escorted him up to the board room. It soon became obvious that Bill Forsythe-Jones was worried that James might have come to claim his inheritance. He liked Forsythe-Jones, who was a decent dull man, deeply knowledgeable about chemistry and geology, who had come up in the company through the minion route. He was an exceptionally good-looking man, tall, spare with fine features, but without the unmistakable mark, the embalming fluid, of the middle-aged roué. He has never made love to a black woman, thought James.

'Are you proposing to take any active part?' he asked deferentially. 'You'll be on the board of the holding company, it goes without saying, but I mean in the day to day running?'

'I don't think so, Bill. As you know I've never been very interested in the business. Or any good at it for that matter. But perhaps I can learn.'

'There's no need to rush it,' he said without irony.

'No. But I'm not about to burn my boats. Not just yet anyway. We won't change anything for the moment.'

'No, no, quite.'

Forsythe-Jones smoked a pipe. He was sitting beneath a workmanlike portrait of Frank Thompson, staring out as if at the races, with his eyes fixed on some distant object.

'Can I ask you a question, Bill?'

'Of course.'

'Was my grandfather a great man in any sense?'

'I think the answer must be yes. I used to believe, whether it was true or not, that he had a cosmic view.'

'A cosmic view? What is that?'

'Sorry, James. I mean that he thought about our enterprise in relation to world events, to historical events, even to philosophy.'

'And what was his conclusion?'

'He never lost faith in what he called the irresistible economic logic to improve the world.

'Was he right? I don't see things looking too good just now, do you?'

'He would have said that this was politics. He looked down on politics rather. To him there is a great distinction between politics, which is essentially the selfish instinct competing, and ideals. He had the power and the means to put some of his ideals into practice.'

'That's the arrogance of all philanthropists,' said James cruelly.

Forsythe-Jones drew on his pipe, tapped it, and drew again.

'It wasn't so much in philanthropy, as in setting processes in motion that he wanted to realise his ideals.'

'He must have died a sadder man.'

'I don't believe so. He never lost faith in the ability of well-run industry to improve the world.'

'Where did Hitler and Krupp fit into this theory?'

Forsythe-Jones smiled, refusing to be drawn.

'James, I can't answer for his every contradiction and peculiarity. I am just a mining engineer. But to answer your question as truthfully as I can: yes, he was a great man, and the proof is in what he has built.'

There was more than a hint of reproach in that. Forsythe-Jones had worked steadily in the company for thirty years. James felt that he was justified in his reproval.

'Bill, tell me frankly, would you prefer it if I gave over all my votes to you.'

'Frankly, yes, I would.'

'I'll think seriously about it. I've got some things I need to sort out first. Personal things.'

'I can imagine, with your father dying.'

'Well, yes, and other things too.'

'Understood. I've got plenty to do too. This unrest is not helping the share price.'

'Just one thing, if I may. Don't pretend we're on the side of law and order. We're on the side of orderly progress towards greater freedom. Will you say that?'

'Yes. Of course.'

'Can I make one more suggestion?'

'Of course. After all, you soon will be the major single shareholder,' said Forsythe-Jones amiably.

'Let's get that portrait of my grandfather from London for the boardroom. This one makes him look like a man with a cosmic view.'

James went shopping for Daisy. He walked down to the Indian market, where the shops had a profusion of vegetables, blankets, tin baths, and most curiously, African medicines. One of these had drying animals hanging from the roof; birds, crocodiles, aardvarks, cervals, genets, turtles, bats. There were trays of bark and powdered roots; horns, hooves, dried skins and ready-mixed concoctions in old pill bottles.

Nearby was a shop selling wigs, where he made his furtive purchase.

'You upset Bill Forsythe-Jones,' said his mother over dinner.

She was dressed dramatically in a black turban and a pleated dress, also in black.

'He phoned?'

'Yes.'

'You're right, I haven't got any business telling him what to do.'

'Why did you do it then?'

'I don't have a good answer. I just felt I should.'

'The truth is you really think he's a bit of an ass that your father put in so as to make sure he wouldn't rock the boat, don't you?'

'I suppose so. I also wonder if he knows how to handle what he calls 'the politics.' '

'Do you have any special insights you could offer him after your two months' living in the bush?' she asked acidly.

'I don't think so.'

She ate a fig while he was still eating his lamb.

'What irked him most, I think, was that you reminded him of your grandfather,' she said.

'How?' he asked, warmed by her smile.

'He said you were feigning humility as you did it. That was old Frank's trick. There may be hope for you yet. I must go, I've got some things to do.'

'Ma, why are you always up and off?'

'God knows. I suppose I'm scared of tedium. Have you seen your father today?'

'Yes, I saw him this morning before going into the office.'

'How is he?'

'He's gone a dreadful purple colour as though his face had been burned. And there's Solomon sitting guard.'

'Do you know what it reminds me of?' she asked from the doorway.

'What's that?'

'Rider Haggard and Umslopogaas. Your grandfather knew him well.'

'I know what you mean. Also it reminds me that this is still Africa.'

'Goodnight, my boy.'

'Ma, do you have to go?'

'I think so.'

She went to another part of the huge house and he sat alone in the drawing room of a mausoleum. Eventually he took his coffee to the library.

I do not need to tell you, I am sure, that when you recite the Lord's Prayer at bed-time, you do not the following day test its efficacy as you would an internal combustion engine. In the same way the Native who performs a magic ritual, does not literally expect to see his crops grown or his enemy die upon demand.

It was nearly midnight. James was reading his grandfather's correspondence, neatly bound in volumes in the library.

I follow, I believe, Malinowski's guide in dividing ritual practices into three classes: the Productive, the Protective and the Destructive. The truth is, I believe, that we do much the same in our own society in our own time.

His grandfather's correspondence with academics and politicians was surprisingly wide. Of course his philanthropical leanings had given him a foot in the door; the price of a new building or laboratory was, it seemed, a protracted correspondence. He had letters from universities and institutes all over the place, and ten honorary degrees.

Ritual murder is both protective and productive. To take a defenceless life and sacrifice it as medicine seems to the European a barbarous and selfish cruelty. Yet to the Native, I believe, it appears quite different, the act of sacrifice itself having a noble and symbolic value, which derives from the awfulness of the act. Incidentally, the word 'awful' has the meaning of 'numinous' which will not have escaped you. The two closest analogies I can find in our practice are the Holy Eucharist and the value we place upon death in action. In the first instance the nature of the sacrifice is similar. In the second we believe that death can have a symbolic value far greater than the mere fact of dying. We pretend to see in death in battle a sign of an inward grace. The Native sees death in battle in more mundane terms.

His grandfather had perhaps been misrepresented; he seemed to be wrestling here with the intractable problem, the old chestnut, of whether an individual is indeed the best judge of his own happiness, and therefore the best judge of his own state of freedom.

It is my belief in industry, that the Native of South Africa, if sufficient allowance be made for his traditional beliefs, which, I have argued, are not dissimilar in origin to our own, is perfectly adaptable to the demands necessary for his continued progress.

This letter was written to Jan Smuts, in 1938. Jan Smuts believed in holism.

The library was a large, solid room, windowless so as to avoid distraction, but with a lovely domed skylight to save it from intimations of claustrophobia. It was lined with books and the bound volumes of correspondence, lectures and notes. For his last thirty years his Grandfather's life had been centred here. Reading through his papers James saw that his grandfather had been trying to incorporate the experiences of his adult life into intelligible and systematic form. He was trying to encompass wars, cruelty, suppression, superstition, magic and ignorance into his belief that life must be progressing to a higher plane and a more advanced form, and by implication to a more perfect state of freedom. It was a hopeless task. It seemed to James that the old man had had his doubts, too. In another letter he found this quotation from D. H. Lawrence:

In the dust where we have buried the silent races and their abominations we have buried so much of the delicate magic of life.

It was late. He climbed up to the little tower with its ornate balcony looking out towards the low range of mountains which rose darkly against the first hints of dawn. An aircraft passed in the middle distance, its wing tips flashing anxiously.

When he thought of Daisy, he thought of her mouth; her mouth eagerly annointing him with the taste of ash; her mouth taking his penis innocently and hungrily; her mouth smiling shyly. She would be lying now in a hut, spread out like the victim of a road accident, her long thin legs with patches of discoloration the size of half crowns, her sparse, scratchy pubic hair, her round breasts, their nipples soused in dark purple, her eyes closed firmly against the light he could see coming now through the chinks in the mud walls, the soles of her feet scallop white. Her woody, wet mouth was what he longed for.

Just before dawn his father died. James had just gone to bed and woke in a confusion as Solomon knocked at his door. His father had died, a man who had never truly existed in Africa or anywhere else. James and his mother, in their dressing-gowns, drank tea in the kitchen as they waited for the doctors and shared a few moments of intimacy. They shared more, a sense of unease. The truth was that the poor man had meant little to either of them. He had lived with them, but not among them; he had been elsewhere. The pity was that there had been no re-kindling of affection and respect. Solomon left the house as the body was taken away.

Despite his protestations that The Chartered Company was completely in the hands of the acting-chairman, James found himself cast in the role of heir to all his grandfather had created. Newspapers and their correspondents looked to him for predictions about the future in these uncertain times. On the day his father's ashes were scattered in the grounds of Hilldrop, beneath some reclining figures in bronze, there was a serious riot near Johannesburg when black workers tried to march into the city centre. The air was heavy with the bitter almond scent of revolution.

His mother returned to Weltevreden and her garden as soon as she decently could and James let it be known that he had made all his voting rights over to Forsythe-Jones and was going off to America, where he would not be involved in the affairs of the company. He drove instead down to the farm, leaving Hilldrop empty. Mr Voss, however, continued motoring around the grounds on his tractor, marshalling his workforce which he feared was becoming restive.

There was a subdued air about the farm. Tshabalala said that the telephone was now in and some other people, some policemen, had come visiting in his absence.

'What did they want?'

'I don't know, sir. They doesn't tell me. They come with Baas Van Rensurg.'

'How are the buck?'

'Not so good.'

'What happened to them?'

'They running away, sir, down that side.'

'Where to?'

'All over.'

Tshabalala was impatient with the details. It seemed most of the antelope had wandered on to the next farm where they had been shot. He walked around the house. The scratchings of a garden had been neglected. The few plants he had put in were dying. The house was tidy; Daisy had been in every day, but none of the others had done anything in his absence. Tshabalala attributed this to the Christmas season. Daisy was in the kitchen, scrubbing the floor. She stood up and wiped her hands on her apron. He held her hand briefly.

'I'll give you your presents tonight.'

'Thank you, sir.'

She made him tea and smiled at him shyly.

'Did you have a good Christmas?' he asked awkwardly.

'Thank you, sir.'

'What did you do?'

'Not so much.'

'My father died. That's why I've been so long.'

'Shame. He died, your father?'

She looked at him with real concern.

'Yes, he was very ill.'

'He is sick in the head.'

'Yes, really I suppose so.'

'I hear before.'

He left her unpacking his things, singing gently to herself, in the bedroom. He walked up the river to his grandfather's arboretum. He would build his own house here one day (if the ancestors permitted) and he would restore the farmhouse below. By then there could well be a black government with Nelson Mandela or Robert Sobukwe as Prime Minister and Albert Luthuli as President. They would have their own version of the more advanced and free society. Everything was changing. What little work had been done here clearing the trees and the brass plates had stopped. Everything was changing, yet he felt in no way responsible.

Van Rensburg arrived in his pick-up to visit him late that afternoon. He had heard that someone had driven off the impala and blesbuck. They sat on the verandah, looking out towards the river, drinking brandy and water.

'That's a bad business,' said Van Rensburg.

'What can I do?'

'Nothing much. You should try to drive them back one day when he's out. He's probably shot most of them already. Unless you catch him opening the fence, there's fuck-all you can do about it. He can just say they jumped over the fence. You must get a game fence. Listen, I wanted to talk to you about something. I suppose now you won't be living down here any longer?'

'You mean since my father died?'

'Ja. If you want me to look after the place, or lease it, I would be interested. It would be a shame to let it go again.'

'Well, I haven't really started yet. As you can see. But at the moment I have got no plans to leave.'

'Well, keep me in mind. People here are talking about it.'

'About what? About my family?'

'Ja. And such things. They're a funny lot of bastards down here.'

Van Rensburg always liked to affect the air of a man who has seen a bit of the world.

'Ja. You know what these people are like,' he said gravely.

James was not sure whether Van Rensburg was warning or threatening him.

'You don't know why the police were here while I was away, do you?'

'No. Just keeping an eye open I suppose. There's a lot of those Pan African bastards coming in from Swazi. No, I don't know, to tell the truth,' he said reflectively.

They drank half a bottle of brandy.

'Do you want something to eat?' said James. 'My maid can get something for us.'

'No, no, I've got a wife and kids at home. Good stuff that French brandy. Bye now.'

He stumbled into the gathering gloom, jumped into his pick-up and roared off, clipping the gate post as he went.

Daisy had made sausages and mash which he ate drunkenly. She was so pleased to see him, yet he could not really talk to her. For a start they could only talk in very simple terms. She also seemed to be reluctant to impose on him in any way. He wanted to possess her more fully, but it was impossible. It was not enough to know that she loved him or was devoted to him. It was a cruel barrier which he could see no way of breaching.

He gave her the presents.

'Put them on. Let's see what you look like.'

The night air was full of the sounds of insistent insects. He sat in the near dark, gazing down to where the river crawled, black now; from down below, from Tshabalala's village, a baby's cry floated up on the night air, as clear as a choirboy's solo against the creaks and squeaks of the night. He went inside so that no one should be party to what was about to happen.

He turned on the radio and sat nervously in the solitary armchair, flanked by packing cases of goods, mostly school memorabilia his mother had sent on from the Cape. God knows what the intended symbolism was; he was surrounded by piles of school pictures of himself in cricket flannels and running shorts and rugby jerseys; on either side of him in these pictures sat other boys with similar little quiffs and slicked down hair. It might have been possible to trace his metamorphosis from child to adolescent to young adult by laying out these absurd pictures, had anyone wished. He turned the wick down in the lamp. The radio played 'Seven little girls sitting in the back seat'; he felt sympathy for the driver: 'Keep your eyes on the road and your hands on the wheel'. Daisy stood in the doorway.

'Oh my God,' he whispered.

She wore a tight straight skirt and a little jacket, in itself shocking enough; on her head she had a black wig, his gift, long and straight, so that the extruded nylon hair just touched her shoulders. Her mouth was vividly slurred with red lipstick.

'I look too nice, sir.'

'Oh Jesus,' he whispered.

The brandy made him reckless. He stood up and they danced clumsily; he kissed her, feeling the synthetic hair brushing the side of his face. She looked as life-like as a child's doll. He began to undo her blouse to see if she was wearing the underwear he had bought. She laughed, delighted by her new things.

'Daisy, I ...' But he could not say it because he did not really know what he felt. He wanted to violate her, to finish the corruption of innocence, to bring all this to some sort of conclusion. He could not wait.

'Lie down.'

They collapsed into the armchair and he pulled at her new clothes. Roughly he tugged her new skirt up to expose her buttocks in sleek black.

'Daisy, Daisy.'

'Don't spoil it.'

'What? What are you talking about?'

He was confused.

'The new clothes, sir.'

She took them off carefully, and knelt down again, naked in the lamplight.

He drew her mouth down on to him; his penis touched her over-red mouth.

'Oh my God, forgive me,' he said to her, or perhaps to himself. He ejaculated almost immediately. He was weeping, but she kissed his face with lips streaked with tears, lipstick and semen.

Days, weeks went by. He no longer bothered to send Daisy home. She slept most nights in his bed. He gave up planning for the farm. A sort of African insouciance came over him. It was enough simply to be alive and go about a few basic tasks. He refused to answer the telephone most of the time; two shorts and a long was his code on the party line. Van Rensburg appeared again, trying to make some sort of deal about the farm. They sat on the verandah, with Van Rensburg doing all the talking. James bought a few things to keep him quiet.

His days fell into a lethargic pattern. Every morning Tshabalala came for a briefing, but every morning James had less for him to do. It became a purely totemistic meeting. Tshabalala with his notebook, painstakingly writing down tasks which could never be carried out: the new cows which would never be ordered (they bought milk now and kept it in the dairy); the three miles of game fencing which would never be erected; the new hen house which would never be delivered; the seed catalogues which were never ordered. Van Rensburg had offered to get these tasks done, but James declined the offer. Tshabalala would place his bicycle by the kitchen door carefully and wait for James to get up. James was drinking brandy every night and found it hard to get up. Daisy would give her father a cup of tea in a tin mug, made from an old Koo apricot jam tin. The old man would drink it slowly, standing just outside the door. Daisy would then wake James. Once he made love to her as her father was standing outside waiting for his orders, pulling her quickly into the bed. Finally James would get up and summon Tshabalala into the kitchen. He would remove the soft felt hat he always wore, revealing his greying hair, and clasp the hat deferentially in front of him. James rarely paid attention. He was looking forward to his swim in Grandpa's pool.

'The policemen come again, sir,' he said one morning.
'When?'
'When you were with Baas Van Rensburg.'
'What did they want?'
'They asking all the people questions, sir.'
'About what? About me?'
'I'm not so sure, sir.'

That night as they lay in bed, the lights of a car flared on the road below the house. By the time he got out of bed and ran down the stony track, all he could see were the tail-lights bobbing in the distance.

In the morning he asked Tshabalala if he had seen anything.
'No, sir. I just hear the cars in the night.'
'What do they want?'
Tshabalala shook his head sadly. He had disappointed Tshabalala; but he was used to disappointing people; he had been practising all his life.

Daisy stood in the corner of the kitchen watching them. Tshabalala said something to her and she went out of the back door to feed the chickens.

'Daisy's husband he's coming back maybe next week.'
'Her husband?'
'Yes, sir.'
'Where's he coming from?'
'The mines, sir. He's working short contract by Chartered.'
'Thank you, Ephraim. I don't think there's anything else this morning, do you?'
'No, sir.'

Tshabalala fastened his bicycle clips and mounted the heavy Hercules with its balloon tyres. When he had gone, James called out.

'Daisy.'
She came around the side of the house, holding the tin which contained the crushed mealies. Her eyes did not meet his.
'Daisy.'
'Yes, sir.'
'You didn't say you were married.'
She did not reply.
He glanced about nervously, but there was nobody. He felt weak.
'Come inside.'
She followed slowly.

'Who is he?'

'He's my husband, sir.'

'I know that. How long have you been married?'

'One year.'

'Daisy, why didn't you tell me?'

'It doesn't matter, sir.'

'Daisy.'

She stood looking at him as he sat slumped at the kitchen table. He looked up at her. She was wearing her nylon housecoat of sky blue, and the doek. What else was she keeping from him? It had never occurred to him that she might be married. Jo-Anne had always accused him of gross insensitivity about other people's lives. Maybe Jo-Anne was right on one thing at least.

'Daisy, what do you want?'

'Beg yours?'

'What do you want from me?'

'Nothing, sir.'

'Are you happy?'

'I'm happy.'

'What about your husband? Will he be happy if they tell him about this? What the hell is he going to do?'

'He is going to beat me, sir.'

'And your father?'

'He hit me many times.'

'Why didn't you tell me?'

'I don't like to tell you, sir.'

Her face was so grave now, a pupil trying to mirror a teacher's sentiments. He stood up and hugged her.

'Daisy, this must stop. I must send you away somewhere with your husband. I'll get you a good job in Johannesburg, and your husband. What's his name?'

'Joshua.'

'Joshua can be a driver. We'll get him a heavy duty licence.'

'No sir, I want to stay with you.'

'Don't be crazy, the police have been coming. Your husband is coming back.'

'It doesn't matter, sir. You are a big man.'

'I'm not a big man. I'm a little man. I'm a fucking little turd. A prick.'

'Beg yours?'

'Forget it. I was talking to myself. When's he coming exactly?'

'Maybe next week.'
'Okay. From tomorrow you don't work in the house any more.'
She began to weep.
'I'll take care of you. I'll give you money.'
'I want to stay with you, sir.'
'No, no. You've got to go. Understand? I can't do this to you. And your husband and old Ephraim. No. no.'
'I must stay with you.'
'Are you pregnant?'
'What you say?'
'Baby. Are you going to have a baby?'
'I want to, sir.'
'Sure, but are you pregnant?'
He made a gesture of roundness.
'No. My husband was too cross before. I don't have baby.'
'Anyway I'll go away next week and you must stay away from the house, okay?'
'No, sir. I must stay with you.'
She held his hand tightly. She was, as he had discovered in bed, very strong.
If I go what will happen to her?

The question was academic as it turned out, because the police came for her the next morning at 4.30.

EPILOGUE
21 March, 1960

Sharpeville. The township is alive with rumour on this, its big day.

This rumour has it that some important people are going to address the inhabitants. The boys from the PAC, many of them filled with a pleasing sense of importance, go around telling people to stay at home. A day of action has been called by Robert Sobukwe. Actually, it's a day of inaction because the only thing the inhabitants of Sharpeville can do to contribute to the day of action is to stay away from work and do nothing. The more daring among them claim to be going to hand in their passes, emancipating themselves for ever. No buses are leaving as the bus drivers have been asked, firmly, not to report for work. The people of Sharpeville begin to mill about. The township is very functional, a dormitory with a few basic amenities around which the little houses are grouped. Most prominent of these amenities is the police station, a group of low buildings surrounded by a small fence. In the no-man's land between the fence and the buildings some small trees have been planted. Many people drift towards the police station, naturally unaware that this is the day that will make their township famous.

Speeding towards Johannesburg in his bright red Maserati are James Thompson and Ephraim Tshabalala. They are going to change cars, courtesy of Mr Voss, for something more sober and responsible from the office, and then make for Sharpeville intent on kidnap.

As the morning advances, a large crowd gathers around the police station, concentrating on the main gate with another group at the side gate. Suddenly, coming from nowhere, Sabre jets scream low over the crowd. Boys throw their hats up in the air because the jets seem to be so low.

It is going to be a hot day. The Presbyterian minister, Mr Robert Maja, goes in search of his Anglican colleague, Father Voyi, to discuss the situation and have a cup of tea. Father Voyi is not at home, so Mr Maja walks to the police station, but he does not find him there in the crowd. The crowd have been told by the leader of the PAC in Sharpeville, Tsolo, who has had a conversation with a Lieutenant Visser of the South African Police, that an important person – a big man – will address them later in the day.

Many people disperse, heading for the shops and café near Seeiso Street or wandering off home. The truth of the matter is that they are not very sure what to do with themselves now that work has been cancelled.

Eventually Mr Maja meets up with Father Voyi at his house and they have a cup of tea. From there they can see the crowds still waiting at the police station for something to happen. Of course if the crowds had known what would happen, they would not have hung about at all, particularly not with so many children hoping to see the jets again. A couple of Saracen armoured cars trundle into the enclosure around the police station as if in response to the need of the aimless for something to look at. More policemen arrive with a senior police officer.

Tshabalala is silent. He is not impressed by this expensive automobile with its fancy Italian interior. If anything he finds it cramped compared with a pick-up. James Thompson is driving very fast. The plan is to call in on Mr Voss, change cars, pick up a blanket and some supplies, and head south for Sharpeville. Tshabalala will find Daisy and bring her to a rendezvous. She will lie in the back covered by a blanket until they reach the outskirts of Soweto. She and Tshabalala will then catch a bus into Soweto and find her uncle's house where she will lie low for a few weeks. James will drive Tshabalala back to the farm. In time papers – if papers are still required after the upheavals – will be purchased for Daisy and she will move to Johannesburg to a new job.

James wonders if all this can succeed. He has always had difficulty translating intentions into actions. He has also not told Tshabalala that he is selling the farm to Van Rensburg and friends at a knock-down price. And yet he is looking forward to the adventure. Above all he wants to see Daisy again, probably for the last time, and explain himself to her and receive her blessing. They are approaching Johannesburg through the straggly semi-rural flatlands. What has Daisy been thinking about these last few days, ripped from his bed, bundled into a cell, shipped across the country and dumped with alien people? His eyes actually well with tears, which do not quite overflow on to his cheek. He stops the car at the Dolls House roadhouse and orders two Cokes and hamburgers. Tshabalala eats his hamburger carefully; James attempts to drive and eat at the same time. They pull into the gates of Hilldrop.

Daisy Tshabalala is polishing the red cement verandah of the deputy superintendent's office. All morning people have been passing. Sharpeville seems to be a busy place, with planes flying overhead, police cars rushing here and there and Saracens rumbling down Zwane Street and so on. And this is a Monday. Somebody tells her that an important person will come from Pretoria and address the people of Sharpeville. That is why they are gathering at the police station. They are hoping to be told that passes are no longer necessary, thanks to the PAC. The pass is a constant worry and constraint.

Joshua Motha, a bus driver, not working today, goes towards the café to buy a drink. The café is doing terrific business, selling drinks, pies, bits of chicken and curry and rice. Motha decides to wait there for news of the big man from Pretoria. The two reverends, Mr Maja and Father Voyi, are drinking tea. Lechael Lusibi, a schoolteacher, cycles past the police station towards his house. He has been to the school, which is deserted, and had a conversation with the Principal. The Principal has come to the conclusion that they might just as well go home.

'What the hell's this?' asks James angrily.
    Mr Voss has provided a Lincoln Continental, flying the standard of the Chartered Goldfields, complete with chauffeur.
    'This is the best office car they could find. I'm sorry.'
    'Okay. We won't need the driver, but ask him to leave his cap behind. He can take the Maserati back to Main Street. I'll get it tomorrow.'
    'Jimmy, if you don't mind me asking, what do you want the car for?'
    'I've got to open a fête in Soweto.'

'You're joking with me. Who's the old man, my boy?'
'That's Tshabalala.'
'Is he any relation?' asks Mr Voss.
'He's the murderer's son.'
'What the heck are you doing, Jimmy? Tell me, man.'
'Is my mother here?'
'She's in the garden, where else would you expect her?'
'Tell her I'll be home tonight quite late. No dinner.'
'Okey dokey, Jimmy.'
'And keep this to yourself, please.'
'Sure thing, Jimmy.'
'Put that flag away,' says James to the chaffeur, who finds a little leather bag for it and slips it over the standard.

In Sharpeville there is now a constant traffic of police cars and Saracens to and from the police station. A few people in the crowd are shouting slogans – *Africa* and *Africa belongs to us* – at the police. The arrival of police cars and Saracens is taken by many to mean that the announcement is going to happen shortly. More people gather at the fence around the police station. Lechael Lusibi, the schoolteacher, mounts his bicycle and sets off for the house of a pupil to fetch some keys.

Vereeniging, the nearest town to Sharpeville, is a difficult place to get to, demanding a tricky drive out from the city, through the mine dumps and compounds to the South; they pass one of his grandfather's earliest mines, now virtually exhausted, its headgear (looking like the wheels on a gun carriage) rarely in use, its workforce on maintenance only. James does not recognise it. Unexpectedly four jet fighters scream over the mine dumps ahead of them. James glances at Tshabalala, who is clutching his notebook, his face expressionless, except perhaps for a slight look of pain, like that of a man suffering bravely from a chronic illness.

'Army aeroplanes,' says James.
'I see it, sir.'
The landscape around them is completely foreign to James. The mine dumps, the waste product of the cyanide process (which saved his grandfather's bacon) rise yellow and furrowed from amongst the dusty blue gum trees, tin-roofed houses, prison-like

compounds and antique mine shafts. It does not look like a rich and properous industry from here.

Tsolo, and another leader called More, are arrested. This seems unfair, as Tsolo, with the help of Elias Lelia, a dress designer and aspiring writer, has been trying to protect the fence from damage. A large group of people wait near the shops and café, to see the arrival of the big man from Pretoria and to march in convoy with him down to the police station in the hope of impressing on him their eagerness, so that he will make some concessions. The big man is acquiring quite a standing with the crowds. Perhaps Dr Verwoerd is sending a minister. Perhaps the head man from Bantu Administration himself will arrive.

Daisy decides to slip away to the shops for a few moments, to buy a cool drink and possibly to catch the announcement, which everyone is talking about, on her way back. The crowds around the police station are in an expectant, festive mood. Men talk to her, mainly in Sotho which she does not understand, but their meaning is clear; she hurries on.

James and Tshabalala reach a crossroads outside Vereeniging. They enquire about the way. They are told that there is trouble down there. James puts the chauffeur's cap on Tshabalala's head and unfurls the standard. It is a pity Tshabalala can't drive because they look rather silly, sitting in the wrong seats. On the road that leads off to Sharpeville there is a roadblock, a Saracen pointing its machine gun down the road and armed policemen walking about. The long black car with its standard – a gilded heraldic animal looking something like a wildebeest – is waved through after a moment's hesitation.

'What's going on, for Chrissake?' asks James rhetorically.

'Too much trouble,' says Tshabalala sadly.

Lechael Lusibi, the schoolteacher, cycles back from the school with his books. The Lincoln passes him.

Joshua Motha, the bus driver, is waiting near the main gate of the police station.

Mr Maja and Father Voyi are worried by the constant movement of men and vehicles at the police station.

James stops the car near the café, around the corner and out of sight of the police station.

Lt. Col. Pienaar, the man in charge, deploys his men in a line and orders them to load five rounds. The men with the sten guns simply clip on a full magazine. There is some movement around the main gate; the crowd is eager and restless.

'Ask them where the Superintendent's Office is,' says James to Tshabalala as the crowd waiting near the café surge round the car.
 'I don't understand them, sir, they speaking Sotho.'
 A young man steps forward.
 'We are waiting for you, baas. All the people are waiting.'
 'Where's the Superintendent's Office?' asks James.
 'Down that way, baas.' He points.
 'Go now, Ephraim, I wait for you here.'
 James does not want to attract the attention of the authorities. Tshabalala gets out of the car. The crowd is puzzled by this shabby figure, clad in brown trousers held up by a thick belt, an old grey shirt and a threadbare tweed jacket. On his head is a black chauffeur's cap with a shiny badge, reading, had anyone been interested, The Chartered Goldfields Company. Tshabalala sets off purposefully, keeping his head low, like a man caught in a shower. The car is now completely surrounded. James can see nothing.
 'Come on, baas.'
 'Africa.'
 'You must tell them.'
 James gets out of the car the better to see what's going on.
 'What do you want with me?' he asks pleasantly, although he is anxious.
 'You must speak to the people, baas. They are waiting for you.'
 'No, no you don't want me.'

It is the Lincoln which has misled them. Cautiously he walks around the car. A huge crowd is gathered down the road. Above the crowd he can see a few policemen standing on Saracens.

'Are you the big man, baas?'

'They waiting for you.'

Someone tugs his sleeve.

'No, no. Don't worry, I'm just here to fetch someone. Tell them that,' he says soothingly.

'You not from the government? You not the big man?'

'No. Shit no. I'm just here to fetch that old man's daughter.'

He points in the direction that Tshabalala was last seen.

His questioner gives him a push. James has disappointed him. James is used to disappointing people. The man shouts at the crowd. They are angry. It's time to go. But the car is being rocked by the crowd. It turns over on its side, exposing its plumbing; someone lights a match. The car is almost instantly aflame, burning with a thick black smoke. The crowd laugh and shout *'Africa belongs to us'* and run off towards the police station, leaving James standing looking at the burning car. It is about to explode; he runs and throws himself flat just outside the Hollywood Stores.

At the police station things are tense. The police are worried that the fence will be pushed over by the crowd. But nobody thinks of asking the crowd what they are waiting for. The children are looking at the guns and Saracens and hoping to see the planes again. The adults are waiting for the Big Man from Pretoria to tell them to throw away their passes. The police are expecting something to happen too. A young constable standing on top of one of the Saracens sees a group of about a hundred men and boys running towards the police station from the direction of the shops. He sees smoke rising. He shouts. There is a dull thud in the distance, behind the shops it seems, as the Lincoln's twenty-four-gallon petrol tank goes up. It's not a loud noise; it sounds like a shotgun from this distance.

'Shoot,' shouts a policeman, never identified but certainly not Lt. Col. Pienaar.

James hears the noise of firing. It takes him a moment to work out what it is; he peers around a brick pillar holding up the galvanised iron roof over the stoep of the Hollywood Stores. People are running towards him, away from the police station. Somehow he has caused all this. For a moment he thinks the running crowd are the disappointed man and his friends coming back for him with reinforcements, all equally angry, but he soon realises that they are running from the firing. It would be a lot more sensible simply to fall flat, because the police are shooting them even as they flee. There is a continuous volley. A man on a bicycle falls off as he rounds the corner from Seeiso Street. His head has exploded. Bullets strike the window of a shop, and it collapses into tiny shards of glass. James lies flat behind the verandah of the shop, but he cannot stop himself looking up at the carnage he has created. People are screaming; the firing is continuous, hundreds and hundreds of rounds popping, thudding, chattering and whining.

Lechael Lesibi is shot in the leg. He falls on top of his bicycle, not sure what has happened. He tries to wheel his bicycle away.

Joshua Motha is shot in the right hip, right outside the police station main entrance, trying to run.

James stands up. *I must stop this. I must stop this.* At that moment he sees Daisy leaving the café carrying a bottle of grape Fanta. She pauses, bewildered.

James runs towards her shouting, but she drops long before he can get there. *She's dead, she's dead,* he says, but when he gets to her and falls on his knees he discovers that she is not yet dead. Her lips are moving, but her eyes are curiously stationary as though they have lost their ability to revolve in their sockets.

Mr Maja stands up. Two people fall right at the front gate of Father Voyi's house. He fills a bottle with water and runs to help the wounded and dying. Many of them are his flock. Within the compound the policemen now stand alone looking out at a desert of bodies. Two tired horses wander down Zwane Street, picking their way through the corpses, shoes, umbrellas and hats that lie everywhere. The dead have fallen in improbable positions; they lie for all the world as though they are carelessly asleep, except they hug the ground more closely. Mr Maja does not know where to turn next.

James tries to lift Daisy, but he is trembling so much that she slips from his grasp and falls gently back on to the bare, baked earth among the bubblegum wrappers and fish and chip papers. He kneels again. He begins to weep with the certainty that he has caused all this.

'James,' she says, 'James, James, James.'

She pronounces his name with the stress on the second syllable. It frightens him because she has never said his name before. Indeed a surge of blood pushes through her knit blouse and her lips grind slowly to a halt. James stands up, looking for help, but Tshabalala is nowhere to be seen.

Gradually the police emerge from their compound. They feel a need to blame someone, and shout at the wounded and dying:

'Get up. We did nothing to you.'

'Here's your Africa for you.'